MW00436817

NATIONAL SECURITY

A VINCE CARVER THRILLER

MATT SLOANE

BLOOD &
TREASURE

Published by Blood & Treasure, Los Angeles
First Edition

This is a work of fiction. Any resemblance to reality is coincidental.

Cover by James T. Egan of Bookfly Design LLC.

Print ISBN: 978-1-946-00851-0

Matt-Sloane.com

Preface

I'm Matt Sloane, I like great stories, and I hope you do too.

The cool thing about stories is they come in all kinds. Everyone has their opinions and nobody's wrong. (Which must mean I'm right.)

So here's what I like in a story: Smart dialog between characters that feel real. Spurts of action, moments to breathe, and plenty to think about. Complex plots that aren't easy to predict, with realistic twists that don't make your eyes roll. And most of all, a satisfying ending, because you can't cheap out on those.

The Vince Carver books are high action, high intrigue spycraft on the world stage, and I hope they're your kind of story.

If you'd like to get in touch to say hi, offer a correction, talk shop, or otherwise gab, feel free to drop me a line:

matt@matt-sloane.com

Or you can get an email from me every time a book is released at: Matt-Sloane.com

Happy reading,

-Matt

National Security by Matt Sloane is stunningly real. A debut espionage thriller packed with intrigue, spycraft, and blistering action. From high-stakes business deals in Taipei to a strategic installation nestled in America's Appalachians, this instant classic doesn't stop to breathe until the last page.

★★★★★ "**Sensational**. A taut thriller that has a great deal more to offer than bullets and brawn."

★★★★★ "The fight scenes are the **best you'll find** in crime fiction."

★★★★★ "Very real and **very very good**."

NATIONAL SECURITY

"Intelligence is about practical knowledge that facilitates decision-making and reduces the uncertainty intrinsic to research and policy."

- *The Science of Military Intelligence,* Chinese Communist Party

1

An armed motorcade is a deceptively elaborate operation, but its core tenets remain simple: protect the principal, plan the route, and—no matter what—keep moving.

A good escort requires four vehicles at least, spacious, and equipped with high-performance engines, run-flats, and sufficient ballistic protection. You map out multiple routes ahead of time, randomize it on the day of so you're not overly predictable, and send a point car ahead to spot any surprises well before the main convoy reaches them.

Firepower is mandatory, the more the better. You can't thwart violence without the capacity to return it, so you need close protection officers with sufficient experience in a firefight.

Vince Carver was one such experienced operator, having served a decade in the US Army where his storied career culminated in the 1st Special Forces Operational Detachment-Delta. Now in his early thirties, Carver was a long way from the dunes of the Middle East and the scrublands of Africa. Absent, too, was the rigid command structure he had so often relied upon. His old life had been traded for private industry back home. Consequently, he now found himself the team leader of an armed convoy of close protection officers driving Range Rovers on the Red Mountain Freeway in Mesa, Arizona.

Private security wasn't as glamorous as national security, but the chances of getting sniped at by insurgents was markedly lower.

Carver absently rubbed the scars on his left bicep. They weren't visible under the sleeve of his black tee, but the marks were forever imprinted in his mind. He sat in the passenger seat, his powerful six-foot-two frame and the Tavor X95 rifle strapped across his chest the primary reasons escort vehicles require ample space.

Mike Davis, his security driver, was the only other close protection officer in the vehicle. Arizona was far from non-permissive territory, unless you counted soccer moms as enemy combatants, so there was little need to line the back seats with extra personnel.

The radio crackled. "Point to Team Leader. Something's goin' on up here. Boxes in the road slowing up traffic. Please advise. Over."

The mechanics of a motorcade: While their escort consisted of three vehicles, a fourth—a point car—was a mile ahead. Point's job was to get an eye on the terrain before the rest of the team, and the principal, were in the zip code of trouble.

Carver leaned into the screen at the center console and checked the nav system. The map displayed no warnings or road hazards, but that wasn't a surprise. Even during periods of smooth traffic, modern multi-lane highways were fickle beasts, and a single minor accident could upset the flow at the drop of a hat. For now Davis kept the speedometer fixed on an easy sixty-five, same as the rest of the convoy.

Carver lifted the radio to his mouth. "It looks all clear from back here. How slow are we talking?"

"It's getting bad," he grumbled back. "I'm doing twenty now, but there's a truck ahead that lost some of its load. Cars slowing to a crawl."

"Can you get past them?"

"Negative. There's no emergency lane due to construction. I'm a sitting duck here."

Carver clenched his jaw. His point man was Nick Shaw, a former SEAL he'd met a couple of years ago in Europe. Shaw was his second-in-command as well as a hard man who didn't spook easily.

"Do you see anything suspicious?" Carver radioed.

A snort. "You mean besides the sudden U-Haul oopsy? I don't like it, boss."

It was probably nothing. The point car was a fully-outfitted black Range Rover, like the rest. If anybody was trying to stop the convoy, they would be better served waiting for the easily recognizable scout to pass before obstructing the road. Still, while it was likely little more than bad luck, the security business was built on taking all precautions.

And besides, every good security plan has contingencies.

Carver checked the map again and radioed back. "Copy that. Lead, we will exit the highway at Gilbert and maintain residential speed. Point, if you can't reverse to the exit, take the next one and rendezvous with us on McDowell. Unless anyone calls out trouble, maintain REDCON 2. How copy?"

Both operatives signaled affirmative and the lead car drifted to the right lane as the convoy diverted. Carver's eyes were calm, the color of smoky-gray ash and just as dead, but the activity within was deceptive. From his vantage at the tail of the motorcade, he didn't miss a detail on the road in front or behind.

The three Rovers settled into the lane and slowed in anticipation of the upcoming exit, and the finer terms of the security detail nagged at Carver. The principal they were protecting was a well-known self-made billionaire, Walter Lachlan, CEO of Crystal Processor Systems. CPS fabricated semiconductors that revolutionized computer chips, motherboards, and the software that drove them. Carver was ignorant of the finer points of the company's products, but their influence in the industry was plain. The CPS logo was emblazoned on stickers affixed to nearly half the computers on sale today.

Walter Lachlan was a Very Important Person, one who took security seriously, and one who already had his own team in place.

Carver's unit had only been enlisted to supplement the local residential security team two weeks ago. Lachlan's office campus and residence were already locked down, and what security measures Carver was able to review were tight. That said, the computer billionaire's properties weren't staffed with the dangerous men found in the special forces, the kind of men that had lived and breathed the harsh terrain amid hostile combatants for weeks at a time. Lachlan's close protection officers were armed and trained, but they were accustomed to searching employee handbags and securing cocktail parties and fundraisers. In short, they lacked the cold experience of hardened killers.

So when CPS's latest innovations warranted an increase in security while Lachlan shopped a cutting-edge algorithm around, Carver and company stepped in to supplement the existing team.

Shaw, in the point car, was stuck in traffic a mile ahead. The convoy veered away as the exit looped off the freeway. The lead car was responsible for maintaining the speed of the motorcade and remaining tactically aware. That was more difficult without a point car but hardly impossible.

The principal vehicle was only a few car-lengths behind. Lachlan was safely within, surrounded by his own personal protection operatives. Carver had looked up his bodyguards and, while they didn't have the chops to be on his own team, they were familiar to the principal and adept at handling him, two qualities that couldn't be discounted in this business. It was Lachlan's insistence that had kept them close, a semblance of routine in his new normal.

Carver stretched in the passenger seat of the last Rover in the convoy, the driver and he protecting the tail and ready to take offensive action if needed. They were the closest thing outside a war zone to a quick reaction force.

As the team leader, Carver preferred manning the follow

car. He didn't care much for face time with the principal. Sucking up to the rich elite wasn't his cup of joe. It was better to remain outside the spotlight, on the fringes of the escort where he could better assess the wider net. Sitting in the back allowed him to focus on his role leading the rest of the team, and it kept him in visual range of the principal at all times. That was a win for the convoy because, without that careful coordination, and much like the fickle traffic itself, one or two minor incidents could quickly lead to disarray.

A safe motorcade was strong, aware, and flexible.

The lead car slowed as it passed a few cars and turned onto the residential street. The stoplight flicked to yellow and Davis, the driver of the follow Rover, flashed his lights to signal his intention to drive through. Lachlan's security driver showed no hesitation getting through the intersection and everyone stuck together without issue.

While the convoy to the airport was unfortunately diverted, they'd been forced off the state road only a few exits early. Their current heading followed the freeway and was the main contingency route. They turned onto the access road and resumed freeway speed. The road was clear but only two lanes going each direction, which meant they had fewer options when navigating past slow-moving vehicles. As the sterile bubble surrounding the convoy necessarily closed in, Carver absently checked the weapon across his chest.

The X95 is the civilian version of the Israel Weapon Industries TAR-21 assault rifle. The bullpup configuration places the action behind the trigger, creating a more compact firearm with reduced length and a closer center of mass, making it perfect for swinging in and out of tight hallways and, say, passenger seats of Range Rovers. It's comfortable to shoot standing, kneeling, and on the move, and sacrifices a shorter sight radius for steadier recoil. Much of Carver's military experience relied heavily on the American M4 and firing at range from a dug-in position, but once he joined the private sector in Europe he had taken a shine to the Tavor's mobility and rugged reliability.

"Team Leader," called Menendez in the lead car, "looks like spotty traffic, but nothing we can't handle. Slowing to residential speed. Over."

"Copy," answered Carver.

The development was expected. The convoy passed a double-long semi before slaloming into the right lane to pass a slow-moving station wagon in the left. As they gained distance from the truck, the deep rumble of a motorcycle caused Carver to turn halfway in his seat. Within seconds, a red racing bike weaved past the semi and then the station wagon. It was doing eighty at least, and there was nothing the convoy could do to avoid being overtaken.

"Be advised," radioed Carver. "One bike passing from behind."

His gray eyes fixed on the unarmed rider who sped past the driver's window. Before he could relax, another motorcycle sped into their rear view. This one wasn't going quite as fast and appeared to be an off-road dirt bike.

"Get in the left lane," he instructed Davis, "and tighten

up our follow distance a bit."

"Just what I was thinking," said the driver. He drifted left and accelerated.

Even though the new formation exposed the rear of the principal car, Carver didn't like being passed on the driver's side, with his view partially obstructed. Not only did the left lane allow their car to get closer to the principal without risking a collision, but it gave him a view of the red super racing bike as it sped past the rest of the convoy and into the distance.

"Bike's clear," called Menendez.

In the meantime, they had nearly reached the bumper of the principal car in the other lane.

"Back off," Carver said to Davis. "Not that close." He lifted the radio to his lips and spoke. "There's another bike in tow," he warned. "Looks unrelated."

With the convoy occupying two lanes and Davis having closed too much, the dirt bike behind them was forced to slow its approach. Carver grimaced because a non-military motorcade shouldn't obstruct faster, more maneuverable vehicles. The security team's eyes were looking for anybody reacting unnaturally to their presence, and they had just forced that reaction. Now there was a bike on their ass without cause for suspicion, which put them in a bind.

Luckily, the road ahead was clear, the first red motorcycle now just a dot on the horizon.

"Come on," said Carver, waving the dirt bike to their right ahead, even though the Rover's tints put his visibility in doubt. His attention turned to a third motorcycle approaching their tail.

"Stupid asshole," grumbled Davis. "He has plenty of space."

The near rider's mirrored visor swiveled to the window, face fully concealed, and Carver clenched his jaw. Something was off. The third motorcycle was still at a distance, so while it appeared to be a similar dirt bike, he couldn't confirm that. Even though he hadn't seen anything overtly threatening, a special operator's training hones them into a confident and decisive machine. Action is better than idleness eight days of the week.

"Two dirt bikes," he radioed the team. "I don't like them. Go to REDCON 1."

The lead car and the principal merged into the left lane, re-forming the convoy into a single line. That was followed by a subtle increase in evasive speed.

The rider on the dirt bike pulled his hand off the handlebar. Carver's grip tensed on his rifle as the biker brandished a middle finger. Then he hit the throttle and zoomed through the cleared right lane.

Davis chuckled. "Told you he was an asshole, Vince."

Carver could appreciate the humor at a later time. His eyes flitted to the passenger mirror and the next dirt bike overtaking them. This one approached at a steadier, less showy speed directly behind them in the left lane. The motorcycle was a different model and different color but still a dirt bike, and Carver noted the identical matte-black helmet with mirrored visor. These guys were together.

He twisted in his seat to look straight out the rear

window. The convoy was far enough ahead of the semi that he had a long view of the road behind. There weren't any more bikes.

The one behind them drifted out of his view as it moved right to pass. Carver felt like a dick for camping in the passing lane, but he had other priorities. He spun back around to the right window and had to lean to get eyes on the motorcycle riding close to the gas tank.

"Evasive action," he barked.

At the same moment, a loud clunk rapped the vehicle. It could've just been a stray kick from an irate biker, but Carver didn't think so.

"Evasive?" asked Davis. "I can't speed up. What do you want me to do, hit him?"

"Wait."

Carver leaned close to the mirror and scanned the Rover for damage. A glint of silver metal above their rear wheel caught his eye. The dirt bike sped forward toward the principal.

The Rover's ballistic windows didn't lower. While the guns weren't just for show, they weren't an option while speeding down the highway. As the motorcycle accelerated, Carver threw open the passenger door into the unsuspecting rider's path. The front wheel twisted as the left handlebar caught the door, the dirt bike veered into their vehicle, and there was a loud crumple as the Rover's rear wheel bounced over the motorcycle. The rider tumbled in the right lane.

Ahead, the first dirt bike rode up on the lead car. With his door still open, Carver leaned out and checked the rear fender. A silver device had been affixed above the wheel.

"We've got a bomb!" he alerted the team over the radio. "Emergency pullover. Bail vehicles one and three."

2

The Rover's tires screeched on the faded blacktop as they swerved to the emergency lane.

Davis, already aware of the brewing danger, was the first to come to a stop. Carver hopped out, hurried to the dirt off the side of the road, and swiveled the X95 to the downed rider some hundred yards behind them. The figure was still so he turned to the device on the Rover as Davis rounded the back hatch, eyes also on the rider as he secured the vehicle.

"Clear out!" yelled Carver, pulling his driver away just as the explosive charge went off.

The blast hit them like a stun grenade. The Range Rover wasn't engulfed in fire and there was barely a flash of light, but the bomb caused the back of the vehicle to hop. As it landed, instead of a gentle bounce on a heavy-duty suspension, the rear wheel bent sideways. The motorcyclist was still immobile, which meant the device had been on a timer.

"Cover the rear biker," ordered Carver, sprinting ahead to the rest of the halted convoy.

He paused to assess the principal vehicle. It appeared

untouched. Ahead, the remaining dirt bike drove back towards them before rounding to the rear of the lead Rover's passenger side. That vehicle was manned only by Menendez exiting on the left.

Carver didn't hesitate. He lifted the Tavor to his shoulder, lined up the target, and fired three rounds.

The helmeted attacker dropped to the ground, but not before affixing a silver device to the lead Rover's fender. The tires of the principal car suddenly spun up, kicking gravel at Carver. The gunfire had spooked the driver into gassing his engine without his escort.

"Stay in place!" Carver instructed into the radio. "Do not move."

Ahead of them in the street, Menendez signaled for them to stop, but the car swerved around him and gunned it down the open road.

"I repeat," called Carver, "stop the vehicle!"

He scowled as he received no reply. The residential security team either lacked wartime discipline or Walter Lachlan himself had ordered his people to move out. Complicating matters, they'd so far shown little desire to use the radio. While their head of security was equipped with one, it was likely turned off. Carver cursed and rushed ahead as Menendez inspected the dead biker and then his vehicle.

"Get back," ordered Carver.

He again raised the rifle to his shoulder. This time he sidestepped behind the Rover so he could see the edge of the bomb. He took careful aim and fired at the device. The second round dislodged it from the fender and skipped it upward, spinning. It exploded in midair, cracking the ballistic windows on the passenger side of the Rover, but leaving it in drivable condition.

Carver eyed the principal car disappearing into the distance, then checked ahead and behind for further threats. "Status," he barked.

Davis answered first. "Rear tango's starting to move a little, but he's unable to stand. Should I secure him?"

"Negative. Our responsibility is the principal. Lead tango is down."

Menendez tried his radio and then said, "Principal Team's not answering."

"Ditch the follow car," Carver ordered. "Load up in the lead."

He marched ahead and opened the rear door as Menendez rounded to his side. Carver jumped in the passenger seat, and Davis followed in the back a few seconds later. The Rover peeled out before his door was closed.

"Point to Team Leader," buzzed the radio. "You guys okay back there?"

Carver held the grab handle over his head as their Rover veered and accelerated aggressively. "A-OK, Point. Two tangos down. Follow car disabled by an explosive device. We're in pursuit of the principal who panicked. Where are you?"

"Still on the freeway but almost past the construction. When the emergency lane opens up I'll ride that to the next exit and come back for you."

Carver shook his head to himself. "Negative. The principal will be headed to Falcon Field. Meet us there."

"Copy that, boss man."

The Rover sped towards light traffic. Carver clipped the radio back to his shoulder and leaned forward in anticipation. His nerves tingled as he, for the first time, began to process the sudden surge of adrenaline flooding his system. It was a familiar rush, and one that was long overdue in his line of work. There's a truth in the security business: no matter how sophisticated your countermeasures are, the ultimate success of a mission comes down to whoever has the greater capacity for violence.

This contract was supposed to be a simple escort. An active threat in the American Southwest was unexpected, especially since this wasn't your average disgruntled employee taking potshots at his boss. They'd used two high-tech charges strong enough to take out armored vehicles. It now seemed likely that the U-Haul dropping boxes was meant to divert their convoy off the freeway. This attack involved a sophisticated level of planning and coordination.

Which meant there was more to it than a couple of unarmed bikers.

The lead car pursued at blistering stints of ninety miles per hour, but the speed was impossible to maintain as they navigated between cars and trucks. Menendez hit the brakes as one overeager semi overtook another, effectively blocking both lanes. He laid on the horn. The Rover slowed, rolled into the emergency lane to the right of both trucks, and illegally passed.

"Team Leader to Principal Team," Carver spoke into the radio. "The threat has been neutralized. I say again, the threat is neutralized. Please resume highway speed so we can fall in. How copy?"

He ground his teeth waiting for a reply, but the residential security team was clearly not answering. Carver shared a grim look with Menendez and Davis, and then went for a long shot. He pulled out his cell phone and dialed Walter Lachlan's direct line. They'd only linked up this way once before when trading numbers. Beyond that most of their long distance coordination had gone through his security team.

"He's not picking up," reported Carver. "They're racing forward like a bat out of hell. Something's wrong."

The intersection for the turnoff to Falcon Field Airport was backed up. They lost almost a full minute before the Rover squeezed onto the sidewalk and rolled past the congestion, scraping an old chain-link fence in the process. By the time they made the turn, the principal car was out of sight.

Luckily, there were a few more intersections to go before the airfield, with the occasional car and light to slow the principal down. Menendez blew through a red light and regained visual contact just as they turned into the airport. Carver scanned the surrounding area for anything out of place. Maybe he was feeling trouble that wasn't there. Maybe they would pull this off without another hitch.

They swerved into the airport, eyes glued to the principal Rover as it made a left.

"That's the wrong turn," noted Davis.

Walter Lachlan's private jet waited on the distant tarmac while his vehicle had turned to a nearby airfield where a black helicopter sat ready, rotors spun up. The principal car ignored the painted lines on the tarmac as it cut a slanted path straight for the chopper.

Vince Carver swapped out his partially empty mag for a full one. "The residential security team is in on it."

"Whoa," said Menendez. "You sure about that?"

"It's the only explanation. They're not answering the radio and they're attempting an alternate exfil. Maybe that's why Lachlan hired us in the first place."

Davis shook his head. "If he didn't trust his own team, why's he in the car with them?"

Carver worked his jaw, unable to provide a good answer. Unfounded suspicion was a nasty thing, sometimes more insidious than outright betrayal because it was more difficult to act on. If Lachlan was worried about loyalty without hard proof, it could explain the half measure of hiring supplemental security.

The principal car skidded to a stop as close to the spinning rotors as they could without turning the Rover into a convertible. The vehicle doors flung open and Carver's suspicions were confirmed. One of Lachlan's bodyguards brandished a pistol and yanked his charge by the arm. The driver rounded the vehicle to the back door and reemerged a moment later with a metal briefcase. Lachlan's assistant and head of security remained in the Rover.

"Take us as close as you can," ordered Carver.

Given the opposition's head start, Menendez could only do so much. Their vehicle couldn't possibly cut off the kidnappers before they reached the chopper. Even if there was room for such a maneuver, they were too far behind.

Carver realized this as the seconds ticked. He opened the sunroof that doubled as an emergency exit in the case of a tipped vehicle. He pushed the Tavor above his head before following it through with his head and shoulders.

"Steady," he called.

He fired several rounds, purposely wide. Lachlan's personal protection operatives flinched and hunched over. Another couple of shots had them taking cover behind the Rover, out of sight but no longer advancing on the chopper.

Their speeding Rover was ten seconds out. Instead of waiting, Carver turned his rifle on the helicopter. He started with a burst before slowing his rate of fire. While the X95 was a civilian weapon without a fully automatic mode, it nonetheless carried a military load of 5.56 NATO ammunition. Still, the probability of disabling a helicopter from a speeding vehicle was low. Carver's shots were designed to harass more than maim, and as a round glanced off the helicopter's windshield, the plan worked.

Menendez skidded to a stop beside the other SUV, and the black helicopter hovered off the ground.

Panicked at seeing their extraction fall apart, the bodyguards emerged from behind their Rover. The driver ran to grab the aircraft's skid, but the attempt was poorly timed and he missed. The other bodyguard swung his arm onto the Rover's hood and fired his pistol.

Carver ducked behind the ballistic windshield as one of the rounds chipped it and ricocheted over his head. Menendez and Davis opened doors on opposite sides of the vehicle and laid covering fire.

"Watch the principal!" Carver warned, but they didn't need to be told. Their rounds hit the tarmac wide left and right of the Rover Lachlan was behind. The helicopter, content to no longer be fired upon, waited for a resolution to the conflict a hundred feet above. Carver squinted through the open sunroof but couldn't see through the reflection of sunlight covering the cockpit.

Up against ballistic glass with only a pistol, and a driver whose only contribution was waving a briefcase over his head for the chopper to come back down, the bodyguard stopped firing. He grabbed Lachlan and held him below the hood of the Rover.

"I'll kill him," he warned. "Put your guns down."

Carver grimaced. Maybe he would have to shoot the chopper down after all.

"Boss man," crackled his radio. "I have a shot."

Carver scanned the far fence line and located Nick Shaw and his point car parked outside the grounds. A desert-colored Mk 11 Sniper Weapon System was propped over the hood, and he had clear line of sight to the kidnapper's back. The shot was less than a hundred yards.

"You can't hit the principal," warned Carver.

"I won't hit the principal," said Shaw.

Carver bit down, ash-colored eyes giving the callous impression of death. It was an impression that missed the true mark. Carver preferred to imagine his eyes were uncolored by the biases of the world. He saw in black and white but operated in the gray. His mind was made in under a second.

"Take the shot."

A hole opened in the bodyguard's chest and he collapsed to the ground. The three of them advanced, Menendez covering the stranded driver, Davis the principal car, and Carver rounding the vehicle and securing a trembling Walter Lachlan.

As he pulled the man to his feet, the billionaire said, "They're dead." Carver didn't hear the words so much as read his lips, but he followed the man's gaze inside the car and found his assistant slumped over the front console with an entrance wound in the back of her head. The head of security in the back seat shared a similar fate. His holster was empty.

Out of reach in the sky above, the helicopter pivoted into the clouds.

Walter Lachlan looked more like the owner of a bank than a tech CEO, but an astute observer could make out the modern flourishes that cemented him a product of this time. His mostly white hair was just slightly unkempt. He wore no tie and left the top button of his shirt open. His blue suit was smartly patterned and well-fitted.

"Are you hurt?" asked Carver.

Lachlan answered only with a thousand-mile stare. Carver did a circle around the principal to confirm he wasn't hit. No physical damage, though the man was clearly in shock.

Carver checked the horizon for incoming threats. This section of the airport was empty. Falcon Field employed private security, but if they were mobilizing they were taking their time. It was Lachlan's personal team who had been responsible for coordinating with them. He felt it a good bet that whatever employees waited at his private jet weren't in on this.

"Did they say what they wanted?" Carver asked.

Nothing but a blank stare from Lachlan.

Carver snapped fingers in front of the billionaire's eyes to refocus them. "You need to work with me, sir."

Walter's head gave a hesitant shake. "N... no. They just told me to stay quiet."

"What do I do with this one?" asked Menendez. The driver was belly down on the tarmac, hands and ankles zip tied. Meanwhile, Shaw's Rover pulled around to the entrance and was quickly closing on their position.

Carver approached the driver. "What's your name?"

The man set his wide jaws and said, "Screw you." He sounded Eastern European.

"He's a new replacement," offered Lachlan.

In another time and place, the blame would fall on the Soviets. Carver knew the type, mercenaries from the various broken states formed after the last Cold War. These guys no longer had identities, much less ideologies. They were true soldiers of fortune, selling their guns to the highest bidder. They could've been hired by anyone, foreign or domestic.

Shaw's Range Rover pulled up. He opened the driver door but made no move to get out. Nick was a country boy with skin tanned red and what could only be described as a special forces beard the color of mahogany. His tactical vest was worn over a sleeveless shirt, and he went nowhere without his black sunglasses and a backwards cap on his head.

"Look who's lucky I was around," he said.

Carver returned a grateful nod. "Davis, contact airport security and wait for them here. Menendez, sit on the driver. Shaw's gonna get us to the plane."

The principal flinched at the suggestion. "We... We can't just leave." He furrowed his brow. "Can we just leave?"

"Sir, I still consider this an active situation."

"We need to call the police."

"My team will manage the local police. Right now my job is to secure your person, and there are too many variables out in the open." Carver grabbed him but the man protested.

"My briefcase!" Lachlan ran over and collected the metal case beside the hogtied driver.

Carver was surprised it hadn't been handcuffed to the principal. "Is that what they wanted?"

"Everyone wants it. It's a prototype wafer with three nanometer semiconductor nodes."

None of that registered with Carver. "Is that important?"

"Well, yes. But... it's not the real prize." Lachlan seemed to gather some confidence as the subject matter turned to something familiar. "They no doubt wanted what's in my head."

Which tracked with a kidnapping. "Technology?" Carver asked.

His head shook. "Algorithms are encoded in digital lockers. They want passwords and access to my company's network."

Carver nodded. "Okay, let's get you out of here."

Lachlan was directed inside the Rover. Carver slid beside him in the back seat while Shaw drove. Lachlan took heavy breaths to steady himself, showing impressive control for a civilian. But then few billionaires were made without a steely resolve.

"What the hell was that?" he whispered to himself.

The relative silence and calm were welcome, but in the security business it was only an illusion. Carver knew the bullets could restart at any moment and without warning. Shaw did too and drove with determined, no-nonsense urgency.

Lachlan began what could only be described as measured trembling. "This is unacceptable..."

The Gulfstream 280 waited on the tarmac, airstair deployed and manned by the security team. It was a small but luxurious private jet, meant for domestic travel. When the Rover parked, Carver placed a hand on Lachlan's shoulder and he refused to budge.

"This is unacceptable," he repeated with more vitriol, cheeks flushing red.

"Not now, sir. My job is to keep—"

"Don't tell me what I need to do, young man. I wouldn't be in this position if you knew how to do your job."

Carver took a breath and calmly met the billionaire's eyes. "Respectfully, sir, if you want to live, you'll shut your pie hole and come with me right now."

Shaw smirked. Lachlan jerked his head back, unaccustomed to being spoken to like that. Something in Carver's smoke-gray eyes warned off a response.

The waiting security team fidgeted while the principal mulled over his options. The last thing they needed was Lachlan becoming a distraction, especially when it was his own security team that had sold him out.

The CEO wisely shook it off. "Yes. You're right."

Carver helped him out of the vehicle while Shaw made sure the jet was clear. They all climbed in. Even though he hadn't been meant to join them on board, there would be no debating it now.

The flight staff rushed to clear their exit with panic in their eyes. Even the security team outside was jittery. All perfectly acceptable after the trade of gunfire. Lachlan's fingers drummed his metal briefcase as he radiated tension and threatened to go supernova.

Carver wouldn't relax till they were in the air. He stood beside the closed hatch and stared out the window. Fortunately, billionaires have more pull than the average citizen and the pilots readied for takeoff. Shaw strolled from the back of the jet and presumptuously sat across from the still-brooding CEO. He leaned close and spoke in a low voice.

"Vince is right, you know. Your own company men were in on this. If it wasn't for us you'd be dead right now. Or worse."

Lachlan swallowed. His eyes flicked to Shaw's for a brief second, but they didn't hold. They fell to his lap before appraising Carver with something akin to awe.

3

The Gulfstream gained altitude, and Walter Lachlan grew more resolute with each mile from the scene of their narrow escape. Men like him, with a net worth in the billions, rarely encountered mistakes without setting their mind to correct them. That was especially true of blunders of this magnitude and import. After settling into his seat with a finger of whiskey, and without offering any around, he spent most of the flight violently berating whoever he could reach on his phone.

Carver and Shaw were all too happy to dispense with conversation. They spent the short flight lounging in luxury at the head of the jet.

San Jose International Airport was a hop and a skip away, and though Carver's contract had technically expired on the tarmac in Arizona, they made sure to see Lachlan safely to the next jet at his destination. They even insisted on securing the interior.

The Bombardier Global 8000 was built for long international voyages. The industry-leading business aircraft had a range capable of crossing the Pacific in one go, and its extensive cabin, which included a galley and three large suites, ensured the ride would be in the height of luxury. Lachlan's security advance party welcomed them and seemed, to Carver's trained eye, more stoic than usual, no doubt a result of Lachlan's numerous angry phone calls.

Carver shared his concerns with Lachlan about his personal team but agreed he was probably safe for now. If the flight crew were compromised, there would have been little sense in attempting the armed kidnapping before boarding the plane. So, after a clipped round of thanks from their principal, Carver and Shaw handed Lachlan off and watched the plane maneuver toward the runway for takeoff.

"With an aircraft like that," mused Shaw, "man should give us his Gulfstream. Least he could do for saving his life."

Carver nodded while holding back a smile. Shaw had a devil-may-care attitude about life. It allowed him to function effectively without dwelling on any complications. Those were reserved for Carver, as their team leader. The logistics of unwrapping this mess had taken seed during the flight. Those seeds were growing by the minute.

"Why don't you head back to the office for debrief?" Carver suggested. "Then take the rest of the day off."

"You buying?"

"I need to chat with our guys in Mesa and make sure they get home. Then, I imagine, my debrief will take quite a bit longer than yours. I'll see you tomorrow."

Shaw sighed. "All work and no play makes Vince a dull boy."

It was a jovial warning, and a fruitless one, as his friend knew. Shaw waved and headed for the terminal. Carver waited outside until the Bombardier took to the air.

The logistics, it turned out, were as familiar as his time in the Army. Mostly out of his hands, and a whole lot of hurry up and wait. Davis and Menendez were embroiled with Mesa police. It would be some time before they were free, and it was entirely possible they wouldn't sniff California till the next morning.

Carver, at least, was home. He loaded the weapons into the bed of his black Dodge Ram 2500 and climbed into the seat with a heavy sigh. The end of any deployment was a relief. Your body crashes after the highs of combat, but it's a good low, a slow burn of satisfaction at another job well done.

He drove a short distance to his office park. Being located in a major Silicon Valley hub, many of his firm's clients worked in the tech sector. Walter Lachlan was no exception, though he was admittedly on another level. And despite his kidnapping being spectacularly thwarted, no businessman, much less tech mogul, appreciates a close call with the bad guys. No, the most successful security work was done behind the scenes, invisible to principal and onlookers alike.

In the shade of the underground garage, Carver slotted his pickup into his personal parking space, climbed up a flight of stairs, and pushed through the glass doors into the first-floor office of Dynamic Security Solutions. It wasn't the most imaginative of company names, but Carver was proud of the kinetic division he'd built over the last year. It was his baby, and he had to defend it. And while Carver wasn't sure if this morning's incident spelled doom for his fledgling protection outfit, there was nothing to do but face the music.

The front office was a series of modern desks laid out in an open floor plan. Dynamic Security Solutions had started its life as an INFOSEC company, and though only half the desks currently buzzed with activity, the employees were all programmers. Carver wasn't good with computers but he understood the need for data security in today's market. This was as true on the battlefield as in the trenches of corporate America. Another truth Carver held was that, no matter how many firewalls, digital vaults, or safeguards you implement, all security eventually comes down to a man with a gun.

This was the value of Carver and his team to Dynamic Security Solutions, and this morning's events had borne out his theory. Most of his twenty employees occupied the field rather than the slick air-conditioned office, so he was surprised when the door to the kinetic division opened and Juliette Morgan filed into the hallway.

The physical demands of the close protection business ensured it was male dominated, and Morgan was one of only two women in Carver's division. A female personal protection operative was handy for certain clients, like children or women who wanted privacy. Juliette Morgan, however, was no token female. She was a Green Beret, an Army Special Operations combat interpreter in Afghanistan, and had served behind enemy lines in Special Reconnaissance. For DSS she coordinated the security advance party to secure escorts on arrival.

Morgan was 5'9" with piercing green eyes and straight brown hair that fell below her chin. She strode down the hall with a grin.

"Missed you out there," said Carver.

"Heard it was a riot," she cooed.

He glanced around and wondered how much Shaw had told her and if he was still around. "How's couples therapy?"

She rolled her eyes. "As brutal as it sounds. My husband is griping about my career not being as stable as his. He wants me to be a mall cop or something. I swear, it's only worth putting up with for the kids."

Carver disguised a frown and nodded encouragingly. He wasn't sure if he should congratulate his coworker on the news or sympathize. This was terrain Carver didn't attempt to navigate. Ten years as a professional soldier and kids were beyond his scope of training.

"I'm sorry I couldn't be there," confided Morgan, mostly to fill the silence. "This stupid spat is dragging out and—"

"Lachlan's team was in charge of the advance party," he interrupted. "There was nothing for you to do on this one."

She huffed. "Maybe there should have been."

"No argument from me there. But you're doing what needs to be done for your family. Nobody thinks less of you for that. Work it out. When I need you in the field, you'll get the call."

She nodded a lackluster thanks, still distracted by her family drama. Then mirth entered her eyes as she met his. "Did you really tell Walter Lachlan to shut his pie hole?"

Carver snorted. "It's as bad as high school in here." He waved her off and continued down the hall, regretting his choice of words with the billionaire. In the heat of the moment it was the best thing to say to get him to comply, but he now wondered if he should've used less memorable language. He was the product of the military, he could say that much.

Carver marched past the kinetic division to the closed door of the large corner office and knocked.

"Come," said his boss.

Carver entered to find Mark Marino behind his desk. His boss stood as soon as he was recognized. "Vince, glad to hear you made out." He circled his desk and offered his hand.

"Hooah, sir."

The formality was a throwback to the Army, where Marino had also served in the 75th. It was before Carver's time, and Marino was now in his early fifties. He had been a Ranger Communicator, though it wasn't obvious by looking at the guy. Broad shouldered, with a large crooked nose and a boxer's jaw, but a just-as-prominent amiable smile showing a set of perfect teeth. He was shorter than Carver but shook his hand with the strength and paws of a bear. Though he didn't do field work anymore, he mostly kept in shape and retained a youthful appearance that extended to his hair, still more pepper than salt.

Marino had leveraged a successful career in the Army into a data security business. Dynamic Security Solutions was veteran-owned and founded in COMSEC and

INFOSEC. It was only after the two men met a little over a year ago, when Carver had been contracted for a short job, that DSS picked him up for good and branched into OPSEC.

Mark remained standing and tucked his arms across his chest. "I hear it was hairy out there. Was there any indication a strike was likely?"

"None at all," assured Carver. "They hit us in the street. The only hole in our net was Lachlan's own people. Euro mercenaries. From what I could gather, they were new hires. That leaves most of his team intact, except for the ones who were killed."

"Police are sorting through that," said Mark. "I hope you don't mind, but I've been coordinating with them for you. They're pissed you left the ground. Screw 'em." He signaled to the leather couch along the wall and took position in a lounge seat. "You're gonna need to fly out there in a day or two."

"You're serious."

"There's no getting around it. Morgan can do that security sweep for JenTech tomorrow." Mark stalled protest with a raised hand. "I know they're a new client and you like to get a look at things yourself, but Juliette's more than capable."

Carver leaned back and put a boot on the small table. "Fine, I get it. She's been itching to get back to work anyway."

"Glad you agree. Unloading your week will allow you to focus on your after-action report and make nice with the police. Cooperation will help them find out who was behind this. Which"—he raised a pointed finger—"would go a long way toward damage control with Lachlan."

"Damage?" Carver asked innocently.

Mark's eyes narrowed. "I don't want to hear anything else about pies and holes. Got it?"

Carver rolled his eyes and caught Mark fighting off a grin.

"Walter's been out of reach in the air and it's another twelve hours till he touches down. That means you can turn in your report in the morning and fix this in the afternoon."

"What is there to fix?" asked Carver. "I was under the impression the contract with Lachlan was a one-off while he toured the new facilities in the Arizona desert."

"No, no, no," urged Mark. "Don't you see, Vince? This is an opportunity. We've proven our value. Some assholes with a grudge proved the need. If we angle this correctly, we could secure a permanent contract with Crystal Processor Systems."

"DSS and CPS together, huh?"

"It's a coup. We're based in the same city, and his own team is compromised. And if we can get Walter on board with our data protection suite, we'd become a premium brand overnight. Not bad for a part owner, huh?"

It wasn't bad at all. But if Carver's team were to continue shadowing Lachlan, he would need to move into investigative operations. Whoever had struck out at the billionaire would try again. Aside from a protective detail, the best way to stay ahead of the perpetrators was to find out who they were and go after them first.

"But," said Marino, interrupting Carver's rapidly spinning thoughts, "we're getting ahead of ourselves. Don't miss what's in front of you, right? Nick gave me the highlights but he wasn't with the escort team. I want to hear from you exactly what happened, beat by beat, so we can nail these bastards."

4

That night Carver went home to his one-bedroom apartment where he enjoyed a couple of lagers. The beer helped him relax, but he rarely overindulged. The part of him that maintained combat readiness would've been exhausting if it hadn't been drilled into a mindless habit, and a habit it had been for years. So the two beers did what they were supposed to do to help him unwind, and he woke early the next morning, eager to tackle his administrative tasks so he could get back in the field.

Carver's desk rested alongside several at the end of the kinetic division's back office where he had eyes on his entire team. There weren't enough desks for each of them, but that was okay. Their job didn't require a lot of butt-in-chair time. He made sure Juliette Morgan was prepped for the JenTech assessment, and once she was out he had the office to himself.

While finishing his report, Davis messaged with updates. He and Menendez were on their way home. Apparently Lachlan's driver, now in police custody, was a gun for hire lucky enough to have avoided a criminal record until now. That explained how he passed Lachlan's background check.

Of the two dirt bikers, one had gotten away and the other was a corpse who remained unidentified. The U-Haul was never tracked down.

It seemed the only guy who could have told anyone anything, who'd been close to Lachlan for some months and might've known what they were after, had a hole in his chest from a high-powered rifle. The shot had been ordered by Carver and, in retrospect, he didn't see any other way the showdown could have played out.

When the after-action report was complete, Carver went to Mark's office to drop it off but found the door locked and the blinds closed. Multiple voices murmured inside. A couple of the programmers whispered about a meeting with law enforcement, but they were just as much in the dark as he was. So Carver dropped the report back on his desk and took an early lunch.

When he got back the main office was empty. That wasn't unusual for the normal lunch hour, though usually a tech or two would be scarfing down instant noodles at their computer. Mark's blinds were open, but so was the door to the kinetic division. Carver approached with curiosity, again finding no employees present, but—

"Vince," called Mark, hurrying from his office, "I'm glad you're back. These—"

"People are going through my desk," he finished loudly enough for everyone to hear.

The man and woman rummaging through Carver's papers straightened and turned to face him, and Mark was clearly tense.

"Yes," he said in a conciliatory tone. "Sorry about that. I wasn't sure if you were around."

"I'm around."

Mark followed Carver into the back office. "I want you to work with them," he hastily explained.

The man looked like something out of a seventies police drama, a balding head matched by a weathered, mustached face. His gray suit was a size too large and did a poor job of hiding his excess bulk. The woman was a curiosity. Black, somehow stocky yet trim, a power skirt, a garnet leather jacket, and a resting bitch face that would make her mother blush.

"You're not police," he said to them with a frown.

The man stepped forward. "We're FBI, Mr. Carver. We'd like a word with you."

"And here I thought you wanted me to leave so you could keep rifling through my desk."

The woman bit down, jaw flexing with either resentment or chagrin. The man raised his hands in a you-got-us gesture. "Fair enough," he said. "I think we'll just talk. I'm Arthur Gunn."

"Of course you are."

Mark Marino smacked his lips. "I'd really appreciate it if we could get along here. We're all on the same side of this thing, Vince. I've been speaking with Agents Gunn and Williams and they've assured me all they ask for is cooperation." He turned to Gunn. "For your part I'd ask that you respect the privacy of our employees and their workplace. As you can imagine, we have a lot of headstrong personalities in this wing of the office. It would be great to focus that tenacity on the bad guys."

Carver eyed the agents for a long moment before turning to his friend with a sigh. "Fine with me," he said.

"Good. Now, they don't need me around so I'm gonna get out of everyone's hair. Play nice, fellas."

Mark lingered at the door a moment to see if anyone might accidentally drop a grenade, but all weapons remained holstered. He shut the door when he left.

Carver knew if the FBI had insisted on speaking to him alone, it was to see if they could find inconsistencies in his story. It was the first rule of interrogation: separate the suspects. That, right off the bat, showed the agents were suspicious of him. He supposed that was judicious in light of the two already-compromised security personnel that were involved.

What did surprise him was the speed of their visit. Walter Lachlan obviously had a lot of pull because his flight had only touched down in Asia hours ago, yet the FBI was already loitering in his office.

Carver was an imposing man and he knew it. He used his frame to brush between the two special agents, forcing them to step back without making contact. He straightened the papers on his desk until his point was sufficiently drawn out, then reclined comfortably in his Eames office chair. It was tan vintage leather, with a low back for unrestricted support. It was the only nice thing he had in his office.

"What can I do for you?" he finally asked.

The two agents glanced at each other.

"Special Agent Williams and I have spoken with Mesa PD, Falcon Field security, and Mr. Marino at length," started Agent Gunn.

"Don't forget that you read my report while I had a double cheeseburger," replied Carver, sliding it across the table on offer.

Gunn winced. "And we read your report." He took the chair beside the desk but the other remained empty as Williams chose to stand. "I spoke with Michael Davis and Herman Menendez yesterday. We reviewed their police statements and may wish to follow up with them and the other shooter who flew over with you."

"Nick Shaw," Carver disclosed, though he was sure they already had the information. "He assisted me in escorting the principal to San Jose International. I can make him available to you, as well as Davis and Menendez, starting tomorrow."

He nodded. "That would be appreciated."

The man seemed congenial enough, if a little listless, like he had something to say but didn't know how to say it. Agent Williams, meanwhile, watched him like a hawk might a field mouse, quiet and from a distance, but ready to swoop in at any moment.

"It's my understanding," Gunn continued, "that you were the team leader out of state, handling all security to and from the airport."

Carver shook his head. "I led Lachlan's personal escort section. That's the outer cordon around his entourage when he's on the move. All residential security was handled by the

CPS house teams, including the aircraft, two fabrication plants, and the principal's desert residence."

Gunn nodded. "Sure, I got that. You're saying you were only responsible for Walter Lachlan during specific limited periods of transport."

"That's correct."

"Why do you think that was?"

"Excuse me?"

"Why do you think Walter only used you for limited periods?" Gunn clarified.

Carver blinked at the agents, unsure what they were getting at. He spoke slowly and with emphasis. "I'm not sure, Agent Gunn. That sounds like a question for Walter Lachlan."

"Speculate," Williams said tersely.

They locked eyes.

The FBI agents were slow-playing him, which was why his answers were dry and innocuous. Apparently they weren't ready to give him the goods just yet. Carver decided it didn't hurt to play along a bit.

"Well," he started, "on the face of it, Lachlan's moving into new territory and is taking additional precautions. The fabrication plants are a new project, still under construction, and his desert residence is barely moved in. I assume it's a case of his reach outgrowing his army."

"Army?" prodded Williams.

"Just an expression. I probably should have said arm. He only has so many security personnel at his various properties. Winding up new teams takes time. For all I know we were a temporary supplementary measure. There's also the consideration that Lachlan's working on something especially sensitive."

Agent Gunn nodded. "What do you know about that?"

"Not much. Some kind of prototype chip. I think he called it a wafer."

"Is that what was in the briefcase?"

"That's my understanding. Apparently the chip is cutting edge, something to do with nanometers, though I wouldn't know the difference between ten and two."

"I hear ya," replied Gunn with what Carver believed was forced camaraderie. "Those new desert facilities aren't spun up yet but they're very important. They're part of a strategic joint venture between CPS and Taipei Semiconductors."

Carver nodded carefully. He was beginning to understand why the FBI was interested. The agents seemed to be waiting for a reply. Carver took a long breath and said, "Just to head you off, my team and I have no knowledge of Lachlan's dealings or technology. We weren't allowed inside the plants and were never invited into the residence. Although Dynamic Security Solutions would no doubt like a contract managing Lachlan's info security, we don't currently have one. I'm in charge of physical protection."

"Let's talk about that then," Williams broke in, walking around the empty chair and finally sitting beside her partner. "Why did you get into private security?"

This was starting to feel like a bad job interview. "Isn't being good at something reason enough?"

Agent Williams barely hid a contemptuous snort. "Is that

your only consideration? Anything for a paycheck?"

It was obvious she didn't like him or what he did. It wasn't a new attitude for Carver, especially from law enforcement. "Special Agent Williams," he stated with measure, "there are over two million full-time security workers in the US today." He ticked his fingers. "We provide access control, patrol, and protection services. It's a three-hundred-and-fifty-billion-dollar-a-year industry, and the private sector accounts for eighty percent of that."

Agent Gunn was nodding as if he wanted to move on. Williams said, "And Dynamic Security Solutions is your piece of the pie. You didn't start the company but you founded the kinetic division a year ago. What would you say you bring to the table?"

Carver shrugged matter-of-factly. "High-end special operations expertise and protection." His answer was confident, not so much a boast as the unequivocal truth.

"It probably pays well, if you don't mind me saying."

If she intended to ruffle him by infringing on personal matters, it wouldn't work. "I get by," he answered, "and I don't mind."

She crossed her fingers in her lap. "You're not just paid well, you're a minority owner."

He gave a knowing nod. "Moving into kinetics was a whole new ballgame for DSS. I'm not just throwing bodies at existing problems. The company underwent a marked evolution when I came aboard, and Mark Marino recognizes that. INFOSEC, firewalls, and vaults can only do so much. If you want to be an elite security company today, you must have the capacity for violence."

She simpered. "Spoken like a true soldier."

Carver wasn't sure whether she thought she was making a point or not. Thankfully, Gunn took the baton.

"Nothing wrong with that," he said. "Special Agent Williams is just teasing. She knows I'm an Army man myself. Let's talk about your military career." He pulled out his phone and referred to his notes.

"We should start earlier than that," suggested Williams. "After graduating high school, your best friend was killed in a drunk drag racing accident. You ran away and enlisted as soon as you turned eighteen."

Carver bit down. "I didn't run away," he said strongly.

"Let's all relax," tempered Gunn. "I imagine this is a sensitive topic that has no bearing on this interview, so we'll leave it alone."

He looked to Carver for agreement. Carver returned a single nod and Gunn continued.

"No college. You joined the Army at the bottom where you deployed to Africa. As private first class you saved your sergeant's life during an incident involving insurgents outside Addis Ababa, Ethiopia. But as corporal your promising career stalled due to disciplinary issues."

Carver blinked evenly. "My record is spotless."

Gunn canted his head in concession. "Our investigation goes beyond the public record, Mr. Carver. We spoke with Major Gunderson as Fort Jackson."

Carver scoffed. "He's a major now? No comment."

Agent Gunn studied him a moment before continuing

down his list. "This... clash of personalities, let's call it, might have had something to do with your volunteering for the 75th Ranger Regiment and deploying to Iraq, where your star shone once again. You'd barely earned your paratrooper wings when you transferred to the 1st Special Forces Operational Detachment-Delta. How'd you manage that so fast?"

"Every once in a blue moon the Army actually recognizes aptitude."

"Not my experience," he laughed, "but maybe you're on to something. Great marks in the Operators Training Course. Proficient in close-quarters battle, close target reconnaissance, free-fall parachuting, offensive driving..."

Carver leaned back while Gunn listed his accolades. It seemed overly thorough for the FBI, and he wondered at the point, but he did enjoy Agent Williams shifting uncomfortably while avoiding eye contact. It was as if she refused to give him his due.

"In your six years with Delta," Gunn went on, "you deployed all over the Middle East, Asia, and Africa. It was a storybook career until you took two bullets and retired."

Carver's hand massaged his left bicep before he realized what he was doing. The two agents noticed the action, and his answer was almost defensive. "I served my country."

"And you figured you were done?" asked Williams pointedly.

"I was sick of acting on bad intel and decided to strike out on my own, with lower stakes where friends don't die."

"You're referring to Sergeant First Class Driscoll," she

returned. "He was one of your best friends too, if I understand correctly."

"He was," said Carver with more heat. "And he was a great operative, wasted in the shitshow the Middle East became."

"No hard feelings?" she pressed.

Carver bit down the implication and spoke with a gravelly voice. "We knew what we signed up for, but my time was done. I almost lost my arm. Now I'm a civilian just like everybody else. I've earned that right."

"Nobody's saying you haven't," rejoined Agent Gunn. "A Bronze Star, a Soldier's Medal, a Silver Star, even a Purple Heart for your injury. Some people might call you a hero."

"Would you mind unpuckering your lips from my asshole and quit the good-cop, bad-cop routine?"

Gunn smiled, but Williams was unreadable. They conferred by trading a silent glance and Gunn nodded, his decision made. "I'm satisfied."

"You can't be serious, Arthur. He's a gorilla."

Agent Williams had shamelessly made her counterargument in Carver's presence. He normally would've objected, but he was too angry and curious to stop them.

Agent Gunn sighed. "This is my call, Laney, and I'm calling it. Now read him in."

5

"Do you know," began Special Agent Williams, "what the world's most important natural resource is?"

Carver frowned. The FBI agents had turned some kind of corner, but he wasn't sure what it was. Williams certainly wasn't thrilled about the development, dutifully going through the motions with a veneer of irritation. Carver proceeded ahead with whatever they were proceeding with.

"Oil?"

"Sand," she answered with a cock of her head. "Oil had a good run. It dominated the twentieth century, but the twenty-first is about sand. It's needed to reinforce eroding beaches and to build islands. You've probably read about how much sand the world uses for concrete and the predicted shortages in the future. You even need it for fracking in order to get to that oil you're talking about."

Carver waited for her to get to the point.

"But the most vital application of sand is for computer chips. Silicon is the second most abundant element in the Earth's crust, after oxygen, and controlling its supply is vital for a healthy and continuing economy in the digital age."

She took a momentous breath and Carver asked, "Are we

still allowed to build sand castles with it?"

Agent Gunn snickered. "No reason to be a tough guy. Have you heard of SEMICON Taiwan?"

Carver was sick of the trivia questions so he just shook his head.

"It's a global meeting of the minds in the industry. It's why you escorted Walter Lachlan to a jet bound for Asia." He pulled his sleeve back and checked his watch, which must've been an old habit because he still held his phone. "The big man landed in Taipei six hours ago."

Carver nodded as he put the pieces together: the Arizona joint venture with Taipei Semiconductors, the prototype wafer, and the trip to Taiwan. "When's the conference?"

"It starts Wednesday and runs to the weekend. As with a lot of these events, all types of people show up. Exhibitors, speakers, press, consumers, managers, engineers—"

"I get the picture."

He gave a single nod. "The point being that most of the pivotal meetings take place behind closed doors, away from the rabble, where, say, a billionaire could meet and deal with the CEO of the world's leading semiconductor company. Microchips, Mr. Carver, made from that silica sand that is so in demand, are a valuable geopolitical commodity. Just look around." He waved his smartphone before slipping it into his jacket pocket. "They're in phones and data hubs, toy trucks and hypersonic aircraft, personal computers, pacemakers, thermostats, and just about every other device you can think of. Ten years ago I thought it unnecessary to have a computer chip in my coffee maker. Today there's one in my toothbrush."

"You must have some teeth," said Carver.

Williams snorted with impatience. "At least try to wrap your head around the strategic importance, Mr. Carver. While the US played war in the Middle East, China has been slowly but steadily gaining a leg up in production dominance. Now that we've caught on to the problem, we're stuck playing catch-up."

Carver burned slightly at the pointed critique of his involvement in the Middle East, but he understood the gist. "Too much worry about oil, not enough about sand."

"That's exactly right," she said. "Covid only exacerbated the need for technological autonomy. That's why Taipei Semiconductors, in coordination with the US government, and Walter Lachlan, spurred by the Chips for America bill, are building a twelve-billion-dollar facility in the Arizona desert."

Agent Williams was, in essence, saying that not only had his job involved protecting company interests, but US interests as well, and Walter Lachlan was at the head of that list. "Billionaires are important," Carver conceded. "So are microchips and nanometers."

She saw he was keeping up and ignored the flippant remark. "Every iteration to make chips smaller and more powerful takes billions in investment capital. More and more countries and suppliers are choosing not to compete, and the field continues to thin. But Taipei Semiconductors possesses an unrivaled stranglehold on the market, and now they're breaking ground in the US and Japan."

Agent Gunn leaned forward. "How do you think that sits with Big Brother?"

Carver frowned again. "China?"

He pointed a finger gun. "Got it in one."

Agent Williams wouldn't do anything so personable as lean in, so she sat up straighter. "What do you think, Mr. Carver, is China's most important import?"

"I'm not gonna say oil again."

She flashed a thin smile. "Microchips. Most of them end up being exported. China's main contribution to the market has historically been testing and assembly, just one of the stops between A and Z. For the last twenty years, they've been aggressively maneuvering to change that. They've injected billions in cash and subsidies. The Made in China strategy aims to meet eighty percent of domestic chip demand by 2030. But China's hit a wall with US sanctions. They missed their 2020 interim goal of meeting forty percent of demand. Flagship chip makers are going bust. The CCP's draconian leaders are getting desperate."

Carver swallowed. According to Special Agents Gunn and Williams, China was responsible for the attempted kidnapping of Walter Lachlan. Not a disgruntled employee or a competing business interest, but a sovereign state.

"This is all well and good," he said, despite the bleak outlook being neither, "but I'm no geopolitical strategist and this isn't the Department of Commerce." He tapped on the armrest of his Eames. "We have nicer chairs here." Carver stared at the agents for a minute. They had hit another pivotal turn in the conversation and were hesitating.

"Then again," he added in a light bulb moment, "you're not the FBI, are you?"

Agent Gunn wiped his bald head with a handkerchief and laughed it off, neither confirming nor denying. Williams was a different story. She went cold and rigid, eyes lasered on Carver. She hid the reaction well enough, but it was a reaction all the same. The signs pointed to him being in the right ballpark, and it was a small park.

"Come on, Mr. Carver," chuckled Gunn, "what are we talking about here?"

The former operative leaned his elbows onto the surface of his desk as he moved in for the kill. "I was in Delta for six years running off-the-books ops, but then you already know that. It's probably why you're talking to me now. I've worked with some of your operatives in the field. You're CIA."

Their blank faces offered no rebuttal.

He leaned back on the firm leather. "SAC already tried to recruit me. I turned them down and went private for a reason."

The not-so-Special Agent Williams clicked her tongue. "We're not trying to recruit you anymore."

Carver worked his jaw. Her response was a borderline admission that they were not only CIA but part of the Special Activities Center. SAC is the action arm of the CIA's Directorate of Operations, the division for covert and paramilitary ops. Their activities range from various psyops, economic and cyberwarfare, to targeted tactical strikes. Ground Branch puts boots on the ground in small or solo

teams for supreme operational agility, adaptability, and—
perhaps most importantly—deniability.

Carver didn't impress easily, but SAC operatives were,
without a doubt, some of the finest special forces in the
world. Which wasn't to say that these two officers were part
of that elite brotherhood. More likely Gunn was in charge
of operations and Williams was a case officer. In other
words, a handler.

"Are you telling me in so many words," asked Carver
diplomatically, "that my team has somehow stumbled into
your international investigation?"

"Not into," corrected Gunn, "but alongside. We're
giving you the opportunity to take part."

Carver's head shook idly. His heart rate increased. His
body was going through a process not dissimilar to readying
for combat. "You have my attention. Now let's stop
perusing the menu and fucking order dinner already."

Gunn smiled. "I knew I liked you." He turned to his
partner. "Didn't I tell you, Laney? This is the guy."

She took a stilted breath but held her tongue.

Gunn shrugged, checked that the communal office area
was empty and that the door was still shut, and then shifted
in his chair to a more comfortable position. "Intelligence
has come through the wire that China is looking to acquire
new technology." He spoke like it was inconsequential, just
an everyday trifle like his coffee not being hot enough. "You
and I both know the methods the CCP uses to achieve
technical advancements, and it has nothing to do with
blood, sweat, and tears. They isolate the market leader and

copy, steal, or both."

"This is serious stuff," interjected Williams. "The FBI has several thousand counter-intelligence operations ongoing at any given time. Over half of those relate to China."

Gunn nodded. "And they're not all digital. We have so many American companies working in China operating under Chinese law using Chinese workers... It's a sieve. And you have to understand. In their culture, cheating to get ahead isn't looked down on. They have no moral objection to it. Either you're savvy enough to get away with it or you're held back."

"You're talking about the contents of the briefcase," deduced Carver. "Except Lachlan reiterated that the prototypes were of little value without access to his network."

Gunn looked to his partner. She crossed her arms and didn't meet Carver's eyes, but Williams was a trooper and pressed forward. "The design and manufacturing of semiconductors occurs all over the globe, but the vast majority of chips, no matter their country of origin, depend on American software. Aside from US-led sectors like proprietary chip design and manufacturing machinery, software is vitally important. Intellectual property is the lifeblood of the semiconductor industry, and that's what the CCP is targeting."

It all seemed a little far-fetched, that China would attempt to kidnap an American billionaire to get him to spill secrets. Yet someone *had* hired the mercenaries and helicopter. It didn't strike Carver as the CCP's standard operating procedure, but maybe, as Williams had said, they were desperate.

"I assume you want me to look into the attackers?" asked Carver.

Arthur Gunn shook his head. "It goes deeper than the kidnapping. We have it on good authority that someone stateside is selling secrets."

Carver frowned as he pondered the implications. If the Chinese were buying stolen secrets, then it wouldn't have been them behind the attack. The people getting their hands dirty, it followed, were the group that wanted to do the selling. That ticked his concern about it being unlikely for the CCP to attempt such a brazen attack on American soil.

His thoughts turned as he realized the scope of the CIA's investigation, looking into leaks and bad actors.

"So this is why you put a magnifying glass on my career history? I was under investigation?!?" He was angered by the idea. Accusing him of treason was a personal affront, even if it had only been suggested.

"Take it easy," said Gunn. "We reviewed all recent contacts with Lachlan and CPS. That includes the fabs in Arizona, his engineers, members of his security staff, anyone even remotely tied to the Taiwanese joint venture—"

"And my company."

Gunn pressed his lips out and swiped at his mustache.

"How do you know it isn't me?" asked Carver.

Williams took a strained breath and finally met his gaze.

"We've decided, based on your behavior and record, that the leak would literally be every single other person in DSS before it was you." It looked like the admission caused her physical pain.

Carver didn't know how to respond to that, except he couldn't say they were wrong.

"Not to mention," she added matter-of-factly, "it was you and your team who foiled the kidnapping. The way it went down, you easily could've let him be taken if you were part of it."

"If it's any consolation," offered Gunn, "the Taiwanese, and even Lachlan himself, are the most likely culprits. But we can't take anything for granted. Not with the intelligence we have. We need to move slowly and vet everyone every step of the way."

Carver worked his jaw, finally starting to buy what they were selling. "Does Mark Marino know?"

Gunn's face momentarily tensed. "He thinks we're FBI investigating the kidnapping."

"You want DSS cooperation," stated Carver plainly. "He's the owner of the company."

"Yes," said Williams curtly, "but his financial stake is more pronounced than yours. His record is less exemplary, and he's been embedded in the private sector much longer. He has certain..."—she took a diplomatic breath—"conflicts of interest."

"Just say what you mean," Carver grumbled.

"She doesn't mean anything," Gunn said with a glare at his case officer. He sighed and raised an assuaging palm.

"Look... It could be anything. It could be nothing. But Walter Lachlan is the most important client DSS has ever courted. Where would Mr. Marino's loyalties lie?"

There was no certain response to that. Lachlan was a notable billionaire in the security company's backyard. Mark had been itching to sign him for years. The kinetic division had been the next big hope for securing that contract, and it had succeeded. This Arizona job had come a year after formation, with the allure of more handshakes in the future.

The security business is built around protecting its clients. What happens when that client is a traitor?

"Lachlan is a paycheck," explained Williams, striking unerringly close to his own thoughts. "Would Mr. Marino be willing to forgo that? Maybe he looks the other way, or maybe he refuses to believe what's in front of his eyes."

"When you've been in this business long enough," added Gunn, "you learn to keep the circle as small as possible. That means you. Not Mark, who's stuck in the office anyway. Not Nick Shaw and the rest of your team. Just you. And it goes without saying, but especially not Walter Lachlan. You can't rightly walk up to him and ask if he's selling secrets. That would not only compromise the operation but put your life in danger."

Carver grunted. "I think I can handle one overconfident billionaire."

"It's not the money man you need to worry about, it's who his money can send after you. We have to consider that Lachlan himself was responsible for the attack."

Carver blinked. "You think the principal tried to kidnap

himself?"

"We don't think," asserted Williams. "We consider possibilities."

"But this one's ridiculous. Lachlan could have been hurt. His own men were killed."

Gunn canted his head, playing devil's advocate. "Maybe he intended the brunt of the attack to go against a newly hired outside security team. A team he underestimated. The charges meant to disable your vehicles weren't lethal."

"They were shooting real bullets."

"And nine out of ten security teams would never have reached that point."

Williams nodded in agreement. "They diverted or knocked out two of your three vehicles, Mr. Carver, and nearly got the last one. You barely got Lachlan out of there as it was."

He grimaced. The planning and precision of the attack had been tightly orchestrated. As team leader that fell on him. It was difficult to think about how close the situation really was, but there was no denying the truth.

"I don't believe it," said Carver resolutely.

Gunn shrugged. "Lachlan knows his country is relying on him. The spectacle could have been a means of absolving him of blame."

"I saw his eyes. There was real fear in them."

"Maybe the whole thing got out of hand," he returned. "The convoy was meant to be stranded. The helicopter extraction would've been smooth. And then all of a sudden he's in the middle of gunfire. Who wouldn't be scared?"

Point.

This was what happened when you made a living as a spook. You were constantly paranoid about everything and everyone. It was part of the reason Carver had finally gone private, and now he was right back in the middle of the CIA's mind games.

He took several measured breaths. A man like him was trained to act on information quickly. Decisions aren't always perfect, but they're a hell of a lot better than indecision. Carver wasn't sure if he wholly believed the lengths Lachlan would go to, but he decided to hear them out.

"Okay," he said, dropping all pretense of further sniping. If he would be going along with this, it wouldn't be productive to gripe about it. "Why are you bringing me in on this thing?"

"Because you can help us," said Gunn.

"Help you how? Investigate in Arizona? Get my team ready?" Despite his intent to play nice, his questions grew heated as he realized the officers had no intention of answering them. "I'm asking for specifics. How the hell am I supposed to help if you don't share?"

The three of them stared for a stretched moment. Instead of previous silences, where Gunn and Williams had hesitated on how to proceed, they were holding firm. This time their minds were made up. They were just waiting for Carver to come to terms with it.

"Give us a little credit," Williams eventually added with a smile that carried a not inconsequential amount of bite.

"And a little faith. We are the CIA, after all."

"That's what I'm worried about." Carver took a breath. "Is this legal, what we're discussing?"

"SAC operates in a gray area, but it's legal," answered Gunn.

"You're not supposed to operate on US soil."

"We aren't. As far as I'm aware, you're not employed by the CIA."

"That's the type of roundabout answer I'd expect from you guys."

Instead of taking offense, Laney Williams smiled. "Our motto is *tertia optio*, Mr. Carver. Third option. When diplomacy fails and military force is out of the question, we must turn to covert action. As a former operator of Detachment-Delta, I'm not telling you anything you don't already know. We can only tell you what you need to know, when you need to know it. For now, we just need you to tell us if you're in or out."

Carver didn't wait long. "I'm in," he said, even if he sounded grumpy about it.

Gunn clapped his hands in his lap. "Glad to hear it." He rose from the chair and started for the door. "You're doing your country a service, son."

"So what do you want from me?" Carver asked.

"We'll be in touch," said Williams before standing and following Gunn to the door. She didn't look amped to have him on board, but she had accepted the eventuality before ever walking into his office.

"Wait," he protested again. "What do I do until then?"

"Do nothing," iterated Gunn as he retreated. "Go about your day, business as usual. You don't need us to tell you how to do your job. The reason we're talking to you is because you're good at it."

Now that he was snagged on their line, they were being stingy. They were toying with him, making him spin and tire himself out before the coup de grace. He stood and raised his voice. "You guys have a funny way of doing business."

Gunn filed out the door but Williams paused and sighed. She returned to the desk so her words wouldn't be overheard by nosy coworkers.

"Keep something in mind, Mr. Carver, if you ever question your decision to cooperate. You might not like us, and you have your reasons. I, personally, am not thrilled to be working with someone who amounts to a mercenary. But we're both in the security business."

"We're not the same," he replied with some fire.

"You're right about that," she returned coolly. "And welcome to the suck, because you've just been upgraded from private security to national security."

6

The remainder of the workday proceeded with quiet apprehension. How was someone supposed to return to normal after a conversation like that? But Carver found it wasn't all that difficult once he started ticking off his responsibilities.

He handed his after-action report to Mark, and they discussed the various legal and contractual ramifications. Carver played down the visit of Agents Gunn and Williams, even as he felt like a heel for preserving their cover. He didn't like lying to his friend but figured he better get used to it. There'd be more lies to more friends before the day was out.

Given the growing stakes surrounding the contract, Carver personally picked up Davis and Menendez from the airport. They had little insight into the previous day's events and the cops hadn't divulged anything of interest. Carver sat in on their debrief with Mark before putting them to work on their reports and instructing them to take the rest of the week off.

Nick Shaw wasn't so lucky. Because he had fled Arizona with Carver, the police also wanted to talk to him. He passed by the office with his paperwork before Carver let him go, but was mandated to be in the office first thing in the morning. They would fly back to the desert together. The final item on the agenda was confirming their flights the next afternoon.

Tired from a day of exhaustive overthinking, Carver headed home. He slipped into a surprisingly deep and relaxing sleep and woke the next morning refreshed. It was almost as if his body knew he needed it. Carver showered and picked up a breakfast sandwich at the local bagel place before heading into the office for another boring day of admin work. It made no difference whether he was debriefing with Mark or Mesa Police, or if it occurred in San Jose or Arizona. Downtime was downtime.

His first clue that the day wouldn't go according to plan was Mark excitedly herding him into his office. He was moving so fast there wasn't time to sit.

"Vince," he proclaimed, slightly exasperated and out of breath. Over the years Mark had replaced too many breakfast eggs with donuts. "Things are moving fast. The police canceled your interview. I've booked your new flight." He handed Carver an envelope.

"New flight?" he asked as he slipped it open.

"You thought I couldn't do it, but I did it. I got in touch with Lachlan last night and worked my magic. We have an extension."

Carver examined the ticket. It was a commercial flight, first class. The destination was Taipei. Mark had struck like a starving cheetah, though Carver wondered if the magic had been his or the CIA's. He couldn't say he minded the intelligence agency's involvement. This got him off the hook for interviewing with police. He begrudgingly admitted they weren't entirely useless.

"What's the contract?"

"The gist of it is this," explained Mark. "Walter lost his head of security and a pair of close protection officers who tried to kidnap him. He had his own advance team fly out, but his escort is understaffed. More significantly, he's lost faith and trust in them. Walter's come to the conclusion that the men with him aren't up to task."

"And you assured him I was."

"Hooah, soldier." Mark grinned. "Always be closing. It's what I do."

"I would expect nothing less."

"You're to fly in, coordinate with whoever's heading up his security staff now, and tail your principal."

"In a foreign country."

"You've done foreign work for years, and you know Asia."

"Asia's a big place."

"This is the age of globalization."

"Does that mean I'll be armed?"

Mark huffed. "I doubt Walter will be in any danger. Taiwan's very safe. Private ownership of guns is minuscule and dwindling. If you ignore the aboriginal population who use them for hunting, it's on the order of a firearm per two thousand people."

"It sounds like you're trying to convince me I don't need

a weapon." The statistics were little comfort to a trained Delta operative. "Our advance party will need to be on the ball. I can check with Morgan."

"Juliette's in court all week. You know that. This is a one-man job on foreign soil attached to a team already in place. You'll rely on their resources."

Carver scoffed. "That's exactly what I'm worried about. I get that we want this contract, and we can't help it being last second, but my hands will be tied over there if fly in alone."

"I hear you, Vince, but the kidnapping attempt is over with. The bad guys showed their hand and came up short. You're just in Taiwan to make Lachlan feel safe, restore his confidence in us, and hopefully get him to sign a more permanent contract."

"I don't plan for the best, Mark. I plan for the worst."

He took a harried breath. "Come on, don't be a stick in the mud now. It took everything I had to smooth things out with Walter."

"I can't properly do my job if I'm glued to Lachlan. I like to roam. You know that."

"So what do you suggest?"

The two were still standing. The discussion had progressed enough that it seemed too late to sit, so Carver turned to the window and watched a data tech file to her desk with a latte. She was the first to arrive for the morning, though she wasn't alone. A few of the overnight staff were still at their desks. Security doesn't take nights and weekends.

"I assume we're to shadow Lachlan through SEMICON

Taiwan?"

"Yes, for the week," Mark confirmed. "And at his hotel, and wherever else he goes. This is 24/7 personal protection until he's back on his jet. This is like Arizona except you have full scope. Walter's confident of his safety in Silicon Valley; it's everywhere else he's worried about. All you're doing is supplementing his team with a capable operative."

Carver worked his jaw as he considered the mandate. He was to be an extra bodyguard in addition to whatever PPOs were already on staff. Lachlan likely viewed the job simply: hire the guy who saved him once just in case he needed saving again.

The head of the kinetic division didn't see things in the same terms. Despite Mark's optimistic outlook, as a security operator, Carver had to assume the billionaire was an active target. And, once again, he had to rely on an already existing staff. One that might be further compromised. Then there were the added hiccups of operating on foreign soil. This wasn't at all like Arizona. There was conference security, hotel security, and a completely different set of local laws.

In short, the logistics were terrible. But then, if things were always perfect there wouldn't be a need for security in the first place. Every job comes with quirks and difficulties to surmount. Complaining about reality doesn't get you anywhere. Accepting the truth and planning for contingencies is the only practical way forward. So Carver pondered the absolute minimum ask to ensure the contract ran smoothly.

"I need Shaw and Davis on the team," he pronounced.

"Walter doesn't want a whole crew, Vince."

"It's not a full crew, and it's not negotiable. If Lachlan wants round-the-clock protection, we'll need to take shifts."

"That's what the rest of his detail is for."

"They're window dressing. Look, we'll obviously rely on them a great deal, but we can't just hand Lachlan off, say goodnight, and see him in the morning. We'll have one man shadow him at the conference during the day and the other take the night shift in the hotel. That'll leave me to coordinate as a roamer. It's the only way we get proper coverage of the principal. Even then it's thin."

Mark wanted to object but saw the determination on Carver's face. The boss blew out a lungful of air and said, "Fine. I'll write off the expense as goodwill. If we're trying to make a good impression, it wouldn't do to be understaffed."

"That's right. And we'll need guns."

"They're very strict with their permits over there."

"Seems to me, if anybody could grease the wheels, it's an American billionaire with a government contract and a legitimate need for security. It's a long flight." Carver checked the ticket. "Thirteen hours. I have confidence in you."

He scoffed. "I'll do my best. But it would be a handgun, not that Tavor you're so fond of. You're not in Delta anymore and you're not touching down in Iraq. Any more unreasonable demands?"

Carver grinned. "Just the two."

"Good, 'cause I have one of my own. Get in Lachlan's

ear. Remind him that kinetics isn't all we do. If he thinks you're good, tell him about our data vault service."

"He'll get the full advertising brochure."

"Thanks, smart-ass. Now get out of here. You have two men to brief, and I need to buy additional tickets and pull some strings with Taipei. And no guarantees on the guns."

"Guarantees?" muttered Carver on his way out. "No such thing."

* * *

San Francisco International Airport was about half an hour north of San Jose via the 101. Carver, Shaw, and a disgruntled Davis, who was supposed to have the week off, boarded through the United departure gate. The nonstop flight on the Boeing 777 would take off Monday afternoon and land on Tuesday evening, the night before the conference started. It wasn't a lot of time to get their ducks in order, and they had to spend a whole lot more of it confined to close quarters.

Luckily their seats were first class. Carver and Shaw sat in the aisle across from each other, but Davis was two rows ahead due to the last-second ticket purchase.

"Better for us," chuckled Shaw loud enough for the outcast man to hear. "His snoring will be worse than the turbulence. I guarantee it."

"That's not what your momma says," relayed the big man, looking back with a gleaming set of white teeth. "Then again, we don't exactly sleep, if you know what I mean."

The elderly woman in the row between them knew precisely what he meant, and she stared at him with aghast disapproval.

"You come up with that all by yourself?" returned Shaw. He flagged down the passing stewardess. "Hello, darlin'. My associate and I"—he signaled to Carver—"will have bourbons. And my friend up there will take whatever you have with the most bubbles."

Davis sucked his teeth. "Champagne's a dignified drink, man."

Shaw erupted in boisterous laughter that proved infectious. Carver smothered a chuckle and attempted to ignore the man-children. "I'm sorry, ma'am," he offered the flight attendant. "It's their first high school field trip."

She smirked. "I'd like to see whatever school they're pumping you boys out of." She patted Shaw's shoulder and stepped away.

He straightened and brushed his wild beard. "Hey man, how do I look?" he whispered.

"Like a rabid mountain man."

He nodded. "Good."

Carver had met Shaw on a private security gig in Syria, of all places. In an environment like that, rabid mountain men were necessary. But while Shaw was a little rough around the edges, Carver wouldn't have him any other way. He was good at what he did, reliable, and he wore his heart on his sleeve. When Carver had founded the kinetic division of Dynamic Security Systems one year prior, Nick Shaw had been his first phone call.

The rest of his staff were good people too. When it came to tactics, awareness, and firefights, having a trusted team was the only way to get through. That was why he regretted telling Juliette Morgan to take all the time she needed. Sure, at that moment he hadn't been secretly working for a US spy agency. Now that he was, he needed all hands on deck.

Morgan running an advance team could give them the lay of the land, check them in, get them guns and equipment and a schedule. Without that kind of support, they were flying blind.

Which was only exacerbated by the CIA's involvement. It wasn't lost on Carver that they had apparently changed his agenda without having the decency to give him a heads up. He was positive they had a hand in his trip to Taipei. It wasn't Mark but them who were in Lachlan's ear. Had they merely suggested he take on extra security or had they outright dropped his name?

In order to find the puppet, you had to follow the strings being pulled.

Carver snorted. Here he was waxing philosophical about puppets, when every soldier since time immemorial was nothing more than a chess piece. He was in the military life all over again, except now he was told to go about his business as usual. Carver purportedly had full autonomy to do his job. So although he grumbled about it, he had a protection detail to plan. And with the extra hands he'd convinced Mark to send along, Carver would have plenty of agility to handle the job *and* the CIA.

At least, that was his hope.

Until then he could either drive himself mad going over the possibilities or watch a couple of half-interesting movies, eat a spartan dinner, and enjoy his second bourbon before reclining, putting the pillow under his neck, and trying to get some rest.

7

Taoyuan International was a sleek airport of long, glistening halls. Utilitarian braces supported the massive bulk of the roof: an elegant bowed pergola of open white shutters that revealed the sky. The sun streaming through almost tricked you into believing you were outside, but the barrage of cold conditioned air gave up the score.

Next to the immense scale, the first thing Carver noticed was the security officer watching them. Not because he was so memorable or distinct, though maybe precisely because he was neither of those things. A middle-aged Taiwanese man in a suit among a sea of Taiwanese men in suits. The airport was only pleasantly crowded but, while it seemed like everyone else amid the hustle had some place to be or something to do, this man was firmly planted at a far counter pretending to look at his phone.

Normally this behavior in an airport didn't warrant suspicion. The restless, the bored, the loungers—they were a common sight. Onlookers waited to greet loved ones arriving from long flights. But the families waiting on relatives huddled together and eagerly scanned the crowds.

Gazes flitted quickly from person to person until they hit their target and hesitant smiles broke into full-on gleams.

This man didn't seem particularly interested in the crowd. Instead of pushing forward, he waited back. For a brief but obtrusive moment, he'd locked onto Carver and Shaw and Davis, not unlike the others except missing the smile. Now he was attempting to be inconspicuous by keeping his head down and avoiding direct eye contact.

...Or he was playing Sudoku.

It was the curse of the job, Carver mused. After years working covertly in Delta, he was primed to subconsciously scan for any and all threats. The skill had paid off twenty times over, but the heightened awareness could be exhausting.

He reminded himself that their presence in this country was above board. His supposition that the CIA had arranged this little outing hadn't been confirmed. Anyone from the outside looking in would agree that Lachlan's desire for increased security was prudent.

So what if a businessman had noticed a few American tourists in Taiwan?

There were other men greeting new arrivals without smiles on their faces too, though their motives were more apparent. They were business professionals, drivers with neutral faces brandishing signs with their clients' names. Carver was surprised, on inspection, to find a Caucasian man with a sign that read "Dynamic Security Solutions."

"I'm Vince Carver," he said on approach, offering a hand. "I didn't know to expect anyone."

The man seemed startled by the sight of the operator. He was a little older than Carver but still young. The blond crew cut signified some degree of professionalism or discipline, but he didn't carry himself like a military man. His head swiveled between the three of them before finally settling on Carver's hand, which he took.

"Harry Sparroway. I'm Walter Lachlan's interim security coordinator."

Carver's eyebrows betrayed his surprise. "Interim?"

"Yes, erm, in the aftermath of recent events."

"Ah," was all that needed to be said. Carver immediately understood the situation. Lachlan had lost his security leadership two days ago. Sparroway was the next guy in line, at least in a pinch, and the man didn't exactly inspire confidence. Hence DSS getting the call.

Carver eyed the Taiwanese man at the distant counter. Once again his gaze retreated back to his phone.

"There are three of you?" asked Sparroway, still slightly frazzled.

"That's my count," nudged Shaw, "but I enjoyed some refreshments on the plane so I could be seeing triple."

"Didn't you get the email?" replied Carver.

Lachlan's man jerked his phone from his pocket, exasperated. "Oh, I saw the old one when we first brought you on. I thought the new flight confirmation was only for you, but now I see the additional two."

"Does that mean we didn't get three carry permits?"

"One sec here..." Sparroway fumbled through a list of emails. "I didn't handle those... Nope, it looks like those

came through. When you get to the hotel, I'll set you up."
He winced. "There *is* a problem, though. We didn't fly in
with an arsenal. We only have one sidearm for you."

Carver blinked patiently. "But there are three of us."

His phone fled back into the pocket. "What can I say?
We'll try to work it out."

"Does your team have extra?"

"They don't, and the pistols they do have are vital. I
won't ask them to surrender them."

Sparroway wasn't a total pushover, at least. Carver
worked his jaw and glanced at the Taiwanese man. He had
vanished into the sparse crowd, which took some skill.

"I'm sorry," continued Sparroway. "We're still getting
up to speed here, you understand. Let's go get your
luggage."

As the crew followed, Carver caught Shaw's eye roll.
Neither of them had much patience for people in over their
head. Sparroway's first mistake was made before their arrival
and it put them, and their principal, at risk. Carver remained
silent while they walked, keeping an eye out for their
mystery man. He didn't want to say anything in front of
Sparroway, opting instead to discreetly point him out to
Shaw and Davis. Only to do that, he had to spot him again.
Unfortunately, a wake of traffic followed them towards
baggage claim. It would be the same exiting the airport.

They retrieved their bags. Enough for a week except for
the firearms. Carver slung his duffel over his shoulder and
the group headed outside where a wall of humid air
enveloped them. Sparroway led them to a running Toyota

4Runner. There were two additional men in the vehicle, one in the front and the other in the back.

Carver paused at the door, finding the escort strange. He realized they were armed while his people weren't.

"You, uh, have credentials?" he bluntly asked.

Sparroway jerked his head. "What? Sure..."

He dug into his wallet while the man in the back seat watched closely. Carver noticed Shaw and Davis tensing, keying off his own suspicions. Sparroway pulled a card from a small stack and handed it over. It was a slick thing of bright blue, not paper but plastic, with rounded edges and a QR code on the back. Harry Sparroway, Advance Security Liaison, Crystal Processor Systems.

"My official title doesn't reflect my current role," he stammered.

Carver eyed the group and nodded. They seemed more clueless than hostile, and there was ample space in the SUV. He loaded in, aware that his team would now remain alert just in case. The 4Runner maneuvered through airport traffic in silence, hit the road, and sped on its way.

"Who's on the principal?" asked Carver after some time.

"I've got a team," said Sparroway in the front passenger seat.

"Not you?"

"What's that supposed to mean?"

"I'm just wondering what you guys are doing at the airport with us?"

The security coordinator turned in his seat. "I'm getting you up to speed, that's what. And maybe I'm not Walter's favorite person right now."

"You got a story behind that?"

Sparroway chuckled to himself and faced forward. "Just the way he is. You'll see."

They made good time over the highway before entering a dense city of multi-colored buildings. Taipei was both old and new, modern high-rises abutting run-down buildings, sleek lines marred by busy signs and cluttered windows. Not as packed as Tokyo, not as clean either, yet it retained a rustic charm the more famous megalopolis lacked. Taipei was closely nestled against a cushion of thickly forested mountains. Greenery and medians lined many streets, and the occasional traditional temple or statue gave tactile warmth to the remnants of mechanical industry.

The entire drive, Carver kept an eye out the back window as if he were running an op. Some of the multilane stoplights were a little uncomfortable. In one particular instance, a set of three scooters weaved right past their stopped 4Runner, but the riders were merely skipping to the front of the line. Many of the intersections had white boxes painted at the head where scooters and motorcycles pushed ahead into and waited. As soon as the light switched to green, the two-wheelers took off before the slower-accelerating cars followed. After a few such intersections, the ritual became second nature.

No one tailed them as far as he could tell. Then again, there wasn't much point. Anyone who might be interested in doing so would already know precisely where they were headed.

Twilight dimmed the city as they pulled into the Mandarin Oriental. It was the type of place a billionaire would stay. Urban opulence, a model of grand Euro architecture that charged exorbitantly for every one of its five stars. Exterior lights livened up the already impressive stonework, giving the building a magical and timeless feel, not unlike something in Disneyland.

The group unloaded except for the driver, who didn't valet the truck but instead parked elsewhere. They declined to surrender their bags to the bellhop and entered a regal lobby of Grecian columns, a marbled floor, and a galactic chandelier comprised of hundreds of pieces of crystal. Every feature was built to impress, and not one failed.

Sparroway was going over certain protocols, welcoming them to the security team, before Carver cut him off.

"You think you can get me my own vehicle while I'm here?"

"What for?" he asked. "You'll be shadowing Walter."

"My two guys will be on him. I prefer to rove."

One of his eyebrows arched, but he didn't voice his skepticism. "I'll see what I can do. As far as rooms, we only booked you the one, but Walter reserved the entire floor so that's easily remedied. Give me a second with the desk."

As they waited, Davis whistled. "Now this is style."

Carver turned to appreciate the lobby and found his cohorts doing the same. Davis stared wide-eyed at the chandelier, and Shaw plucked a champagne flute from a passing tray. He was mid sip when Carver pulled the glass from his hand.

"Weren't you just giving Davis a hard time about the bubbly stuff?"

Shaw shrugged. "When in Rome."

"No parties tonight," Carver instructed. "I need you on the PM shift. I don't care what other PPOs the principal has on staff, you're glued to him until he closes his door for the night. You hand off to Davis at 5 am and he takes over for the day."

Davis joined them with a nod. "Guess I get to see the sights."

"Guess I'm the night owl again," said Shaw with a sigh.

"Don't pretend it doesn't work for you," said Carver.

Davis chuckled. "That's right. I've never met anyone who can function on less sleep."

"Your jealousy is showing," countered Shaw. "You'll be checking out boring conference rooms and I'll be up late singing karaoke."

"I think they call it KTV here."

"Mr. Carver," spoke a light voice. "I see you're enjoying Taipei already."

He turned to a slight woman in casual business attire, a black blouse with a gray jacket and slacks. Her hair was tied over pearl earrings and she wore her jacket loose and open, which muddied her form but revealed the tight waistline. It was one stylish flair of many in what should've been a boring outfit. She was unerringly pretty.

Carver passed off the champagne flute without looking. "Vince," he insisted. Shaw helpfully set the glass on the front desk.

The woman held out her hand and Carver shook. "Su Yi-An, security director for Taipei Semiconductors."

Despite her smiling eyes and bouncy lips, her expression was firm and her handshake meant business. Even more impressive was the job title. Taipei Semiconductors was a billion-dollar multinational.

Carver's military service had inserted him into limited roles in Asia. He had no working vocabulary of Mandarin, though he liked to think he'd heard enough that his pronunciation wasn't embarrassing. He was also familiar with the Chinese convention of putting surnames first.

"Nice to meet you, Yi-An."

It was barely recognizable, but she stiffened and her chin rose a notch. Carver wondered if he wasn't as familiar with Asia as he thought.

"I understand you're here to supplement Mr. Lachlan's detail?" she asked.

He nodded toward the team behind him. "Nick Shaw and Michael Davis will be on close protection, though I'm not sure that's any concern of Mr. Lin's."

Her thin brows twitched as he named the CEO of Taipei Semiconductors. "Mr. Lin is not concerned, but I make it a habit of personally meeting anyone who attends dinner with him. I believe you have a nine o'clock with Mr. Lachlan and Mr. Lin. Unless I'm mistaken."

The corner of Carver's mouth tightened. "I'm betting that doesn't happen a lot."

She blinked, unsure how to respond to what could only be taken as a compliment. It was evident she expected people to play tough with her. She was so prepared for pushback that she found herself flatfooted now.

It was cute, Carver found himself admitting. Yi-An was cute on top of pretty. His professional interest wondered how tough she was in that small package. She didn't come off as especially petite for a woman of Taiwan, but she was only half of him.

Sparroway approached and passed out room keys. "Three rooms on our floor, as promised. Ah, I see you've met Ms. Su."

Carver's face flattened. "She was gracious enough to inform me about dinner tonight."

The security coordinator's face lit up. "Right. That. Walter will want you there, of course. I hope you're up for it after the flight."

"It's what we're here for. But we should get moving so we can clean up."

"Don't forget to dress to impress," added Yi-An. "I hope you have a suit in that army bag?"

"This isn't my first rodeo," replied Carver.

"So I've heard." She turned with a wave. "If you need anything at all, just ask."

Yi-An strolled away and the four of them watched. It wasn't lost on Carver that she wore flats. He wasn't sure what was fashionable here, but the shoes were more practical than most, and he had a feeling that was on purpose.

"Don't mind her," grumbled Sparroway. "She's a little uptight."

"What's your excuse?" chuckled Shaw.

"I can tell I'm gonna like you guys," returned the interim coordinator.

8

The security contingent took up the entire elevator. Carver didn't bother taking the duffel bag off his shoulder, even as they rode to the fifteenth floor at the top. As they exited into the hall, they passed a pair of Taiwanese men in suits. Carver immediately clocked them for security and wondered if they were provided by the hotel. They stood against the wall without imposing themselves, passively watching the arriving newcomers.

Sparroway walked to his door and reminded them to show up half an hour before dinner. That gave them ample time to prepare but not do much else. Either way, he seemed like an amiable enough guy.

The crew retired to their rooms. Carver dropped his bag in the bedroom and collapsed on the king bed. It was probably the nicest mattress he'd ever been on in his life, but maybe that was the cramped airplane seat talking. He allowed himself a moment to relax after the trek. He was fully rested, and he made a point of being prepared, so it was only a moment. In battle, preparation often trumped manpower and armaments. Not that dinner with a billionaire equated to warfare.

The bathroom was elegant gray marble with a spa tub. Carver showered and shaved. It wasn't until he put on the suit that he realized he was slightly nervous. Sometimes that happened in the hours before a mission, before there was danger to respond to or anything worthwhile to do. It might've just been all the fancy trappings of the hotel and what was sure to be an impressive dinner. More likely it was the players involved.

Billionaires didn't play by the rules everybody else did. While Lachlan's net worth heightened the importance of the contract, it wasn't until the attempted abduction that things became serious. Nine out of ten security gigs were as eventful as waiting at the DMV. The ones that did incur action rarely involved live weapons.

Doubling the intrigue was the very real possibility that Lachlan was a bad actor. A traitor, even. And, of course, it wasn't every day that the CIA knocked on your door looking for favors.

Carver double-checked himself in the mirror. He would never be fully ready without a firearm, but it wasn't as if he was naked. He had his trusty Bravo Company Colonel blade in a concealed-draw sheath on his weak side. It was a small knife with an angled blade, similar to but not a true karambit. All special operations guys had their own knife preferences, and this was Carver's. While the farthest thing from big and showy, it was undeniably lethal. He also had something more conventional as an everyday carry. The Extrema Ratio Police III folding knife and multitool slipped into his opposite pocket.

Davis and Shaw waited in the hallway as he exited. They marched to Sparroway's door and knocked one minute early. He let them in, dressed but still wrangling the tie, and showed them to a table with their carry permits and a single pistol in a holster. Carver checked the weapon. Standard Glock 17, loaded with one extra mag. He returned it to its holster and handed it to Shaw.

"You two pass this like a baton as you switch shifts," he instructed.

"Will do." Shaw fitted the holster to his belt.

Sparroway finally defeated the length of polyester around his neck and led them back outside. "Boss wants to talk to you." He stopped at a room flanked by two members of his team. He nodded at them and knocked.

A man wearing a hotel jacket and best described as a butler answered the door to the presidential suite. He welcomed them into a palatial living room with two wraparound couches, a day bed, a bar fully stocked with expensive bottles, a pair of ceiling-to-floor windows overlooking Taipei 101, and a matching pair of chandeliers because why not. Past the fireplace were two doorways, one leading to a study with curated art pieces and another with an extended dining table, set to impress with ten places and a floral centerpiece.

"There you are!" exclaimed Walter Lachlan as he strode in from yet another adjoining room. This suite was larger than most houses. The principal was dressed in his signature blue suit. He was a lot more put together than the last time they'd seen him, complete with handkerchief and cuff links that could fund a college education. He was still exempt from a tie and, for that matter, buttoning the top button.

Lachlan vociferously shook Carver's hand. "I can't thank you enough for making the trip. I know how last second it was."

"All part of the job, sir. I'd like you to meet Mr. Shaw and Mr. Davis. I'll have one of them stationed with your close protection team at all times."

"Yes, I recognize you boys. The only reason I'm enjoying the amenities of the Mandarin Oriental is because of you. Thank you. That was good work." He shook their hands too, and for once Shaw didn't ruin it by saying something uncouth.

Lachlan turned to Carver and straightened his jacket. "I hope their presence here doesn't mean you won't be joining us for dinner."

"I'll be in lockstep," assured Carver.

"Good." He rested a finger under his nose for a few seconds of indecision. "Listen, I want to apologize for my behavior on the tarmac. I can be a little pigheaded."

"Not necessary, Mr. Lachlan. It was an extreme situation and you pushed through admirably."

He waved dismissively. "First of all, call me Walter. I'm not much for ceremony, and I hope I can call you Vince."

"Of course."

He nodded. "And don't shine me on about being admirable. You boys were decisive and handled the threat. I could use people of your caliber."

Shaw and Davis exchanged a hesitant glance. Carver was

similarly stunned. He had walked in with the expectation of needing to apologize on behalf of Mark Marino and Dynamic Security Solutions for telling their VIP to shut his pie hole. Instead it was the billionaire apologizing to him.

"We're glad to hear it, Walter," said Carver blandly. "DSS is at your service."

Lachlan snorted. "DSS... CPS... The man is the asset, not the company. Remember that."

He strode away before Carver could agree. They loitered through a few minutes of final preparations before heading out together. One of the bodyguards remained at the door of the presidential suite and the other joined them. With Carver, Shaw, and Sparroway, that put four officers on the principal.

As they approached the elevator, Lachlan spoke to the unassuming Taiwanese guards posted there. "Thank Mr. Lin for his concern, but your services are no longer necessary. My staff has been properly reinforced."

The men looked shocked to have been addressed directly. One mustered a weak objection. "It's not a problem, sir. Mr. Lin wants us to stay—"

"I can handle my own security," interrupted Lachlan. "And I'd take it as an insult if anyone thought otherwise."

Shaw stepped forward with just the slightest hint of menace. The bodyguards appraised the bearded man with apprehensive eyes, but they remained cool customers.

Lachlan ignored the theatrics and moved to the elevator. "Take care of it, Sparroway, will you?"

"Of course, sir."

They rode down without him. As they exited, Davis waved them off as well. Introductions complete, he was no longer on duty and had his own mission to find local street food.

Walter Lachlan knew where he was going and led the way. The restaurant was situated in the hotel and he'd had a couple of days to familiarize himself with it. Their destination was a hot pot joint. While small, it hosted a private table in the back where the other party greeted them.

Carver stopped dead as a woman turned to face him. Su Yi-An's hair twirled and they locked eyes. The stern woman he'd met not two hours before in the lobby had been replaced with a stunning figure in an elegant, strapless black evening gown. A slit up the side showed her leg to just below the hip. A diamond bracelet hung on one wrist, drawing attention to slight fingers with nails painted scarlet. Her pale cheeks flushed against the dim lighting, and her large lashes quivered ever so slightly.

Carver cleared his throat as he fumbled for something to say. "Looks like I'm not the only one who cleans up nicely."

Her nostrils flared. She was momentarily speechless as he apparently had a similar effect on her. She liked men in suits, he decided. She must've noticed how long she was staring because she suddenly averted her gaze. "And I was told you didn't know how to follow directions."

"Who told you that?"

She met his eyes again and arched an eyebrow. "That isn't a denial."

Carver watched her curiously, and he found himself leaning closer as he tried to figure her out. She confidently stood her ground and, for a protracted moment, nobody else existed.

Lachlan broke in on their moment. "Vince, there's someone I want you to meet."

Yi-An retreated before he could stop her. Lachlan dragged an Indian man forward.

"This is Panesh, my executive assistant. I want you to exchange numbers. If you need anything regarding security logistics talk to Harry, but for anything else Panesh is your guy."

Carver shook hands. Panesh wore black dot-com frames and a small beard lined his jaw. He looked like the type of guy who'd be at home giving a TED Talk on the psychology of social media.

"Absolutely," chimed Panesh. "Harry has the conference schedule, but if you need insight into any of the players or events on our agenda, I'd be happy to discuss."

"I appreciate it," said Carver.

"And of course," pivoted Lachlan, "our esteemed co-host."

He pulled Carver toward a robust middle-aged man with styled black hair and a strong jaw. His carefree eyes and easygoing smile made him seem like your everyday everyman, not the undisputed head of Taiwan's vital semiconductor industry.

Carver offered his hand. "Mr. Lin, I presume."

The man, though amiable, was surprised by the gesture.

Carver wondered what a close protection officer was doing meeting a CEO, and no doubt he wondered the same thing. Still, Mr. Lin flashed a pleasant smile and took his hand.

"I am sorry," he said. "You find me at a loss..."

Lachlan slapped Carver's back. "This is Vince, our guest of honor. He's the man who put me on the plane to your fine country. You should've seen him, firing a machine gun out of a sunroof."

Mr. Lin's eyes widened in recognition. "Ah, yes. You left quite an impression on Walter."

The fellow billionaire laughed. "Okay, don't go blowing up his ego, Chen-Han."

Mr. Lin laughed and waved his business partner to the round table seated for six. He sat beside a young man, presumably his own assistant, opposite Panesh and Lachlan in mirror formation. To Lin's left sat Yi-An, leaving a setting between her and Lachlan. Carver moved to take his place along the wall with the security detail.

"No, no," berated Lachlan. "Not today you don't. This seat's for you."

Carver paused and assessed the table. Mr. Lin was taken aback by the offer, and Yi-An had gone still. His first thought was wondering what Lachlan's game was. CPOs weren't usually included among the winers and diners.

Then again, Lin's security director was also strangely at the table. Granted, she looked better in a dress than Carver did, but it was an odd concession that couldn't be written off as a cultural difference.

As much as Carver wanted to push back against the idea,

he knew that, absent somebody's life being in danger, a security officer's job was to make the principal look good. If Lachlan wanted a tough-guy prop at the dinner table, he'd be at the dinner table.

Carver's weighing of the situation was done in the blink of an eye, and he graciously accepted his seat without a hint of outward hesitation. He pulled the chair away just as Sparroway entered the dining room. The interim coordinator had been heading to the table but, upon seeing Carver take the chair, detoured and joined his guy at the wall.

While this was interesting, it was hard for Carver to care as he squeezed into the seat beside Yi-An. She kept her face forward, though clearly aware of him, and he tried not to stare. The field was ready now, three versus three. An entirely new kind of chess match, one Carver was unaccustomed to, was about to begin.

9

Although the round table meant everyone had two neighbors, Panesh and the other assistant had a large gulf between them, and in a minute it was apparent why. A waitress greeted the table and took her station there. She addressed Lin in Mandarin and then Lachlan in English, leaving only smiling eyes for the rest of the guests. She placed a large copper pot on the table's central burner and started the gas. Lin ordered a Spartan round of waters for the group. Shaw innocuously rolled his eyes, and Carver warned him with a glare.

The waitress left the table as the pot heated. The yellow broth contained a variety of chopped vegetables. Lachlan leaned forward and took in a breath. "I can already tell this is going to be great."

Mr. Lin asked, "Have you had shabu-shabu, Mr. Carver?"

"Not in Taiwan."

The answer quieted the table for a second, as if a follow-up was expected. Carver didn't wish to expound and was sorry he brought it up.

Lin grinned magnanimously. "You lucked out then

because this is the best in Taipei. It's not the most expensive," he noted with a glance at Lachlan, "but sometimes I find price a poor indicator of quality."

"Hasn't been my experience," chuckled Lachlan. "Anything can be overpriced, of course. It's just that there are some things that can't be had without paying a premium."

"People don't want premiums, they want reliability."

"Bullshit. People pay premiums *for* reliability."

The CEO of Taipei Semiconductors shook his head. "They pay for glitz and glamour. Status is a side effect of the free market, but it's not the driving force."

"You see, Chen-Han, that's where you and I disagree. The movers and shakers set the tone. That starts from the top."

"I often find the real action at the bottom."

Yi-An betrayed her presence with a light laugh, attracting the eyes of the table. Lin smiled at her and they shared a few words in Chinese. Then he reverted to English.

"Ms. Su is the most practical woman I know. She won't say it, but she finds our ideological discussions of trade to be a lot of hot air."

Her lips pursed. "That's not the case at all, Mr. Lin."

"I rest my case."

Another smile. It was strange to see her so accommodating, and Carver wondered if theirs was a purely business relationship.

Deliveries of raw beef stole the attention of the table.

The waitress prepared slices of Australian Wagyu and Black Pearl pork alongside small plates of leafy vegetables, fish cakes, and tofu. It was enough to keep conversation sparse. After the main course, the flavorful broth was cooked down with rice and served as a final course.

It was then, as dinner winded down, that Lachlan and Lin began discussing the meat of their deal. The facilities in Arizona, the timetable to full production, and their current capabilities. Panesh and the other assistant entered the conversation when requested, delivering mundane details and numbers from prepared sheets with robotic efficiency. Yi-An and Carver were a bit out of their depth and exchanged covert glances between sips of tea, the only remaining sustenance on the table. Carver kept an ear out for discussion of proprietary technology or data access.

"But you keep falling back to Arizona," protested Lin. "I've seen Arizona."

Lachlan nodded. "And we're on target, so I don't understand the sticking point."

"Arizona's not being questioned. It's the capabilities of North Carolina that concern me."

"Ridiculous," asserted Lachlan. "Why bring this up so late in the game?"

"Perhaps because I feel I may have been shined on."

"Panesh?"

The assistant obediently responded. "We have every confidence in our output capabilities, but this isn't about confidence. It's a contract with the federal government. Our facilities in Arizona stake a permanent claim on Spruce

Pine's resources. It's impossible to get a better deal."

"I appreciate that, Mr. Mehta," countered Lin, "but my worry doesn't lie with the contract. This is about fulfillment."

"Volume's never been a problem before," insisted Lachlan.

"Yet our new venture will place unprecedented demands on the quarry. This is a valid concern that shouldn't be minimized. Our partnership requires open access."

Walter Lachlan huffed. "I don't own the Spruce Pine facilities."

"Ownership is trivial," countered Lin. "They will respond to our collective bargaining power, let me assure you. I require a tour of their facilities before further sign-off."

"Chen-Han, where is this coming from? We've been working at this for years. You can't delay approval of the next milestone because of cold feet."

"I will move ahead only if what I see at Spruce Pine satisfies me."

"Then sign off and schedule a visit whenever's convenient. What does next month look like, Panesh?"

"No," interrupted Lin. "I won't sign until I visit. The sooner the better."

The table silenced as the business moguls stared each other down. Whatever partnership they'd cultivated was being strained. Ultimately, a tour wasn't much of a sticking point.

"Fine," Lachlan barked, sliding his mug of tea away. "As

soon as the conference ends then. How does that sound? We can fly straight to Spruce Pine."

A nod. "That is satisfactory."

"Good," declared Lachlan, immediately standing. "Panesh will take care of the bill."

Lin shook his head. "I cannot allow that. I'm your host in Taipei."

"Fine, thank you." The words were cordial but the tone agitated. "Have a good night."

Everyone stood but Lachlan didn't wait. He stormed out of the restaurant with Shaw and Sparroway hurrying to keep up. Panesh flashed a nervous smile and mumbled a weak excuse about his boss being on edge since Arizona. He thanked Mr. Lin for dinner and added a few other compliments, but they were hollow and forced. Lin hastily nodded him off.

Yi-An looked up at Carver, backing away. "Night," he said, more to her since Lin was no longer paying attention. Her face was straight, emotionless, and she didn't answer. Carver considered hanging around but didn't want to overplay his hand. He was no longer welcome.

So much for being the guest of honor.

He exited the private dining room. Instead of retreating to his room, he found a surreptitious spot at the bar and ordered a Japanese whiskey on the rocks.

It was getting late, it wasn't the weekend, and the Mandarin was too pricey to host regular conference attendees. Only a few tables in the restaurant had guests, and the only other person at the bar was an old man nursing a hot sake. The bartender set down a glass with a single large ice cube, procured a bottle of the good stuff, and delivered a healthy pour.

Lin's assistant left the back room and walked out of the restaurant alone. Carver waited for Lin and Su to follow, but they didn't. He stared at the glass a few moments, wondering what the hell was going on. He finally took a sip and barely noticed the bite.

Carver soon received a text message from Shaw. The principal was checked into the presidential suite and tucked away. Nick would be posted in the hallway overnight. Carver asked for a menu and browsed for something that suited the burly man. He settled on sending up a box of Chianti-braised Wagyu ribs, a bottled water, and a black coffee.

Meanwhile, Lin and Su were still in their private room. Carver bristled at the thought, which he found strange. He wasn't a jealous person by nature. Jealousy was a poison. It was friendly fire, inflicted upon yourself. Rarely did good come of it. But something about the way Yi-An looked at him made him wonder.

Halfway through his glass, Lin's assistant returned and Carver realized he'd been holding his breath. He kept his head down to avoid notice. Within a minute, the three emerged from the back in the middle of discussion. Yi-An's gaze locked on him. She was vigilant, he had to admit. He raised his glass her way so nothing seemed amiss, and then he turned away as if uninterested.

Through an obstructed mirror behind shelved liquor

bottles, Carver caught their movement to the door. The bartender blocked his view as he returned the bill with Carver's credit card.

"Leaving so soon?" asked Yi-An.

She was radiant up close, sparkling like the diamonds on her wrist. Carver suspected it had something to do with the change of company. Lin and his assistant were gone.

"Hey there. I didn't mean to overstay my welcome. Just picking up dinner for my guy." He signed the check and slid it away.

"You should have said something earlier. Mr. Lin would have been happy to provide it."

"That's okay. I can take care of my team. I shouldn't have been sitting at that table anyway." Carver turned in the seat to better study her. "Why were you?"

She pressed her lips tight and sighed through her nose. At first he thought she ignored the question. Yi-An slid between him and the next empty seat, leaned on the bar, and ordered in Mandarin. The black hair straddling her shoulder smelled of lavender, and his pulse quickened in her proximity. His eyes traced down her back, where the dress was so tight-fitting it seemed it would burst if not for the slit up the side.

"Is it so strange," she asked, still facing away, "to enjoy the comforts of company?"

"Is that what you two call it?" Carver caught her eyes in the mirror behind the bar. She spun to him.

"We don't call it anything." Her eyes flared. "I know what you're thinking."

"I doubt it."

"You think I'm sleeping with him."

"Are you?"

"You think the only reason I hold my position is because I'm pretty."

Carver chuckled dryly. "Can we agree that you're pretty and drop it?"

The bartender placed a flute with gin, champagne, and some other stuff in front of her, and she thanked him.

"You can put it on my tab," Carver told him.

"It's already paid for by Mr. Lin."

"Of course it is."

She lifted her glass before him with a satisfied smile. "What are we drinking to, Mr. Carver?"

He put his hand around the whiskey but left it on the bar top. "I'm still trying to figure that out, Ms. Su."

Her lashes closed almost imperceptibly. She waited, as if in challenge, and Carver decided not to disappoint. He lifted his glass to hers.

"How about we drink to being on a first-name basis? It's terribly unprofessional, but I suspect you can handle it."

Her lips parted. "It's a deal... *Vince*." The glasses clinked and they drank.

Introduced once again, Yi-An boosted up and sat on the stool. With them facing each other, their knees touched. The dress rode up her leg and exposed the pink flesh of her upper thigh.

"I gotta tell you," said Carver, "that's some dress."

"Thank you, but it's not as fun as it looks. I wear it more

for business than pleasure."

"That's too bad."

"For you as well. I expected you to show up in a cheap wrinkled suit. Instead I find you in... What is that, Brioni?"

"Brooks Brothers."

She smirked. "That makes a lot of sense. It's well pressed and tailored, regardless."

He nodded at the compliment. "Surprised I'm not just dumb muscle?"

"That's not it at all. I read up on you. I know what you're capable of. I have great respect for special operations soldiers."

Carver nodded along, unfazed. "You do background checks on all the guys staying at the Mandarin?"

"I do when they'll be in the same room as Mr. Lin."

"Fair enough. You're thorough."

"You don't know the half of it," she said with a cock of her head.

Carver decided he had better get another whiskey. He signaled the bartender for another one, which would be his last. It would be plenty seeing as how Yi-An had only taken a light sip of hers.

"So tell me what tomorrow's gonna be like," he prompted.

"The conference? Don't tell me Mr. Sparroway hasn't given you the agenda yet."

He hadn't, but Carver thought better than to reveal the oversight. "That's not what I mean. Do you foresee any problems? Any threats to Mr. Lin?"

"You mean like an attempted kidnapping in broad daylight?" She smirked. "I don't mean offense, Vince, but this isn't the United States. Weapons are strictly controlled here. And there'll be private security all over the expo center."

"So you predict things going smoothly?"

She pondered that for an honest moment before returning a confident nod. "I do. Nearly all of Taipei Semiconductor's business is behind closed doors, with companies we're previously partnered with. I understand your concern, but you should worry about your eventual return to your country more than anything else."

Carver leaned in to gloat. "If I didn't worry then I wouldn't be doing my job."

She stiffened, holding his eye contact but eventually breaking away and going for her glass. After a sip, "Do you have any reason to believe your attackers followed you?"

"You mean besides the fact that they didn't get what they came for?" He shook his head. "No, I don't have anything solid. Lachlan only signed me on two weeks ago, and no one's been able to identify the perpetrators yet. Eastern European mercenaries is my guess. The FBI's looking into it."

She blinked. "You can't stop there..."

He chuckled. "What do you want me to say?"

"Were they good?"

"Not really."

The edge of her lip curled up. "Not really?"

Carver shrugged. "I didn't get the feeling they were real

professionals, you know?"

She laughed lightly, and it was charming. "Don't show off."

"I'm not. It's the truth of things."

"I was under the impression they almost absconded with Mr. Lachlan."

"Well, you heard what you heard, but they were already in the car with him. Credit where it's due: the strike was well planned. But when it comes down to their guys with guns versus mine, they didn't stand a chance."

"You must be some man," she teased. Then she breathed deeply and dipped into her bubbly drink.

Carver was still trying to guess at her game. Yi-An was noticeably less defensive than she was in the lobby. What had really changed since then? Now she was speeding right past congenial and straight to flirty. He figured someone in her position would be more cautious.

But there was an undeniable magnetism between them. The sheer physicality of it tickled his skin. He could wrap her up right there and she would shrink within him.

Back as a Delta operative, Carver was given a lot of freedom to behave as he thought best. That was a pretty wide margin at times. While it wasn't in intelligence, he had *worked* for intelligence. When dealing with assets, you had to blend in, to find common ground. That could mean anything.

As soon as he became a security officer in the private sector, the whole ballgame changed. At DSS he had the autonomy to lead his division as he saw fit, of course, but it wasn't the free-for-all that special operations could be. Maybe he no longer took orders, but he had a new mandate of professionalism. It was a lot of planning and watching from a distance, making moves in the background but letting the main stage play out as if he wasn't involved.

Now, as a CIA asset himself, Carver's hands were untied. Perhaps more than ever before. And he saw no reason not to play along with Yi-An's advances.

He wasn't sure he could stop himself if he wanted to.

Carver slid his stool closer. Her hand dropped to his knee to protest, but then she relaxed. Instead of saying anything, she took another sip and watched him with large eyes. Her hand remained where it was.

"Why do I get the feeling you've been in a firefight before?" he asked.

Her eyes flashed. "You pride yourself on reading people, don't you?"

"Now who's reading who?"

Her lilting laugh made a return appearance. "I'm not a man so my service wasn't mandatory."

"You volunteered?"

She nodded. "But I'm afraid most of my experience is based on training."

"It's a good basis," returned Carver.

"It doesn't limit what I'm capable of."

"I wouldn't dream of assuming your capabilities."

Her hand tightened a bit on his leg. "I have to confess, I... am curious to know exactly what you're capable of."

"It's the kind of thing that's easier to show than explain."

Her lashes fluttered. She swallowed and downed the rest of her glass. "Maybe we have some things we can show each other."

Carver set his glass down.

"But first," she said, hopping off the barstool and twisting away, "you can spare me the indignity of walking out of here alone."

Carver put the last drink on his room tab and left it unfinished. The two of them strolled to the elevator.

"Do you like working for Mr. Lin?" he asked. She was visibly annoyed at the subject change. "I mean, is he a straight dealer?"

She snorted. "Are you asking if he was involved with what happened to Lachlan?"

"Of course not. That wouldn't make sense, them being fast friends and all."

She studied him a moment. "Why are we talking about my boss?"

"Sorry. Force of habit. From now on, instead of engaging in conversation, I'll just stare at your dress." He pushed the elevator call button.

Yi-An snickered. "Are you a sensitive man, Vince? I can see you're big and strong and in control, but what are you hiding on the inside?"

The elevator doors opened and he waved her in first. He pushed the button for fifteen and leaned against the wall. She smirked, brushed past him, and pushed fourteen.

They watched each other for a moment as the elevator door closed. Her skin flushed pink in the cold light. She leaned close. "You didn't answer my question."

The elevator kicked into gear and she swayed forward, bracing a hand on his chest. He caught her waist and they stared into each other's eyes, her body on his.

"I don't understand your implication," he answered. "Do you think I'm hiding something?"

Her eyes were wide. She didn't answer.

"Isn't it enough," he said, "that I am big, I am strong, and I am in control?"

She took in a breath and squirmed slightly in his arms. For the briefest moment he thought he saw a flicker in her eyes, something raw and bare and honest, and he was suddenly worried why that would be the exception.

The elevator dinged and opened. Yi-An hastily pulled away and backed out. "Thanks for the company," she said a little breathlessly.

She started to turn down the hall. Carver stepped out with his hand holding the door, and she snorted. "I had a good time, Vince, but don't presume you're getting farther than that. I can walk myself to my room."

He nodded. "Good night, then."

The hall was empty except for two men standing at the far bend. No doubt they were Mr. Lin's and his quarters were that direction. Yi-An's room was in the same block, which only made sense. Carver watched her walk past them and disappear.

He re-entered the elevator and rode up to fifteen. Lin's two guards had cleared out as Lachlan had requested. Two of Sparroway's men were posted outside the door of the presidential suite, with Shaw hanging out a few rooms up beside a room service cart.

"Thanks for the grub, boss," he said. "You coming back from a nightcap?"

"Something like that. Everything straight on this end?"

"Straighter than a yard stick. This job's gonna be a piece of cake."

"Maybe."

Carver might agree if this was just about Lachlan's protection. He had half a mind to tell Shaw and Davis what was really going on, but his head was still spinning from his close encounter with Yi-An.

"You need anything?" Carver asked.

"It's only a few hours till the morning. I'll pass the Glock off when Davis relieves me."

Carver patted his shoulder. "Good man." Then he headed into his room where he could keep his troubles to himself.

10

Carver woke early, restless. He checked in with Davis before returning to his room and doing a series of push ups, crunches, and lunges. It felt good to get his muscles working, and even better to give them a hot shower. He called room service and ordered two plates of breakfast sausages and eggs before joining Davis in the hall.

"Just what the doctor ordered," said Davis, happily accepting his portion. "My stomach's all upside down after last night."

Carver chuckled. "What did you eat?"

"I don't even know, man, but it was spicy as hell. Some real food will do me good."

"Then don't ask what they put in the sausage."

After eating, Carver checked in with Sparroway. They went over the agenda while referring to a map of the expo center, and the security detail readied as Walter Lachlan emerged from his suite. Outside at the valet, the interim coordinator handed Carver a set of keys to his own vehicle. It was just a Rav4 rental, without the ballistic protection of Lachlan's 4Runner, but Carver was appreciative to be on his own. He took up position in the follow car.

The streets were moderately busy, and the drive to the Nangang Exhibition Center was only fifteen minutes along Huandong Boulevard. They arrived at a pair of large, multistory buildings. The lot as well as the adjacent terminal metro station were crowded, but not to the levels of an overblown event like Comic-Con. The attendees were business professionals in manufacturing, assembly, and design. They were engineers, technicians, scientists, managers, and members of the sales force. More important, and key to Lachlan's agenda, were meetings with attending executives.

The security detail was escorted through a special VIP entrance and herded to a lounge for preparation. Davis made sure the area was secure while Carver tagged along with Sparroway to coordinate with conference security. It was all very routine and the staff looked to be on top of things. Sparroway raised several concerns about access to the private meeting rooms, and they were satisfied with the answers.

Lachlan went over notes with Panesh. After more than an hour, they were ushered into a backstage room. Carver peeked out to a crowded floor, watching the in-progress keynote kickoff of SEMICON Taiwan. He swept through the mass of people to get a handle on event security. Once again, it was solid. Guards lined the makeshift stage. Metal gates separated them from the spectators. There was an easy escape hatch to the back rooms if anything got out of hand.

By the time Lachlan came onstage, Carver barely noticed his words. There were a lot of platitudes about every single person in the room being a visionary. How this was the premier gathering of the chip industry's manufacturing and supply chain, with participation of market leaders like Taipei Semiconductors, TSMC, and Nanya Technology. He touched on artificial intelligence, green manufacturing, strategic materials, machine learning, 5G, and even the Internet of Things. It was a dense presentation that was somehow flighty, covering a multitude of topics without saying much at all. Carver could only assume by the applause that the speech was a hit.

With Lachlan's role in the keynote complete, Carver returned to Davis at the side of the stage. It was only then that he spotted a familiar face among the crowd.

"Huh," he muttered aloud.

"You got something, boss?" asked Davis.

"That man. Black suit, white shirt, short black hair. I saw him at the airport."

"You just described half the attendees."

"I suppose it wouldn't help if I said he was Asian." Carver pointed him out. "That one there. He's not clapping."

The PPO squinted. "I see him. Is it so strange to see a business traveler attending a conference?"

"I don't know," he conceded. "I'm gonna check it out."

The man in the audience glanced at them while they were both looking. Lachlan strolled by and pointed at Davis without stopping.

"I'll catch up," said Carver, breaking away as they retreated backstage.

A new speaker strolled out and applause once again erupted. A third of the crowd retreated after Lachlan's presentation while another third pressed forward to view the next, and lost in the center of it all was his mystery man who was quickly hurrying away.

Carver cursed for having been so obvious. It was a good thing he was tall. At 6' 2", he stood above the vast majority of attendees. But there were signs and cameras held in the air, and the man he was following was short. Carver weaved through an oncoming rush and hit the far wall. He checked the entrance to the hall as well as the exit to the street. The man was gone.

Going with his instincts, Carver rushed outside. A line of attendees collecting entrance badges stretched fifty-long. There weren't many wanderers, and Carver quickly assessed that the man wasn't among them. He marched back inside and to the hall entrance, but he knew he'd missed his shot. At least now he confirmed the man was suspicious. His actions had been too evasive to be anything else.

Carver returned backstage, showing his credentials to gain access, and was surprised to find his contingent had already moved on. He texted Davis for an update and met them upstairs. The entire third floor was closed for private functions.

Lachlan kept busy. People often begrudge billionaires and stars their excesses of wealth, but most are unaware of their work ethic. The rest of the day was a production, numerous meet-and-greets with various executives. Carver got the sense that Lachlan was acting differently today, but maybe it was just the grind.

He was glad he only had to watch because the whole thing was exhausting. He swapped on and off with Davis to give him a few breaks, and both security details could rely on each other as necessary. The blandness of it all was a net positive. It was a security officer's dream: boring, contained, and uneventful.

At the end of the day, the procession relocated several blocks away to a hotel lounge. Although Carver would have enjoyed the walk through a foreign city, vehicles were much more secure. Plus he suspected billionaires didn't operate with his mindset. The bar was wide open, taking most of the lobby's ground floor, with an endless maze of low tables, sofas, and ottomans. He got the sense this was the place business people let off steam after a long day at the expo center.

Shaw met them at the 5 pm takeover, having ridden from the Mandarin with some of Sparroway's staff. He surreptitiously accepted the pistol from Davis and hid it under his jacket.

"Relaxing day?" asked Carver.

"You have no idea," said Shaw. "I found this massage place—"

"Actually, I like the 'not having an idea' part."

"Didn't take you for a prude, Vince."

Carver turned to Davis. "You should be able to catch a ride with Sparroway's crew."

"I have a better idea," he countered. "There's a dinner joint I spotted across the street that looks legit. But if you don't mind I'm gonna sit at the bar and have a drink here first."

Carver clapped his shoulder. "It was a long day. You earned it."

They split off to their duties, with Shaw becoming an imposing presence while Carver disappeared on the fringes. He circled around a lot because the turnover in the lobby was high. Davis ended up getting a second drink because he hadn't snagged a reservation early enough, but he eventually made it out and the lounge grew busier as the sun receded.

As the night wore on, there was no doubt about it. Lachlan was colder than the day before. Now that he was surrounded with his own people, the absence of certain gestures was noticeable. Gone were the praises of Carver's security team or the subtle attempts to hire him. Lachlan's mood had definitely soured, and it likely had to do with the dinner with Lin.

The business crowd was rapacious but fleeting, and the lobby started to thin. Yelling broke out across the floor. Lachlan chewed out Panesh, his words slurred and difficult to make out. Carver walked around the bar to get a better view, but by then Sparroway was having a conversation with his boss and Panesh was making for the exit with his tail between his legs. Shaw stood nearby with a neutral expression and a relaxed stance, indicating there was no actual threat.

Carver had heard snippets about the billionaire's temper. Maybe this was a sneak peak, emerging under the influence of alcohol. He took a breath and turned, settling his back on the bar. Across the lounge a woman leaned against the wall of the elevator bay, watching him. Instead of a skirt she wore slacks, but the garnet jacket was the same. Lanelle Williams, the hard-ass case officer.

"You've got to be kidding me," he muttered under his breath.

It seemed she could read lips because she flashed a "whatever" face before idly turning around and strolling into the hall. Carver checked if anyone was watching before wandering her way without any appearance of urgency. The elevator bay was open on both ends, and as he entered she rounded the corner at the other end. He followed her at a distance down another turn and headed down a hallway with public bathrooms. She skipped the men's and women's doors and headed into a family bathroom.

When Carver reached the same door, the latch was still displayed as vacant. He checked up and down the empty hall before pushing in and locking up behind him. Williams waited beside a baby-changing table.

"I was wondering when you'd notice me," she said.

"Bullshit. You couldn't have been there longer than a minute."

She held a straight face for a bit. "Thirty seconds, but who's counting?"

"What are you doing here?"

"Is that a serious question?"

"Where's Gunn?"

She blinked. "Don't worry about him. You were supposed to come alone."

Carver bristled. "Was I? I must have missed that in my mission briefing."

"Don't get snippy. Remember, if it were up to me, I wouldn't have tasked any of you cowboys with work at all. I'd have kept up the FBI front and investigated every single one of you."

"That's a funny way of asking for my help. I'm here for a job. I brought the necessary manpower to see it through."

Her eyes narrowed. "This is about more than personal security. What you did increases our risk. The extra eyes could expose us."

"Without them I'd be glued to Lachlan all day. I need them to provide me room to maneuver in case anything comes up."

She forced her lips to one side as if failing to come up with a counter argument. "You didn't read them in, did you?"

"Am I allowed to?"

"Of course not. Did you read them in, Vince?"

"Of course not."

Her eyes squeezed into a smarmy expression.

"Why am I here?" pivoted Carver.

"I thought we went over this."

"Get real, Williams. They're talking about computer chips and production logistics. How am I supposed to separate legitimate business from a national security breach?"

For once she took the question seriously. "Stick to the illegal sale of data. That means a purchase and a product."

"That makes sense, but I don't have access to their bank records. Lachlan so far hasn't been interested in our DATASEC department, and I'm not a data guy anyway. I'm one-hundred-percent kinetic."

She shrugged. "This isn't so esoteric. There's a good chance any data being sold is air gapped. That means it won't be online and traceable, but physically transported. Is that kinetic enough for you?"

Carver conceded a nod. "Like the briefcase."

"Like the briefcase. Then again, as you've been told, the briefcase could be a prop. But in situations like this there's almost always a physical transfer. More importantly, there'll be a negotiation first. A handshake before payment. Your vigilance can stop that money from ever changing hands."

He worked his jaw as he thought it over and decided she was probably right. There were edge cases, of course, where Carver wouldn't have a chance to prevent the sale. He was one guy who couldn't be everywhere at once. But if it was Lachlan's data that was getting sold, sticking close to him increased the likelihood of uncovering something.

"You've been here a day," prodded Williams. "What do you know so far?"

He crossed his arms and leaned on the wall beside her. "Not a whole lot. Lachlan's a tireless hustler at the center of many business negotiations. Like I said, it's hard to separate the wheat from the chaff. But if anything stands out, it's his meeting with Mr. Lin last night."

Her eyes lit up. "What happened?"

"So they're going over their joint venture, right?

Everything feels routine, tiresome even. But then they hit a sticking point. Mr. Lin wants to see the manufacturing facilities in Spruce Pine, North Carolina."

Her brow scrunched as if the information didn't jive with her take on things. "Spruce Pine is a quarry. It's the source of the silica that makes the chips. Crystal Processor Systems and Taipei Semiconductors source their wafers there, as does the rest of the world, but they have no ownership stake or access to proprietary methods. Have you heard otherwise?"

"No," admitted Carver with a sigh. He frowned momentarily. "Lachlan relies on his assistant, Panesh, to stay on top of these things. He had the numbers ready at dinner. He might have access to what we need."

She didn't seem entirely convinced, but didn't have a better idea. "Okay, you can work him, but don't think for a minute he'll betray his meal ticket for you. He can't be trusted."

"I've worked assets before, Williams. And what about Chen-Han Lin?"

"What about him?"

"If anyone would benefit from Lachlan's proprietary technology, it's the largest semiconductor company in the world."

"I'm not sure that tracks. Taipei Semiconductors benefits from the joint venture. Why would they need to buy secrets when they already have profitable access?"

"What if he's selling?"

"Our intelligence suggests the seller was stateside."

"He was. Lin already toured the Arizona facilities and is insisting on going to North Carolina. The attempted kidnapping went down in Mesa. The thing has holes but some of the pieces fit."

"Except the biggest one: Mr. Lin is Taiwanese, and the chatter indicates the buyer works for the People's Republic of China."

It was a definite conflict, but not insurmountable. "What can I say? Maybe Lin's for reunification. Maybe he sees the writing on the wall."

She scoffed, but at the possibilities rather than his suggestion. "It's not impossible that Chen-Han is an asset himself. It is, however, unlikely. Otherwise China would already know everything he does."

"Fine, then you tell me who it is because it sounds like you don't have a better idea."

Her hands splayed upwards. "We only know what we know."

"I got that. Can you be more specific?"

Williams sighed. "We have active intel that a meeting will occur during this conference."

"What intel?"

"A tip about a buy, money being moved, expectation of new technology."

"That's very vague."

Her cheeks tightened defensively.

"Is this HUMINT?" he pressed.

Her eyelids fluttered in concession. "It's SIGINT."

Carver grumbled. Human intelligence was imperfect, but

it was pliable, and he preferred to operate with it. Humans lie, but you can look them in the eye and judge for yourself. The look also makes them think twice before setting you up. With that kind of closeness, they know they can be held accountable.

Signals intelligence is based on intercepts. Purported non-friendlies putting information into the world. It comes in snippets and gets puzzled together. You rarely get the big picture, and you only have a recording to determine whether the channel is compromised. It's a cheap source of intel, but an even cheaper disinformation engine.

"This has the NSA written all over it," Carver muttered.

The NSA link explained why Williams and Gunn were active within the United States border. Despite the Agency's mandate to not operate domestically, data-sharing laws imposed in the wake of 9/11 enabled the various alphabet agencies to collaborate. This effectively allowed the CIA to spy on American citizens.

"The intel is solid," Williams assured. "There are people within the CCP waiting to receive files of a strategic nature. We're ninety-nine percent sure this will come in the form of stolen intellectual property."

The scars on Carver's arm burned. "Doesn't sound so sure to me."

She released a patient breath. "Look, I know you've been burned by bad intel. But in statecraft, this is as sure as it gets. There are no absolute certainties. We aren't aware of all the moving parts, but the big picture is clear. We need to find out *who* is selling *what* to *whom*, get *proof* if possible, and, above all, *prevent the sale*. The CIA believes you can find the bad actor, Vince."

He paced to the other end of the small bathroom. He'd hoped for more to go on, but the reality on the ground was never ideal. Men like him are trained to act where others freeze up, to operate in non-permissive environments, and to succeed in their mission by any means necessary.

"Fine," he said, "but this needs to be a two-way street."

"I thought it was..."

Carver emphatically shook his head. "I get that I don't have the security clearance for you to tell me everything, but you need to be open about what I'm walking my team into. I need to know the players, the dangers, and what to look out for."

"It's just a data sale."

He glared. "Get me a gun."

"You don't need a gun, Vince." Her assurance was calm and measured, like a psychiatrist speaking to a patient. "You're here to observe Lachlan."

"Yeah? Does that mean you've tracked down who those mercenaries in Arizona were?"

She huffed. "Unaffiliated Balkan veterans who grew up amid revolutions and parlayed their limited talents to the free market."

"It's the unaffiliated part that concerns me. Who hired them?"

Her face remained stoic, but she couldn't avoid the truth. "We don't know."

"You don't know or you won't tell me?"

"We don't know."

The Central Intelligence Agency didn't know. He shook his head. "Well then, I've made my point. Don't forget that I'm tasked with keeping Lachlan safe. We need to be ready for another physical attempt."

"Fine," she conceded with impatience. "We'll get you a gun."

"A SIG Sauer P320."

She rolled her eyes and nodded curtly. "Are we done here? Is your head screwed on right for this?"

He ignored the jibe. "How do I get in touch with you?"

"You call. This isn't a spy movie. Just don't tie me up with every detail." She texted him so he had the number of what was likely a burner. "Give me an update at end-of-day, or if something goes down."

"Fine," he said again. Before she could add anything else, he unlatched the door and marched out.

11

Williams lagged in the family bathroom a few minutes so they wouldn't be seen leaving together. When she finally did emerge, Carver was already on the other side of the lobby, with as much distance between them as possible. That didn't mean she was out of mind, however. He innocently rested against the front window wearing a single earbud and playing a video on his phone.

Officer Williams strolled through the lobby without a care, looking like a woman who'd had a long day of work and was tired of the grind. Carver wondered how much of it was an act. She didn't glance Carver's way as she passed toward the exit, though he put it ten to one she knew exactly where he was.

Lachlan was docile now, drowsy in a comfortable chair. His security detail appeared bored, and Shaw was no exception. Outside the window, Williams stopped at the corner crosswalk. The movement was echoed by a man twenty yards away walking her direction. He didn't stop, exactly, but he suddenly slowed his pace and dawdled. It wasn't until the light changed and Williams started across the street that he walked with purpose again. Carver stared at his phone as the man passed the window, inches from him. As soon as he hurried into the crosswalk, there was no question: Williams had acquired tail.

Carver scanned the lobby. The crowd wasn't paying attention, either to him or the man outside. The only exception was Shaw looking his way. They'd worked together enough to notice each other's cues. Shaw could tell something was up. Carver gave the hand signal to keep watch before heading out the glass doors.

The follow man looked like most of the Taiwanese businessmen around, if dressed on the casual side. Ahead, Williams reached the sidewalk across the busy street and turned to backtrack, passing across the hotel again and walking right by the restaurant Carver hoped Davis was still at.

He reached his team member just after he'd plowed through a double-chocolate bread pudding.

"Good," Carver texted back. "There's someone I want you to follow, double time."

Davis said it was no problem and Carver sent details. The follow man had, to Carver's lack of surprise, turned to follow Williams, though his pursuit was now less aggressive. The circuitous maneuver may have been intentional on Williams' part to sniff out a tail so the man waited until she was almost out of sight to resume pursuit. It was a fortunate development. As he reached the end of the block, Davis exited the restaurant and Carver pointed out who they were tracking.

"I'll catch up," texted Carver. Davis nodded confirmation

and started on his way.

Carver gave his ticket to the valet and offered to tip extra if they could make it quick. They couldn't, as they were backed up by a line of businessmen calling it a night, and he wasn't on the street until a full five minutes later. Periodic updates from Davis kept him keyed on their position. He slid into the Rav4 and drove off to intercept.

His phone rang.

"He's getting into a car," relayed Davis. "I'm flagging down a taxi."

"Belay that. I'm a block away. Just don't lose visual." Carver honked as a car slowed ahead of him. He groaned as two more passed in the adjacent lane before gunning it ahead of a van and swerving around the obstacle. He skidded to a stop beside a waiting Davis, who loaded in.

"Gold Hyundai, two blocks up. Someone else picked him up, just like you did me."

Carver accelerated. He was more concerned with losing the tail than being spotted. The switch to a vehicle would make it almost impossible for them to notice, so long as he didn't crowd them.

At this point, he had no idea where Williams was. He could only assume she'd been parked several blocks away and had walked to her car. If the guys they were following were following her, it didn't matter whether he had eyes on Williams or not. They were all going to the same place.

"Who are we tailing again?" asked Davis in the passenger seat.

"A suspicious character," Carver replied flatly.

"Suspicious how? Was he scoping out the principal?"

"His behavior's off. The way he got in that vehicle confirms it."

Carver hated deceiving his own guy, but what he had said was true enough. He couldn't rightly tell Davis they were tailing a CIA officer. Not yet at least. If it came to that, he would need to know more first. And if, for any reason at all, he suspected that Williams couldn't be trusted, he would have no choice but to bring in Davis and Shaw and suffer any consequences later.

As they closed on the Hyundai, Carver eased off the gas. The gold car slowed as it encountered thickening foot traffic and turned into an outdoor parking lot. The abundance of pedestrians obstructed their view as they neared.

Carver passed the entrance and pulled to the curb. The man they were following exited the Hyundai alone and walked toward the building attracting the crowd. Its large, warehouse-like entrance had bright neon above the archway, Chinese characters with English underneath: Shilin Market.

It was time to continue the pursuit on foot. This was the end of the line for Davis. Carver popped open the door. "You're already doing overtime. I want you to pull out."

"You kidding me?" he barked. "What is all this?"

"It's probably nothing, like you said. I'm gonna do some recon. Maybe pick up a bite. Take the car. I'll find my way back to the hotel."

"You sure, Vince? I can—"

"I'll be fine," he said sternly, the guilt he felt for his tone buried by cold practicality. It wasn't fair to get Davis involved without his knowledge. "Go rest up for tomorrow. That's an order."

Davis just stared ahead and snorted. Carver stepped out of the vehicle and headed into the crowd of shoppers. He caught sight of the man delving through the main hallway. It was populated with stalls you'd see at any Western mall selling T-shirts, leggings, and jewelry. The large, bustling complex gave him some measure of cover, though his stature worked against him.

The man turned down a stairway and Carver followed. A waft of meat and seafood revealed the market's true draw. The underground was loud and cramped, with double the crowd density as above. Fluorescent lights on the low ceiling revealed an endless hallway. People navigated past booths under backlit menus displaying a multitude of exotic dishes. Every other stall had an alcove for limited seating on plastic tables and stools, many of them in use. The experience was exciting and claustrophobic and a full assault on the senses.

Carver pressed after the tail, past counters covered with pastries, tidbits on wooden sticks, and large balls of dough hiding whole crabs, indistinguishable except for their protruding red legs. Carver had been to outdoor night markets before, but those had more of a carnival vibe. This was a permanent installation, an eclectic fusion of a food hall and arcade and basement.

The man ahead turned down a perpendicular path, looking more and more like an experienced operator as he advanced through the mazelike environs. On several occasions he checked his tail. Carver simply huddled low and turned away. It made Carver wonder what the man's objective was. He still hadn't seen Williams and was worried this whole thing was a bust.

A few minutes and two corridors later, a boisterous group of college-aged kids brushed past him. They wrestled in that way that was more about impressing women than actual contest, and the girls strolling alongside rolled their eyes in that way that disapproved of the childishness while being simultaneously flattered to be part of it.

One of the guys was pushed into Carver. He sidestepped and attempted to continue pursuit, but the guy snapped at him, his curse cutting sharply above the rest of the droning chatter.

Carver backed to the wall, using a tall freezer as cover from the man ahead. People in the hall paused or scurried away, eyes on the commotion. The college kid yelled again, face flushed in misplaced anger. His Mandarin was biting and harsh and entirely unintelligible. Carver couldn't speak in return. Aside from not knowing the language, whoever he was following would be alerted to an American's presence. All Carver could do was raise his hands in a universal gesture of apology.

The boy was bolstered by drink. He stepped closer, lowering his voice in what could only be construed as a challenge.

Carver couldn't risk glancing ahead with all eyes on him, but he likewise couldn't hide here forever. The stupid kid wasn't the problem. Getting into a fight in the middle of a night market during his recon was. It put too much visibility on him.

One of the girls tried to calm the guy down. He snapped at her too and moved closer. Carver unhunched to his full height, readied a fist, and met the kid's eyes with the stare of a killer.

The boy blinked. Some neuron in his brain, some latent survival instinct, finally fired. The college kid suddenly realized the man he berated was larger and more capable of a fight. In that moment, the performative display had run its course. Pressing further would be his undoing, no matter how many of his bros were behind him.

The kid decided to save face with one last insult, one Carver happily absorbed, and then the group moved on. Stray glances lingered his way for only a moment before the hall went back to normal, the commotion consumed by the crowd as if nothing had ever occurred.

Carver grimaced and peeked around the freezer. The man he was following had moved on. Out of sight with no way to know for how long. Carver burst ahead and into an intersection with another corridor, searching both directions without reacquiring his target.

His gaze locked on a stairway. Carver sprinted up and found himself outdoors again, on the edge of the building, with only one line of stalls opposite the exterior wall. Fewer people browsed the merchandise here, and a man who could've been his target rounded into a side street some distance ahead. Carver ran the length of the building and peeked around the corner. Several shoppers dined at picnic tables. Carver didn't see the man but he had to be nearby. There was no longer a crowd to provide either of them cover. He walked out in the open while sticking close to the wall, turning down the only alley the tail could've escaped into.

He retreated when he spotted Williams at the far end. She *was* here. She was alone, having navigated the labyrinthine night market only to emerge at the other end. Carver peeked around the edge again. There was nothing to indicate what she was doing. Possibly heading to an illicit meeting or attempting to lose her tail. Gravel scraped behind Carver, and he pulled away from the wall just as a two-by-four slammed into it.

The man he'd been following reversed the club and swung it back around. Carver hopped away from the blow, exposing himself to the alley as Williams turned onto the street at the far end. The two-by-four came at him again, this time from overhead.

Carver sidestepped and the lumber slammed the pavement. He stomped his boot down and tore it from the man's grip before leaning into a follow-up punch. Carver was surprised when his fist whiffed through the air as the man bobbed his head backward.

There wasn't time to think. His opponent immediately returned a punch to the ribs. Carver pulled his elbow in, absorbing the hit with his left arm while striking with his right. The man batted the fist down and backed away.

The operators stood two yards from each other, narrowing eyes as they realized each was a capable fighter.

The Asian man had close-cropped hair, was well-trained, and carried the unmistakable air of ex-military.

"Who are you?" demanded Carver.

The man lunged. He feinted with his right and Carver missed the left that pounded into his side once, twice. Carver bashed the hand down and blocked a blow to his head, then propelled his knee into the man's gut. Instead of absorbing the blow's full damage, the man rolled with it and grabbed Carver's leg. He yanked him off balance before reversing and driving Carver to the asphalt.

Onlookers screamed as fists rained down. While Carver's forearms intercepted the blows, he was unsettled by the ferocity and strength of his attacker. The man tried to straddle him to gain control, but Carver slid his knee between them. When his attacker attempted to deal with that obstacle, Carver grabbed the two-by-four beside him and swung.

The wood clunked perfectly on the side of the man's skull. He stumbled backward and Carver hopped to his feet, squaring off against the unsteady opponent. The sight of blood streaming down his temple convinced anyone still watching from the tables to clear the area. Carver winced as more screams joined the fracas. Williams would have to be deaf to not be alerted to their presence.

As for the man, he was still on his feet. Carver's blow from the ground hadn't carried the necessary force to end the fight. His grip tightened on the plank of wood and the man reached into his jacket.

Carver pounced as the gun came out, swatting at it with

the two-by-four. The man pulled away to avoid contact but jumped as Carver released the club. It rocketed through the air toward him. Once again the attack was easily avoided, but it had served its purpose. By the time the operator recovered and brought the gun around, Carver got his hand on it. Their dual grips pushed the gun to the sky as it went off.

Flashbacks from Africa and the Middle East surged through Carver as he suddenly faced an intimate threat in close-quarters battle. He wrestled for control of the gun as the enemy pounded his face. Despite the man's strength, Carver had the weight advantage. He set his back into the man and spun him by his arm, pointing the pistol at the alley wall as it fired again. He tried to spin the arm away but his opponent turned with him, maintaining control of the weapon.

Carver spun them both around and forced their backs into the wall. The man, sandwiched in the middle, grunted in pain so Carver did it again. Finally the pistol fell away. Except now the man's hands were both free and pivoted into a choke hold.

Carver snuck his left hand into the grip before it was set. He tried a reverse headbutt but the man leaned to the side. That gave the opening to his right elbow, which hammered the operator's ribs.

The man kicked them off the wall, separating them slightly, and kneed Carver's side. The blows hurt. As Carver worked to avoid them, his hand slipped and the choke locked around his neck.

He kicked up his legs and his full weight pulled them to the ground. The man was familiar with the counter and came down willingly. Carver gulped up a momentary respite of air before the choke tightened again. His fingers scraped the asphalt searching for the gun. The man twisted away and brought his back to the ground so Carver was lying on top of him. Their legs kicked, and Carver's spirits sank when he heard the metal pistol bounce out of reach.

He went lightheaded and knew his lungs weren't the problem. His carotid was being clamped, cutting off oxygen to his brain. It left him in a dreamy state, the seconds of consciousness he had remaining feeling like an eternity. Carver clawed at the man's face over his shoulder, but that was just to keep him looking away while he made his real play.

Carver's weak hand slipped the Colonel from its quick-draw sheath on his hip. The small angled blade punched into the tender flesh of the man's side. He had no choice but to release the choke or be gutted.

He tossed Carver away, who gasped and rolled on the asphalt. A curse in Chinese was followed by a kick to his face. Carver caught the strike and sunk the knife into the man's inner thigh. He snarled and batted the back of Carver's head. Carver was still in a daze, but the fingered grip kept the knife locked in his hands. The angled blade ripped through flesh as the man broke contact and went for his gun.

Carver jumped forward. The man stumbled two steps before collapsing. Carver grabbed his leg to keep him from escaping, but by the time he walked on all fours to the man's face, his eyes rolled up. The Asian operator stiffened, extending his whole body into a curl like a fish, and then relaxed with a muted sigh. Blood gushed from the punctured femoral artery in his thigh. He was dead in seconds.

12

Staring emptily, Carver wondered what the man had been after. Who did he work for, and why did he waste his life?

A strange cocktail of emotions washed through him. He hadn't killed a man in four years. Which wasn't to say he was wracked with guilt about it.

It was the warrior code.

The man had been a warrior. The more you lean into that sword, the more it leans into you. Men like him, men like Carver and Shaw, once they chose this life, they each knew it might end with a bullet.

Panicked screams in the distance were strangely muffled. In the middle of close-quarters battle nothing else had mattered, but now reality was rushing back like a tidal wave. His senses once again attuned to the outside world. People yelled and scrambled in the distance. Luckily, possible eyewitnesses had long fled around the corner.

Carver wiped his knife on the dead agent's pants and sheathed it. He considered the dropped pistol. With the prominent star on the grip, he identified it as a Chinese Norinco. It was a compact pistol, meant for being hidden, maybe a QSZ-11. He didn't examine it too closely because there was ballistic evidence everywhere: a round in the wall, powder on the man's hands, and fingerprints on the weapon.

He cursed. Taipei was a first-world city, not a war zone. He wasn't supposed to run into enemy combatants. He didn't even know who the enemy was. While the immediate area was clear for now, Carver needed to be as far away from the gun, and the dead man, as possible.

He scrambled down the empty alley after Officer Williams. As he neared the end, a car rolled past before screeching to a halt and reversing. The driver's window slid down and Davis yelled, "Get in!"

Carver dove inside the back. Davis hit the gas, and the sudden acceleration slammed the door shut. The Toyota rocked hard as it hit the street and peeled through a red light. Carver groaned while prone on the back seat. His ribs were sore and his throat felt like he'd smoked a box of cigars. He slowly sat up and scanned the traffic through the back window. Nobody followed them.

"Vince, man, what the hell?"

Carver tried to speak but his throat knotted up. He cleared his throat a few times to loosen his voice box before saying, "I ordered you back to the hotel."

"Sorry, man. That Hyundai stuck around and I was keeping an eye on it. I didn't want to leave you outnumbered. Then I heard the reports and drove around back."

The team leader swallowed and sighed. "Thanks."

"You gonna tell me what's going on?"

Carver shook his head in response. "The guy got the

drop on me. He had a gun."

"Who was he?"

"I don't know."

"*Vince*."

"That's the truth. He was trained. Ex-military. Could've been undercover police or a private contractor."

Davis glared into the rearview mirror. "What do you mean 'could have been?' "

Carver winced. "He was trying to kill me, Mike."

Davis stifled a frown as the car swerved a lane over to make a sudden turn. "This is heavy shit, man. What are we gonna do?"

"We can't go to the police."

"Don't tell me we can't go to the police right now."

"We can't."

Davis shook his head. "Don't tell me that, Vince."

"Just... Just give me a minute."

"It's standard procedure," he pressed. "We did it after Arizona and didn't have a problem."

"In case you noticed, this isn't Arizona."

"All the more reason not to start an international incident."

"*Just give me a minute.*"

This was all wrong. Carver wasn't in shock. He was sore and a little bruised, both his body and his ego, but he wasn't a stranger to combat. It was just that his Delta days were supposed to be behind him. This thing—whatever it was—had him operating outside the usual parameters of the urban security business.

He checked his phone, staring at the number Williams had given him. Instead he dialed Shaw.

"What's up, boss?"

"What's your status?" wheezed Carver.

"Pulling into the hotel as we speak. Walter's gonna order in. Why'd you leave so suddenly?"

"It's a long story and I can't talk over the phone. Just go to REDCON 2. Watch out for local hostiles."

"You serious?"

"Very. And don't tell the principal about it. I'm not sure who we can trust out here. Know what I mean?"

"Loud and clear, boss."

Carver disconnected the call and again considered contacting Williams. It didn't make sense for her to be a part of this since she was the one being followed. Still, the circumstances neither incriminated nor vindicated her. It was always possible she was dirty and things were catching up to her. That Carver had seen something he wasn't supposed to.

They finally merged into a steady stream of traffic. While forced to a slower pace, they were now protected by the herd of vehicles, lost among the many.

"Talk to me, Vince," urged Davis.

"I..." He sighed. "Did the FBI interview you in Arizona?"

"They sure did. A detective-looking guy. Going bald but refuses to rock it like I do. I remember him because his name was Gunn."

Carver nodded. "What about a woman?"

"No, it was only the one guy. I figured he worked local since he was on the scene within the hour of you lifting off."

It made sense that the investigation started at the airport. It wasn't until Day Two that Gunn and Williams entered his office, which was the next logical step in the investigation. Gunn and Williams had followed the plane to San Jose. Of course, they also got in touch with Lachlan as he crossed the Pacific.

"Are you telling me this is government business, Vince?"

Carver was still catching breath that never seemed to fully return, but by now his pulse was slowing down. He leaned forward between the two front seats and looked at his friend in the mirror. "I'm not supposed to talk about it."

Davis returned a knowing look. "Are we not talking about this being linked to Arizona?"

"I don't know. It would make sense."

"And the FBI asked for your eyes on this?"

"*Somebody* did, anyway."

"Somebody who?"

Carver sighed. "Look, I really can't say. I'm torn between being straight with my team and being a patriot."

"A patriot." Davis stared. "That doesn't mean what I think it means, does it?"

"Just give me a little plausible deniability till I get a handle on things."

"You killed someone, Vince."

"I never said that. You didn't witness anything. You're not a party to what happened at the night market. You just picked me up. Can you trust me and play dumb?"

"That's asking a lot."

"It is and I know it. I need to wrap my head around this first. Let me figure out what's going on, and I'll bring you and Nick in on it. Are you with me?"

Davis quietly hissed. He was frustrated, and Carver knew he was pulling a dirty card. His men trusted him, and he trusted them. If push came to shove, they would each die for the other. In retrospect, keeping quiet was a minor ask.

"Let's just get back to the hotel," he muttered. "That bread pudding is doing things to my stomach."

They didn't speak about it for the rest of the drive. After the car was valeted, Carver took the ticket and told Davis to go on in. Meanwhile he strolled past the curved front facade of the Mandarin and dialed Williams. One way or another he was going to get answers. Oftentimes being direct was the best course of action.

Williams, it seemed, disagreed, and the call went to voice mail. Carver grumbled, waited a few minutes, and called again. Same result.

There were two possibilities. One was that she was ghosting him. The other scenario was worse. Something could have happened to her. Williams was, after all, the one that had originally been followed. And the driver of the Hyundai was still in the wind.

Carver waited in the shadows of the Mandarin Oriental, watching all newcomers. Davis had driven from the night market like a bat out of hell. If anybody was to follow them back, they'd be arriving shortly.

After half an hour without suspicious guests or a callback

from Williams, he decided to call it a night. There wasn't a whole lot he could do, and there was something to be said for blending in rather than sticking out. Carver strolled back inside and up to the fifteenth floor.

Shaw approached as he exited the elevator. "Davis told me some shit went down. You okay?"

Carver massaged his throat. "I've had better days. The principal?"

"Tucked away for the night. Don't change the subject."

"I'm not."

"Then what happened at that hotel bar?"

Carver sighed and made sure the hallway was clear. He nodded Shaw further down the hall, away from Sparroway's room, and spoke in a conspiratorial voice. "We followed a man who looked out of place to a night market. He was doing classic recon stuff. He must've spotted me. We got into it."

Shaw frowned. "And?"

"And he'll no longer be a problem. We had to clear out of there before I could learn anything, though."

Shaw scratched the thick hair on his cheek. "This means we have tangos in Taipei."

"Probably. But the guy was well trained. He wasn't your usual merc for hire."

"What's Marino say?"

Carver grimaced at the mention of their boss. "I haven't brought Mark in on this yet, and I don't know if it's a good idea. I'm trying to keep a low profile, and our comms aren't secure."

He nodded. "Better safe than sorry. But are we gonna need backup?"

"That's what I'm trying to determine. We'd need Lachlan to approve additional assets, which means explaining our concerns. And it'd be twenty-four hours at least before anyone arrived, and the conference ends in a day and a half."

"So we're in the shit."

Carver nodded and started to back away. Perhaps the best course of action was getting out of Dodge at the first convenient opportunity. "I'm trying to get answers. Just keep an eye out."

"Wait up. Does any of this have to do with that black lady you clocked leaving the bar?" Carver paused, and Shaw shrugged. "What? She kinda sticks out like a sore thumb round these parts, know what I mean?"

Damn it. Unlike Davis, Shaw had seen Williams. The supposed FBI agents hadn't had a chance to interview Shaw, so the visual alone didn't tip him off. Comparing notes with Davis shouldn't lead to anything since he'd only met Gunn, but it was a precarious house of cards.

"I don't know," Carver lied.

"Vince."

Carver's phone rang, and he bit down. It was Williams, at the worst possible moment.

"Let me get back to you, Nick. Just trust me on this." He answered the phone with a "One second" and then disappeared inside his room.

"When I said to contact me at end-of-day," said

138

Williams flatly, "I didn't mean tonight."

"Cut the crap, Williams. There were shots fired."

She hesitated before answering. "How do you know about that? Was something on the news?"

"Someone followed you from the hotel. Could be a local."

Another beat. "I wasn't followed."

"The hell you weren't. I tailed the guy." Carver went to the desk and woke up his laptop as he spoke. "There were two of them in a car."

"I would've made a tail," Williams assured.

"Then how do I know you went to the night market?"

She was gracious enough to stop denying it. "You followed me?"

"No," he said gruffly, "I followed your tail."

Carver hadn't checked his computer all day and had received a few innocuous emails. One from Mark Marino asking for an update. He inserted a reminder at the end to get Lachlan on board with their data vault. Another email from Sparroway attached tomorrow's conference itinerary. More private presentations on the third floor.

"This guy didn't look like anything special," said Carver, "but he was pretty good. He was onto you, and he spotted me too."

"What happened?"

"I can't exactly discuss it over the phone, know what I mean?"

Williams must have. She'd been within earshot when the gun had gone off. A panicking stampede attracts attention too. Perhaps she'd only had clues and Carver was filling in the rest of the story, but she was in intelligence. It wasn't a leap to put two and two together.

"Are we compromised?" she asked.

"That's what I was going to ask you. We're not on my end. The asset that clocked me is off the table."

"Right. I'll look into it. In the meantime, sit tight and keep on it."

"Copy that," he said sarcastically. He bristled as the call disconnected halfway through.

A shuffling sound caught his attention at the door. The small spot of light in the peephole blacked out for a moment before shining again. Carver drew his knife and darted to the door, peeking through the lens. No one was there at first, but then Shaw paced by looking bored. After half a minute, he came around again, twirling at his waist to stretch his back.

Carver pulled away from the door with a frown.

13

Carver woke early to study the conference schedule Sparroway had forwarded over. He skipped breakfast and used the free time to take an extra long shower. Aside from notable bruising over his ribs and some minor scrapes on his arms, he was visually unscathed. The injuries were nothing long sleeves couldn't fix.

With the intent of avoiding the topic of the night market, he ignored Mark Marino's email requesting updates and didn't emerge from his room until it was time to hit the road. Davis waited in the hall with Sparroway.

"Didn't take you for the type to sleep in," said the interim coordinator.

"Long night," replied Carver with a knowing glance at his associate. Davis simply nodded in the presence of Lachlan's security team. "Before we get started, I'd like to discuss the length of Walter's visit. The itinerary is to stay the weekend, but—"

"That's old news," said Sparroway. "We're diverting to North Carolina. Something to do with showing Chen-Han Lin around."

Carver bit down. That decision must have been made

two nights ago. "What about my services?"

He shrugged. "I assume your team is to stay on. Why, did you hear anything different?"

"I didn't hear anything at all. That's the problem."

"Oh," he said without a hint of culpability. "I'll get you the schedule at the end of the day."

"I appreciate it."

Carver told himself it wasn't Sparroway's fault he was in over his head. A job he wasn't qualified for was shoved onto his plate at the last second. It was the very reason Carver was brought on. He just had to learn not to rely on the guy. At the very least, he agreed the details could wait and that the more pressing concern was getting the day started.

From a risk standpoint, the next two days of the SEMICON were ideal. The private meetings with investors and other collaborators on the cordoned-off floor presented little risk. From the perspective of the CIA, however, it was an entirely different ball game. Back rooms were incubators for illegal deals and, judging from the schedule, Carver already had a solid lead.

They arrived at the expo center with little fanfare and made it through two meetings, both brief yet mind-numbing. Lachlan was in a foul mood as he instructed his assistant to "not fuck this one up." Panesh nodded obediently and his boss decided he would skip the next presentation to take an early lunch.

"I don't want a damned production for once," berated Lachlan. "There's a food court and I'll eat in an empty conference room if that's the only way I'll get some peace around here." Sparroway hurried away at his side.

"You go on," Carver told Davis. "Keep an eye out."

The reminder carried real weight after the incident at the night market. While Davis looked like he wanted to raise a concern, all he said was, "Sure thing."

Carver crossed his arms and leaned against the wall as an unsettled Panesh prepared slides for the next presentation. They were finally alone. The assistant paused and looked up at the only remaining member of the security team.

"Are you sticking around for the presentation?" chuckled Panesh.

"I just might," said Carver unironically.

The assistant was nonplussed. "Oh? I didn't take you for the type to have an interest in chip production."

Carver shrugged, lifted off the wall, and grabbed a paper from a stack Panesh had just set down. They were handouts with the heading, "High Purity Quartz in Spruce Pine, North Carolina."

"You might be surprised," replied Carver, pretending to peruse the paper.

Panesh's smile was robotic, without feeling, but his nod was honest enough. "It's good that I have you here, actually. I'm assuming Mr. Sparroway broached the issue of extending your contract?"

"You have details?" he asked diplomatically.

"They're right in front of you," Panesh answered, pointing to the sheet. "We fly out tomorrow evening."

Carver widened his eyes at the news. On one hand, it was exactly what he'd hoped for. Taipei was an unknown quantity, he didn't have a gun, and after the incident at the night market, returning to the United States was a welcome development.

On the flip side was his progress with the CIA investigation. Carver still had more questions than answers, and he now had a rapidly approaching deadline. Which was precisely why Carver had picked this opportunity to learn a little bit more about their destination.

"Isn't tomorrow night a bit rushed?" he asked.

"It's business," Panesh said matter-of-factly. "Walter wants this deal closed as soon as possible. Once his commitments to the conference are satisfied, we're taking a red-eye to North Carolina to finalize the next stage. Mr. Lin is doing the same."

"I mean from a security standpoint."

"Oh." Panesh smiled and nodded. "I guess that's your department, isn't it? But Walter has a great reputation with Spruce Pine. We've pulled strings with security access. They'll have the fabs locked down and ready for us."

Carver nodded along as he made small talk. "You've been before then?"

"Of course. It's our main supply line."

"Right. For quartz."

He grinned in the way only an academic could to a layman. "It's not just any quartz."

Carver glanced at the presentation handout. It was a fact sheet with bullet points proclaiming the greatness of the Spruce Pine quarries. But his curiosity lay elsewhere. "This is a good sell."

"I should hope so," said Panesh. "The product speaks for itself."

"Who are we pitching to?"

"A group of investors from a variety of companies. We give them a small amount of buy-in and they tie their fates to ours. Everybody wins."

"International?"

He shrugged. "Sure. Taiwan is fertile soil, not just for East Asia, but for Indian and Russian interests as well."

Carver's ears perked. This mention of Russia was the first possible link to the Eastern European mercs that had attacked them in Arizona. It was purely circumstantial, of course, but the association raised some questions.

"Hey, Panesh," he said slyly as he approached the assistant. "When our convoy was attacked on the way to Walter's plane, why weren't you with us?"

The assistant stiffened as Carver drew close. "Um, I don't understand the question."

"Sure you do."

He blinked unsteadily. "What I mean is I don't understand why you would ask it?"

"Humor me."

"Okay. As part of the advance team, I flew in a day earlier along with Sparroway and some others. When the whole group didn't arrive intact, Sparroway and I had to fill new roles."

"You were promoted too?"

"Yes. Gail—Walter's previous executive assistant—was murdered in Arizona. And I don't think I like your implication..."

Carver didn't back away. He figured Panesh was a small enough player that he could afford to make him nervous. It was a good first step in turning him. If he was indeed an enemy asset, he had a lot to lose. Putting the fear of God in him might force him to re-examine his options. And then, when things seemed most hopeless, Carver would swoop in at the last second with a lifeline.

Panesh wrested his gaze away, but before Carver could say anything a man tapped lightly on the open door.

"Panesh Mehta? It is nice to meet you."

Carver backed away and took an unassuming position against the wall as a pair of Indian businessmen entered and introduced themselves. Panesh was slightly shaken and made awkward small talk until three Russians entered next. Individual representatives from Thailand, Norway, and Belgium also filed in. Most took only casual notice of the security officer in the back, but one of the Russians kept glancing at Carver with a curious expression.

Welcoming his guests and handing out papers seemed to help Panesh regain his composure.

"Where is Mr. Lachlan?" asked one of the Russians.

"I'm afraid he won't be joining us this morning, but I assure everyone that you will leave here happy. Spruce Pine is home to the purest quartz in the world. High in silica and low in contaminants."

And just like that the executive assistant seamlessly segued into his presentation about how one sleepy town in North Carolina supplies eighty percent of the world's high-purity quartz.

"This quartz isn't just quartz," he explained. "Spruce Pine has set the purity benchmark for the world. It's a true global standard which no other country has been able to match. China is the next largest quartz supplier at only ten percent, but their product isn't as pure. They are, admittedly, getting better at refining the lower grade source material they do have, but their infrastructure is not robust. Your countries, India and Russia, the next market leaders, lag even further behind."

He went on extolling the virtues of HPQ. "Because of its sheer purity, nearly every computer chip on the planet is manufactured using product from Spruce Pine. That's just about every desktop, laptop, cell phone, tablet, music player, and watch. It dominates the exploding photovoltaic industry as well."

The international audience listened with not-exactly rapt attention as Panesh broke down the entire Spruce Pine operation. Carver imagined Mr. Lin sitting in a similar presentation years earlier and wondered what had gone wrong to make him lose faith.

Though illuminating, the presentation continued for far too long and waded through mundanities like the washing process of the quartz sand. This included stages of crushing, scrubbing, magnetic separation, flotation, thermal processing, and several proprietary finishers to hit that coveted standard of ultra purity.

It was the first part of his speech where foul play was possible, where there were secrets that sounded worth stealing. But Panesh himself claimed ignorance of the specific methods when asked, and the subject matter moved away from the topic without objection. By the time Panesh hit the final slide, everybody was ready for lunch, and Carver wondered if there was anything here at all.

He lingered as Panesh took final questions from the investors, traded details, and set up future contacts. Carver approached after the last man stepped out. The assistant studiously organized his attaché case. It was probably nervous energy, worry over a repeat of their chat before the presentation.

"What is this?" asked Carver as he grabbed a folder that had been set aside.

Panesh continued putting his documents away. "I've taken the liberty of creating a schedule for the Taipei Semiconductors tour of Spruce Pine."

"This is for Mr. Lin."

"Yes. I'm to deliver it to him today."

"I'll do it," offered Carver. Panesh looked at him uncertainly. "I'm going to be part of the security detail so I'd like to be involved. And I need to coordinate with his team anyway. I won't have another Arizona happening on my watch."

Panesh blinked and hurriedly nodded. "Of course not. Whatever you want."

Carver got the feeling Panesh was a little frightened of him. "You know where he is?"

The assistant zipped up his attaché case and appeared startled at the possibility of being helpful. "Supposedly he's preparing for his big speech on smart manufacturing this afternoon, but I happen to know he has an off-books lunch with Asia Pacific Quartz. It's why Walter's so insistent on flying to Spruce Pine. He's afraid of losing control of this thing."

Carver chortled. "What happened to Spruce Pine and the purest quartz in the world?"

"Mr. Lin's tactics are just hardball, Mr. Carver, but we still need to take them seriously. There's always someone going after the alpha. Remember that."

The team leader wondered if there was subtext to the comment, but he let it pass. Carver looked up Asia Pacific Quartz on his phone. They were a fully integrated multinational company, from mine to customer.

"This is a Chinese-backed enterprise," he said with dismay.

"Don't be so naive. China is about as capitalist a nation as they come. They won't let something as little as an old revolution stand in the way of profit." Panesh made for the door.

"Do you know where this meeting is taking place?"

"I don't. Sorry." He gladly escaped down the hall.

Carver frowned and strolled the other way as he pondered his options. Davis and a member of Lachlan's detail stood outside a closed door. "Good news," said the team leader. "It looks like we're going to North Carolina." He went to knock.

"I wouldn't do that," warned Davis. "The principal's not in a good mood."

"Liquid lunch?"

"Not a drop."

Carver got the feeling Davis would've said more if Lachlan's man wasn't there. "I'll just need to risk it," he said, and knocked.

"You see?" screamed the billionaire behind the door. "This is what I'm talking about." The volume grew louder as he neared. "How incompetent do you have to be to misunderstand the meaning of peace and—"

The door flung open and a red-faced Lachlan stared up at Carver. His change was immediate, though not total. Anger merely detoured to annoyance. "Excuse me, I'm getting a headache in here." He pointed a thumb at Sparroway sitting at the table with his gaze on the floor. "What do you want?"

"I'll try not to bother you, Walter," said Carver. "I just needed to confirm with you about transitioning my team to Spruce Pine. Will we all be flying with you?"

"Of course. Is Panesh dropping the ball too?"

"I just needed to hear it from you before informing my boss."

"Mark," he snorted. "How do you work with that car salesman? Be honest with me. He wants you pitching me on your data vault?"

Carver chuckled. "You've got us dead to rights."

"Well I suppose I ought to thank you for not doing that. As if I couldn't manage my own IP."

"There was one thing, though, that Panesh couldn't help me with. Do you happen to know where Mr. Lin is now? I have a packet to deliver to him."

He shook his head and scoffed. "Cloak and dagger, that man. Your guess is as good as mine. That it?"

"Yes, Walter. Thanks for your time."

The billionaire spun to Sparroway. "Come on, you're done too. Get out of here and let me think."

Davis rolled his eyes so only his team leader could see. Carver nodded and left before a glum Sparroway could slow him down. He went for the stairway and dialed his boss.

"Vince."

"Mark, I'm glad I got you. What time is it over there?"

"Just after nine at night. I'm at home. How are things going over there? Any more incidents?"

"The principal is well insulated," deflected Carver. "In fact, he wants to extend our contract. The three of us will continue with him stateside in North Carolina. I'll email you the timeline when I have it."

"That's great work. And if you need any more assets, just call them in. This is a coup for us. It has the potential to be our biggest account. Keep this up and he'll sign on a permanent basis."

"Yeah," said Carver in a manner that implied he was unconvinced.

"What did Walter say about our data vault? Did you tell him it was secured with block chain?"

"It's gonna be a tough sell, Mark. Let's just say he's considering it."

"Okay, okay. Just mention the block chain. People like block chain."

"Whatever you say. Talk to you later."

Carver exited the stairway as the call ended. Once past security on the ground floor, he was again in the thick of a crowd that was... if not boisterous then dedicated. It was a short walk to the same stage where Lachlan had given his keynote.

The space was mostly empty this lunch hour, with a few groups camped on the floor eating from bags. Carver badged backstage and found Yi-An with her security team. She caught Carver's gaze from afar and excused herself.

"No diamonds today?" he asked when she neared.

"Believe it or not, I'm here for business not pleasure."

"You say that a lot."

She crossed her arms. "What's on your mind?"

"Just wondering if you want to get out of here, you know..."

"You want to take me to lunch?"

"I want to take you to the United States."

She paused mid smirk, speechless for a moment.

"How does Spruce Pine, North Carolina sound?"

She blinked at him and settled into an easy smile. "For you? I'll be there with bells on."

"That's good to hear. You happen to know where your boss is? I have a schedule Panesh wants to get to him." He waved the folder like the prop it was.

"You're out of luck. My team cleared a steakhouse down the street so you won't see him for a bit. Mr. Lin enjoys his cocktail hour."

"What happened to the Spartan businessman at dinner?"

"The middle of the day is about gathering energy. The end of the day just wastes it. You can leave that folder with me."

"It's okay, I'll wait." When she was about to insist, he said, "I just do what they tell me, you know?"

Yi-An, while appeased by the explanation, couldn't leave it at that. "Somehow I doubt that, Vince. Anyway, I have to get back to it. This afternoon is the big event for Mr. Lin and I can't let anything go wrong. Take me to lunch tomorrow?"

"If you're gonna beg me I won't turn you down."

She rolled her eyes and stomped away. He liked her better in diamonds.

14

There was only one steakhouse within a few blocks of the expo center. It was an easy walk but the humid air made it difficult in the jacket. Carver was just sore enough that he sucked it up instead of stretching to take it off.

The restaurant was a classy joint with smooth jazz and dim lighting, except everything was a little too polished. Mass-market decor, top-40 hits, and without the expected smoke of a respectable old-time establishment. The place felt like the Disneyland version of the real thing. At least the food smelled good.

They sat centrally in the dining room: Lin, his assistant, and two CPOs standing in the background. The balding Asian man sitting with them had a couple of bodyguards of his own.

Carver casually approached the bar spanning the length of the steakhouse. The countertop was a mirror, and there were several of the Victorian fashion along the walls. He took a seat across one between bar shelves where he could comfortably watch Lin's table in the reflection. He ordered an old fashioned with rye.

On the surface, there was nothing strange about a lunch

meeting between Taipei Semiconductors and Asia Pacific Quartz. The fact that it wasn't on Lin's official schedule was unusual, perhaps, but not altogether suspicious. What caught Carver's attention was the stark contrast between the behavior of the security officers.

Yi-An's team was standard private industry. They were attentive and mostly looked the part, but if someone pulled a gun they'd probably be too flatfooted to properly respond. It wasn't even Yi-An's fault so much as a question of available talent. Security in the business sector rarely met the operational standards of a military hot zone. Even an outspoken billionaire like Walter Lachlan had apparently gotten lazy in that department, which explained why he'd taken a shine to Carver's team.

The Asia Pacific fellows were different. The guards had clocked Carver as soon as he walked in. Even now, Carver found himself averting his eyes at their constant spot checks. No doubt about it, he was a suspicious character, even with his back turned to them.

Then there was their principal. The balding man had a belly and a whitening goatee, but he wasn't your average good-natured grandpa. He learned forward in a stance of authority, pounding a finger on the table as he spoke with hushed certainty. In the face of such conviction, even a man like Lin grew submissive.

Carver wanted to get closer to listen in on the discussion, but it was a nonstarter. Not only would the CPOs spot him, but the language made any eavesdropping impossible. And unlike his time in the military, Carver didn't have recording or translating assets at his disposal.

He scanned the other parties in the mostly empty steakhouse, and then his gaze traced over the window to the pedestrians on the sidewalk and crossing the street to the subway station. He sighed and took a sip of the old fashioned. This was one of those cases where surveilling wasn't good enough. Carver slid off the barstool and re-buttoned his jacket.

One of Lin's men backed away from the table, eyes fixed on the subway station across the street. In the security business, constantly scanning for threats was a practiced skill. Something had caught his interest. Carver followed his gaze to where a man stood at the top of an escalator. When Carver turned back to the bodyguard, he was staring right at him.

Maybe he'd underestimated Lin's security. And maybe his hand had just been forced.

Carver approached the table, drink in hand. Within seconds the Asia Pacific guards obstructed his path, each with one arm forward and the other on the grip of a holstered firearm. Lin's bodyguard returned to the table and whispered in his boss's ear.

"Identify yourself," commanded one of the guards. The balding man sat coiled in his chair as if ready to take evasive action. It was a curious stance for a businessman.

"It's okay," said Mr. Lin with a hand in the air. "This is an acquaintance of mine, one of Walter Lachlan's men. Isn't that right?"

"Vince Carver, sir. I have something for you."

The assurance did little to relax the posture of the Asia Pacific guards. "Arms up!" one instructed.

Carver sighed and raised his arms. One of the Asia Pacific CPOs covered him while the other patted him down. He brushed over the knife sheath under the jacket without concern. After not finding a gun, he whispered to his boss. The other guy still hadn't backed away.

Carver made a show of slowly unbuttoning his jacket and pulling out the folder. "It's a schedule for your Spruce Pine tour."

The location earned a reaction from the balding man. He turned to Lin with raised brows.

"I hope I'm not intruding, Mr. Lin," Carver added.

"Not at all," he said, waving him over. "Let me take a look."

The Asia Pacific guards looked to their principal, only backing away after his subtle nod. Carver approached the table and handed the folder to Lin's assistant, who opened it and placed it on the table. Carver was quiet as they skimmed the documents, but couldn't help feeling the other man's eyes on him.

"I'm sorry," said Carver, "we haven't met. Asia Pacific Quartz, am I right?"

The businessman sat up straighter. This nod wasn't as subtle. It came with a congenial smile but no complementary introduction. The quiet type, then.

Carver caught Lin's bodyguard glancing across the street again. That's when he looked closer and saw it. The man was the same one he'd first seen in the airport, and again yesterday at the conference. Which meant Carver had a tail of his own.

"Anyway," he announced, "I don't mean to interrupt your lunch." He backed away.

"Very good, Mr. Carver. Thank you for the prompt delivery. I do have one question, however."

Carver lingered. "What's that?"

"I don't understand why you felt the need to deliver this yourself." Lin and his mysterious associate seemed invested in the answer.

Carver held up the remainder of his old fashioned. "Just needed a little afternoon energy, sir." He drained the glass and headed to the exit.

No one stopped him. As he hit the sidewalk, instead of walking back to the Nangang Expo Center, he dawdled and went the opposite way just as the crosswalk light flipped. When he started across the street, the man who'd followed him to the restaurant turned down the escalator.

Carver quickened his pace and reached the top as his target was halfway down. A few seconds passed and the man made an unassuming glance upward. He spotted Carver and brushed past the people standing in his way.

Both men advanced down the extended metal steps descending into the bowels of the city. Carver was held up by a family toting all their worldly possessions in luggage. At the bottom, the man scurried out of sight. Carver vaulted onto the sidewall and slid unsteadily on his boots, carefully avoiding the obstacles meant to discourage such behavior. He reached the bottom and hurried forward as the man scanned a card through the entry kiosks.

Carver sneered as he approached. There were not one but two security guards overlooking the terminal entry. Kiosks on the near wall supplied admission cards, but there was no time. The station rumbled with the approach of a train, and the mystery man was yet again pulling his disappearing act.

Carver pulled a twenty-dollar bill and slapped it down on a kiosk as a man attempted to scan his card. Carver snatched the card without asking, scanned himself through, and then placed it back on the twenty.

"Thanks."

The action earned only a sideways glance from the distracted guards, and Carver pushed forward as the train arrived. Passengers exited in an orderly fashion before the others loaded up. Carver kept his head down as the man he was following looked around the station before boarding the train near the front. Carver snuck into the back and the doors closed.

They started on their way. He headed to the door of the next car. A chime sounded as he pressed through, making it into the next car and earning a lot of curious looks. His luck ran out at the next door. A uniformed conductor came through ahead of him and said something he didn't understand. It was clear he was being asked not to use the doors.

It didn't matter. The train began to slow and Carver positioned by the exit. Passengers lined up as the train stopped. He waved them ahead to provide cover. Then he peeked out and caught the other man exiting in a hurry. After a few beats, Carver hunched down and joined the crowd heading to the surface. It was an easy wave to get lost in. At the top of the escalator, the man doubled back toward the expo center along the sidewalk, speaking into a radio on his collar.

They both walked with urgency, but Carver's stride was larger. He hugged the storefronts and gained on the man, but there was nowhere to adequately hide and his luck ran out. The man checked his tail and spotted him. Then he broke into a sprint.

All pretenses cast aside, they broke into a foot chase. They whipped past startled onlookers, disrupting the orderly bliss of pedestrian traffic. Carver burst across the street. A car honked. Vehicles momentarily impeded him and the man sped away. Carver grunted and continued to give chase. At the end of the next block, the man fled down a bustling cross street. He wasn't especially fast and had no hope of escaping the Delta operative. It took the length of another block before he spun around in panic and reached for his jacket.

"No you don't."

Carver tackled him into the wall. The man hit hard but fought back, clearing some room with an elbow and spinning around to strike. After the fiasco at the night market, Carver wasn't taking chances. He swatted the blow aside and returned a gut punch that doubled the man over.

"Why are you following me?"

Carver only gave him a second before standing him up

and rocking him with another blow to his side. The man collapsed to his haunches.

"Who are you?" Carver demanded, face red with fury.

The man met his eyes with fierce defiance.

"You don't want to go this route," Carver warned. "You've been on my ass since the airport and I'm not letting you go again. You speak English?"

The man's eyes narrowed.

"Of course you do. Now are you going to tell me what I want to know, or do you want some more boxing lessons?"

An SUV swerved to the curb. Carver pivoted away from the man so he could watch both fronts. The doors opened and men in suits exited. Carver recognized them. One of them had been posted on Lachlan's floor the night he arrived. Another had been standing at the wall during dinner. They stomped toward the man on the ground and helped him to his feet.

"You're Lin's men?" Carver said angrily.

They ignored him as they escorted their team member to the vehicle.

"Hey!" snapped Carver, "I'm talking to you." He marched toward them as they loaded up. "Hey!" He balled his fist.

Begrudgingly, one of them turned around. "Sir," he said, "you cannot do this."

"He's with you?" asked Carver. He stepped into the face of the reticent guard. "He's one of you?"

"Yes," he answered. "This is all a misunderstanding. You cannot do this."

"Why are you following me?"

He shook his head. "You cannot do this. Please."

Carver didn't stop them from backing into the vehicle. They shut the doors and sped away. He threw his hands in the air and shouted, "Unbelievable!"

He paced the sidewalk, ignoring the astonished faces of the locals. Lin had him followed, which meant he was worried about something. It seemed far-fetched that he knew about the CIA, but then, Williams had been followed too. Besides, he'd waded knee-deep in sloppier intelligence in the past. What other reason was there to follow a private security contractor?

Unless this wasn't tied to the CIA at all. If not that then the only curious aspect of Carver's presence was the fact that he had prevented the abduction in Arizona. Whoever had masterminded that operation would be wary of him in its aftermath. It was possible they were keeping tabs on him to look for an opening.

Carver dialed Davis. "Status report."

"A-OK, Team Leader."

"No threats to the principal? Unexpected visitors?"

"Nope. One sec." Davis lowered the phone and excused himself. There were sounds of jostling as he separated from the others before continuing in a lowered voice. "The only thing off-plan right now, besides you disappearing, is we're returning to the hotel early."

"Something came up?"

"More like Lachlan turned everything else down. He was supposed to stick around for the Taipei Semiconductors presentation, but he's in a foul mood. He wants to stew in the hotel spa."

"Maybe it will be an early night."

"I think we could all use one of those," noted Davis. "Where have you been?"

Carver sighed. "Following up with Chen-Han Lin. Turns out he's been keeping tabs on us. That man from the airport, the one I pointed out to you in the keynote audience? He's on their security staff. I ran him down in the street and nearly beat him senseless before they scooped him up."

"What the hell? Does that have anything to do with—"

"No," he interrupted, paranoid about speaking on the open line. "I don't know. I don't think so, but it might. I just wanted you to know about the suspicious activity."

"Roger that, but have you considered your contribution?"

"Meaning?"

"I mean you're wandering around Taipei getting into fistfights. You're following Lin instead of your employer. It looks suspicious from any angle."

Carver gritted his teeth. "I'm just doing my job. Make sure to let Nick know you're heading back early."

He disconnected the call and returned to the underground, this time properly purchasing a subway card. Two train stops to the terminal station later and he emerged in the sun in front of the expo hall. A missed call from Williams popped up on his phone.

"What's up?" he said when she picked up.

"Where are you?"

"The Nangang Exhibition Center."

"We need to talk. Can you meet me?"

He checked his watch. "Sure. I was just about to hop in my car. Same place?"

"No. I'll text you the address. Twenty minutes?"

"If it's close."

15

Carver hunted down his rental in the lot and made it to the cafe five minutes early. He stepped inside and found Williams at a table in the back. She blew into a mug of tea on a saucer beside a bakery box.

"I see you're enjoying the local culture," said Carver.

She pointedly ignored the remark. "Sorry for the cloak and dagger. I'm taking precautions after last night."

"Makes sense." She wasn't wearing her favorite jacket so she must have been serious. He sat down.

"The tea's good here," she said.

"Not my thing."

She nodded to the box. "Try the milk bread at least. It's better than it sounds."

"I'm not interested, Williams. Why am I here?"

She sighed as if he was the most insufferable person she'd ever had the misfortune of working with. The moment passed after a rejuvenating sip from her mug and she got down to it. "I looked into the night market for you. There was no word of a dead man. Are you sure you killed him?"

He stared at her with the certainty of a mountain.

"Right. Well, it's not every day something like that goes unnoticed in a crowded night market. This reads like a professional organization covering their tracks."

"You can appreciate my skepticism," said Carver.

She studied his expression. "What are you talking about?"

"I'm talking about you, Williams. You were there. We both followed you. What were you doing going for a stroll at the night market?"

"That doesn't concern you."

"It very much concerns me. What better clandestine organization to make a body disappear than the CIA?"

They stiffened as a waitress approached. They both waved her off and waited a minute.

"I had nothing to do with what happened," she calmly continued. "I think you know that. Now, all things considered, you came out of this cleanly."

"You call that clean?"

"I do. You were never supposed to be there, and it doesn't sound like you were identified. Given the lack evidence, no authorities will come looking. My advice to you is to pretend the whole thing never happened."

"The cops are only half the problem."

"And we're here to discuss the rest. Have you had any developments?"

Carver grimaced. She was just working him, keeping him settled and moving him along in an endless information pump. "Sure. I just caught one of Lin's security team tailing me. He'd been watching us since we landed."

Her eyes flashed. "You caught him red-handed? Do they know you know?"

"Well, seeing as I softened the guy up for his trouble..."

"Always the blunt instrument," she sighed.

"I'm the instrument you recruited."

"Fair enough. What did they say about you getting into it with their guy?"

"I simply let them know my feelings about being followed. I didn't give them a reason to be suspicious, if that's what you mean, but they wouldn't be following me if they didn't already have an interest."

"It just means they're up to something."

His thoughts exactly. "Speaking of which," he said. "Chen-Han Lin just had an off-books meeting with Asia Pacific Quartz. Their discussions have Lachlan in some kind of state, but my concerns are less business oriented. There's something off about them. The older gentleman, in particular, was out of place. He was overly aggressive with Lin. Confident but flighty about my presence."

She chewed her lip and nodded. "Okay, that's good work, Vince. Asia Pacific is a Chinese company. They're more on the supply side of things, but they're in a related industry. More importantly, they're government sponsored. It wouldn't surprise me to discover some of their representatives working for the MSS."

Carver jerked his head to attention. "The Ministry of State Security?"

"It's how operatives get information, especially in this part of the world. Not Lin's security staff. They're different teams. But the guys on my tail, the man at the meeting... It would make sense if the CCP had a local team overseeing the data sale."

Carver frowned. "Overseeing isn't the right word. It was more like a shakedown."

"Which would suggest Lin is compromised. He's suspicious, so he's watching you."

"Except I don't know if the sale is happening here. Everyone's rushing off to Spruce Pine."

"Asia Pacific too?"

Carver shook his head. "I don't think so. I saw Lin's schedule and they weren't included. I think the whole point is they're the competition."

Williams studied her tea for a protracted moment. "We need to be careful because things may move fast from here on out. It's very unlikely MSS agents will cross the Pacific. It's too much of a risk. We need to keep our eyes on Taipei." She took a long sip and set her mug down. "Okay, so we have Lachlan at Crystal Processing Systems making a deal with Lin and Taipei Semiconductors. Spruce Pine is a potential sticking point, with Asia Pacific Quartz as potential buyers. Any of them could be bad actors."

He nodded agreement. The way Lin's man took a beating, he clearly wasn't special ops. The man at the night market was in a different league. "What doesn't make sense to me is why have muscle like this on the ground for what is essentially an INFOSEC operation? The CCP has a legion of hackers and brokers and spies. You don't need boots for a digital trail. Why risk weapons when cash will do?"

"You already answered that question," she said. "Lin is an uncooperative asset. It's entirely possible he's moving the stage to North Carolina to get the CCP off his back."

"Which means they're going to double down."

She finished her tea and checked her phone. "I've been here too long. If this is MSS, they may know who I am and may be tracking our phones." She stood. "Keep doing what you're doing, Vince, but try to keep a low profile. Right now you have deniability. Lin has his suspicions, but his team will be equally suspicious about everyone. It's the curse of being a criminal."

"I need my gun."

"You need to try the milk bread," she insisted. Williams walked away without taking the box and Carver felt a little insufferable himself.

He switched seats so his back was to the wall and slid the bakery box over. He sliced the strip of invisible tape with his nail and opened the box. A matte black SIG Sauer P320 rested in a crumple of wax paper. Maybe he could get used to pastries.

Carver took the box to the privacy of his rental vehicle, where he emptied it and checked the pair of magazines. He slid one into the pistol and fit it into his waistband until he could get his holster from the hotel.

Chinese State Security. He didn't know why he was surprised. It explained the aggressiveness of the man at the night market. With the full scope of the threat out in the open, the assurances of Williams fell flat. They knew she was a CIA case officer. That meant she had an asset in place.

They'd be onto him. This was Ankara all over again.

With Lachlan ending his day early, there was little need to return to the expo center. Instead he drove to the steakhouse where Lin was still enjoying his cocktail hour. Carver parked a block down and waited. Half an hour later, Lin and his men exited with stoic faces. Carver slid down in his seat as they drove back to the expo center for his big speech.

A few minutes later, the balding pot-bellied man exited, giving his security officers terse instructions. They loaded into a white Defender. Carver waited thirty seconds before following.

It was a ten minute drive and he had to really lag behind. If these guys were intelligence, they likely already knew what Carver drove. Luckily, his presence wasn't noted. They eventually pulled into a small unmarked warehouse. The yard was empty and gave no indication as to the type of work that occurred there, or if any work occurred at all. One thing was certain: with no signage or employees, this wasn't an official Asia Pacific Quartz operation.

Carver parked a good distance away and waited. An hour passed before he received a text message from Sparroway, of all people.

"What's this I hear about you harassing Mr. Lin's security detail?"

Carver set the phone down without answering. He was surprised Lin's team was going on the offensive. He would think being caught following a business partner was embarrassing enough. Carver supposed that, by pressing the issue, Lin was doing his best to guarantee they kept their distance from each other.

Another hour passed without incident until Carver got a call. It was Davis this time, nearing the end of his shift.

"You heard about this shit?" asked Davis.

"What are you talking about?"

"Someone called in a bomb threat at the expo center."

Carver sat up. "Where are you?"

"Don't worry. We left early. The principal's in the hotel."

"You're initiating lockdown?"

"Already on it. But you know how Lachlan is. Would help if you were around. He likes you for some reason."

Carver shifted into drive. "On my way."

Fifteen minutes later, he pulled behind a line of cars in the Mandarin Oriental's driveway. Davis was forcefully yelling at an Asian man in a suit, thick arm raised and pointing away from the front entrance.

"And if I see any of you motherfuckers again, I'm gonna do more than ask nicely."

The man raised his hands innocently and retreated into a waiting sedan that hastily sped off.

Carver exited his running vehicle, thanked the valet, and rounded to the entrance. "What was that about?"

Davis straightened his jacket in a huff. "Caught him sniffing around the fifteenth floor. Maybe I'm being followed too?"

Carver hadn't gotten a clear look at the man or anyone else in the vehicle. "What did he want?"

"He was just looking around. But he was annoying about it, asking me all kinds of questions instead of just leaving. You think he has something to do with the bomb threat?"

"How do you mean?"

He shrugged. "It's coincidental timing."

Carver nodded. "Because Lachlan was scheduled to be at the expo center right now."

"Maybe he didn't expect us to be here. We all were except for you. Lin's men took off already." He snickered. "Said something about an incident in the field, which I took for you kicking their guy's ass. Then the bomb threat came in and they mobilized. Every single member of their team is out securing their boss. I'm not even sure they're coming back tonight."

Carver's brows furrowed. He wasn't sure if this was a problem or an opportunity. "Did they pack?"

"There wasn't time. But Vince, man... this guy I kicked out? He asked about the night market."

"He what?"

"Look, man, the time for bullshit is over. You gotta tell me what we're into, and you gotta tell me now."

Carver worked his jaw. He was used to being decisive, but the damned CIA had him on a gag order. He made a field assessment and concluded his team was more important than national security. "Let's take a walk."

They started a circuit around the hotel exterior, not saying a whole lot of anything while in the vicinity of incoming hotel guests.

"Where's your firearm?" asked Carver.

Davis looked down at his jacket. It bulged from his holster, but it was empty. "How'd you see that? I passed it on to Nick. Due to the threat, he came on shift early."

Carver checked his wristwatch. It was just about five anyway. They were silent another minute until they rounded the corner.

"So here's the deal," said Carver. "After the Arizona job, I was contacted by the CIA."

Davis went stone-faced but didn't respond.

"The details aren't important, but they want me to keep an eye out for an illegal data sale. It's looking like Lin's dirty."

"You know how I feel about the Agency, Vince."

"Mike, I agree with you. After all this I still don't know if I can trust my case officer. She did give me a gun, though." He pulled the spare magazine from his pocket and slid out a round, avoiding stamping it with his fingerprint. The bullet appeared genuine, but he would need to check the gun when he had some privacy.

"So what's the job? Are we expecting wet work?"

"No," Carver asserted, "but you've been a grunt before. We both know there are no guarantees. It gets worse..."

He hissed. "Of course it does."

"Lin's guys aren't the only ones sniffing around. We believe the MSS is in town. They're neck-deep in this thing."

Davis stopped. "The guy from the night market?"

"It would make sense."

"So if this guy was asking about that..."

Carver sighed. "We need to keep our heads down. The principal is still the job. We keep him safe, stay out of the line of fire, and we'll be okay. We fly out tomorrow evening. I've been assured Chinese intelligence won't follow."

Davis worked his jaw over and over, but eventually nodded. "You need to talk to Nick. He's still in the dark about things, and he's pissed off."

"Is he?"

"You've been a ghost, Vince. You need to come clean."

"I know." They passed a service entrance in the back of the hotel, and Carver headed toward it. "Come on. Nick upstairs?"

"No, he's in the spa."

"That's what you call lockdown?"

"What can I say? The principal's an entitled asshole. Short of calling him that to his face, like *some* people I know, Walter Lachlan does what Walter Lachlan wants to do."

Carver frowned. "Does he have enough people there?"

"Security's ramped to capacity. No one's getting to him or his room. Check things out if you want. I'm sure you will anyway."

He sure would, but Carver was inclined to agree. If Lachlan was still a target, he wouldn't be attacked in his hotel surrounded by his men. Not even the MSS would make that much of a spectacle.

As far as letting Shaw in on the CIA plot, it would be impossible to talk to him while he was mobile. It was best to wait until Lachlan was in his room for the night. Until then, the fact that Lin's men had abandoned the hotel might be exactly what the doctor ordered. It afforded a small window of lax hotel security where covering their principal was more important than protecting his assets. If Carver was going to capitalize on that, he had to act now.

16

Davis split off to get dinner while Carver took the elevator up. The doors opened on the fourteenth floor and he peeked out. Lin's men, who normally would've been standing at the turn in the hallway, were gone.

Carver moved furtively to the corner and peeked. Again, the hall was empty. It was a wing of the hotel he hadn't yet visited. He assumed all the rooms past the turnoff were booked for employees of Taipei Semiconductors, whether they were taken or not. Yi-An, Lin's assistant and staff, even his security. It was a more modest setup than Lachlan buying out the entire floor, but modesty only went so far. The prominent suite at the end of the hallway was undoubtedly Lin's.

Carver slowed his approach as he considered the best method of bypassing the electronic lock. And then, quite unexpectedly, when he was ten feet away, the door handle turned and clicked open. A man he didn't recognize stepped out, equally surprised to run into anyone. Carver spoke first.

"Ah, maybe you can help me. Mister... ?"

The door shut behind him, and the man lifted a steadfast chin. "Wu. I'm sorry, but Mr. Lin is unavailable."

They both stood in place for a beat, wary of each other. The man slipped something small from his hand into his pocket. He had a gun under his jacket but hadn't made a threatening move for it.

Carver broke into a grin. "I'm sorry, we haven't met before." He offered his hand and took a single step forward. "I'm leading up Walter Lachlan's security staff. My name is —"

"I know who you are. I'm sorry but Mr. Lin is not here."

Carver waited a moment. The man didn't go for the handshake so he withdrew. "Yeah, you said that..."

Something about the guy didn't feel right. The man looked the part, more or less, but the long hair to his shoulders didn't seem up to Lin's professional standards. The rest of his team had been noticeably clean cut. But it wasn't a lot to go on.

"If you'll excuse me." The man signaled down the hallway without moving. He was waiting for Carver to leave first. Which was exactly what security staff would do.

"Actually," tempered Carver, "my question's for you. It's embarrassing to mention, to be frank, but I do need to keep an eye out for these things, and I'm wondering why you're sneaking around your boss's room while he's away."

The man's jaw clenched, eyes staring hard. He was certainly ready for trouble. His voice found an edge. "Sir, I need to ask you to clear the area. If you don't, I'm afraid Mr. Lachlan will be notified about this indiscretion."

"Maybe Mr. Lachlan and Mr. Lin should both hear about it?"

The security guard took an impatient breath. "Inform whoever you wish. I'm here by request. Now, I hate to do this, but I have a gun, and you don't, so I need to ask you to back away to the elevators before this escalates." He lifted his jacket and placed a hand on his weapon.

Carver blinked coolly and raised a hand to the air. "It's all right. I get it. You're just doing your job."

Carver backed down the hall. The man waited for some additional separation between them before slowly following at a distance of twenty feet. Smart.

It bothered Carver that the man believed he wasn't armed. Sure, it was a tactical advantage over a mistaken enemy, but why make the assumption in the first place? Sparroway and Lachlan's security staff knew he didn't have a gun, but did Lin's men? Did Yi-An?

One other possibility crossed his mind as he moved around the corner back toward the elevators. In the steakhouse earlier, the Asia Pacific guards had searched him. The operating theory was that they were acting MSS officers or assets. They, in turn, could have called in the bomb threat in order to remove Lin's security staff from the hotel and gain access to his room.

Which meant this was an intruder.

Carver stopped after he'd walked too far without the man appearing around the corner. He was no longer being followed. The faint click of a door caught his ear and he charged forward.

Right around the corner was the stairwell for the emergency exit. Carver barreled through the door and heard the man's footsteps a flight below. He sprinted down the stairs in pursuit. Three quarters of the way down, he leapt over the railing onto the next flight, scampered down some more, and repeated the maneuver. It wasn't as fast as he liked but he was gaining on the man. Once he was one flight behind, the man backed away from the railing as Carver made the leap. He kicked the guy's chest as he went for his gun. They tumbled on the concrete steps and Carver pulled his SIG.

"Don't do it," he warned.

Crumpled against the corner wall, the man scowled death at him, though he didn't dare try to make it happen.

"I will kill you if you make me," assured Carver, rising steadily to his feet.

"What are you doing?" demanded the man.

He was no doubt attempting to resume the dialog. As far as Carver was concerned, that ship had sailed.

"You don't work for Lin," said Carver, and the man's eyes flashed recognition. "Who is it, then?"

He merely sneered.

"Right. I'm going to disarm you now. If you make a move I will shoot. No warnings. Understand?"

The stranger thought about it a moment and nodded.

Carver approached cautiously, keeping his SIG against his body so it couldn't be swept from him. He pulled the man's pistol from the holster and tossed it to the side. It was a Norinco, the same make the man at the night market had used.

Next he reached into the man's pants pocket. The

operative flinched but Carver reminded him about the gun. He pulled out a hotel key card and tossed it on the floor. Digging deeper, he found what the man had hidden: a USB drive.

"What's on here?" he asked.

The man shrugged. "Documents Mr. Lin requested. I swear."

"You don't work for Mr. Lin."

"I do. He requested his research on Asia Pacific Quartz. I don't know why, but that's what it is. Check it out if you don't believe me."

"I will." Carver stared at the drive.

The man took a few harried breaths. "Well?"

"Well what?"

"What are you going to do with me? I gave you what I had. I'm telling the truth."

Carver swallowed. Damn the CIA and their bad intel. He was alone over here with nothing but a gut feeling. Still, it was a feeling that had many times been the difference between life and death. And his intuition told him this man was a warrior. A killer. Someone who could only be deterred by extreme violence.

But just because this situation didn't smell right didn't mean he could very well shoot the guy.

"You're not going anywhere till I check this out," he decided.

"Fine. You have a computer with you?"

"I don't."

Another breath. "Mr. Lin's room."

Carver's gaze drifted to the key card on the floor. "That for his room?"

The man nodded.

Carver slipped the USB drive into his pocket and then leaned down to get the key.

The man struck fast, grabbing Carver's gun hand and drawing it to him and past his body. He clamped Carver's wrist and kicked upwards, putting all his weight on the extended arm, trying to get the lock. Once his legs were in place, the leverage could easily break bones. Carver cursed for just about falling for it.

Carver's legs and powerful core strained upward, lifting the man from the floor. He dropped the gun and spun away from the wall, not unlike an Olympic shot-putter. The difference was this shot was holding on with all his might.

He also had a skull which Carver cracked against the center railing. A sound like a home run with an aluminum bat rang out, and the man's muscles went slack.

He wasn't knocked out, though, and he wasn't giving up. After a failed attempt to shake him loose, Carver heaved him into the railing again. This time the man bounced and grasped wildly as he slipped over the edge. His scream cut off as he bucked against the rails like a pinball in the narrow space that led all the way to the ground floor with a final sickening thud.

Carver grimaced and peered down. What was likely another MSS operative was dead. A curse escaped the ground floor and a shadow shifted across the glare on the concrete. Someone else stepped into the center area to look up, but Carver backed away from the opening before either could make visual contact.

There were more men.

He recovered his weapon at the wall, pointed down the next flight of stairs, and listened. No one rushed upstairs. Perhaps more strangely, there was no panic or rustling, no yells or pleas for help.

These were the trained reactions of a professional. Another warrior, no doubt. And one who, for now, didn't have the advantage and wasn't pressing the issue.

Carver scooped up the key card and quietly retreated upstairs, this time to the fifteenth floor. He nodded to Lachlan's security team at the presidential suite and hurried to his room, locking the top latch for good measure.

It wouldn't be accurate to describe Carver as spooked, yet he once again felt the jarring abrasion of the old operative meeting the new civilian. Readiness, training, and preparation were very different from the real thing, and this was about as real as it got.

This wasn't a downtown night market, it was a posh hotel. It was *his* posh hotel. The enemy operatives clearly had access and info. At this point Carver wasn't entirely sure he could even trust the CIA.

Carver pulled the P320 from his belt. He released the mag, cleared the chamber, and checked every round. Then he proceeded to disassemble the weapon to check that too.

It wasn't quite early evening yet, which meant he still had time to reach out to San Jose. Mark had authorized him to call in additional assets. While Taipei was nearly in their rearview mirror, the job was far from over. While Carver worked on the pistol he dialed Morgan. She answered with a tired, "What the hell is it?"

"I've got a job for you, Juliette. Are you free the next few days?"

She cleared her throat in eager attention. "Of course. What are we looking at?"

"Security advance party. Lachlan is flying our team to Spruce Pine, North Carolina tomorrow. I'm concerned about hostiles and want a full loadout, weapons and vests."

"Vehicles too?"

Carver inspected the SIG Sauer firing pin. The weapon was in top working order.

"No vehicles," he said. "We're going to play this one a little differently. Your presence in Spruce Pine won't be public knowledge. Get my drift?"

"Uh... Only about what to do on my end. What's going on with yours?"

Carver smiled. "I'll brief you when we arrive. Until then, keep in touch."

He disconnected and put the P320 back together, wiping the internals down as he did so. The whole time he stared at the USB drive that had come out of the man's pocket.

17

Carver was too wired to make immediate sense of the drive. The contents were a mishmash of documents. Over the next hour, he repeatedly checked the hall to see if anybody was coming after him, but the coast was clear and Shaw reported the same from the spa.

Lachlan was safe surrounded by a full team. As for Carver, just like at the night market, the only person who had seen him didn't live to make the identification. Maybe he was truly still anonymous in this.

Carver broke open a bottle of whiskey from the minibar and drank it neat. In due time he began to make headway with the drive. It was a data dump. A catalog of various business activities, transactions, and initiatives concerning Taipei Semiconductors. The files definitely weren't, as the operative had claimed, related to Asia Pacific Quartz. He browsed through shipment manifests, schedules, presentations, and a timetable for the Arizona fabs.

Without intimate familiarity with the industry, it was impossible for Carver to classify any of the info as illegal. At least that was until he found the schematics for improvised explosive devices. Carver was familiar with those and they had nothing to do with legitimate business. With some digging, he managed to link some of the ingredients to purchase orders made by Lin's company.

It brought to mind the bomb threat at the Nangang Expo Center. Carver checked local news sites for anything related to the SEMICON. Lin's speech had been canceled and the expo evacuated early. Nothing had exploded yet.

It wasn't easy to put two and two together. The man who broke into Lin's room might have stolen these files from Lin's computer. It was also possible that the process was reversed, that the MSS was planting them. Was he holding proof of Lin's wrongdoing or of theirs? The truth would depend on whether the digital work orders for the bomb components were real. It would be difficult for the MSS to fake that.

But try as he might, Carver couldn't figure how Lin or the MSS benefited from bombing the SEMICON.

At least he had something to give the CIA. He went to dial Williams before pausing and reconsidering. China's State Security was capable of hacking cell phones. His communication with Williams had always been risky. After what just happened in the stairwell, he now felt that risk was too high. If he contacted Williams and the MSS were listening, they would know he had killed their men and taken their data. Carver reminded himself that no one had come at him directly. There was a better-than-zero chance his cover was intact.

Disappointed in the quality of whiskey in the minibar, and of the opinion that he had researched the files as much as he could, Carver risked leaving his room. Shaw and Lachlan weren't back yet even though the spa was closed. A quick text exchange revealed them to be at dinner on the third floor. Carver verified the outer cordon around the principal was secure. Rather than approaching Lachlan or Shaw inside, he descended to check the lobby and building exterior as well. All looked well so he returned inside and ordered a drink at the lobby bar.

It grew late as he kept an eye on the comings and goings of hotel guests, and Carver broke his two-drink rule. Finally he heard the commotion only a full security escort could make and he walked to the arch between the bar and the lobby to get eyes on the entrants.

Mr. Lin and his assistant had returned with a full team of ten, including the punk who'd been tailing him since the airport. Yi-An glanced his way as they strode to the elevator. He returned her cold glare with one of his own. They took two elevators up, and Carver licked his lips with distaste before wandering back to the bar and ordering another.

Eventually Shaw reported that Lachlan was locked up tight on the fifteenth floor. Mr. Lin appeared to be done for the night as well, and Sparroway hounded Carver with two more texts. He didn't care and realized he was bitter about the lack of contact by the woman he'd shared a drink with at a bar not two nights ago.

Skulking wasn't in Carver's wheelhouse, but he had a right to be angry. Here he was, supposedly investigating Lachlan, yet the billionaire seemed the only one who'd been straight with him from the start. Sure, the guy was an entitled asshole at times, but that didn't make him a traitor to his country. Meanwhile everybody else was hiding something from him. Yi-An, Lin, and almost definitely the CIA.

He had had it.

He made his way up to fourteen. Extra men were posted in the hall, a few of whom he recognized. Carver sighed as he advanced on them, knowing he was about to make a scene.

"Excuse me, sir, do you have an appointment?" one asked.

"I don't need an appointment," he answered.

"I'm sorry, but you need to call ahead."

"I don't want to see Mr. Lin. Where's Yi-An?"

They glanced at each other. "She's unavailable at the moment. She—"

Carver walked past them. They were stunned for all of two seconds. Then they grabbed him and raised their voices. "Stop, sir! Stop!"

"Let go of me!" Carver shouted.

They attempted to pin him against the wall but he brushed them away. They came at him again, three men grabbing while a fourth called into his radio.

"I'm not leaving until I get some answers," said Carver.

A door opened and Yi-An stepped out in a comfortable dress. "It's all right," she called out.

Carver slackened as the men did. They turned to her. She nodded and they released him.

"It's okay," she repeated more softly. "Come in, Mr.

Carver. We have unfinished business to discuss." She backed into the door to make room for him.

Carver straightened his jacket and strode in, locking rueful eyes as he passed her. Her hair was wet and her makeup was gone, but her skin shone from a healthy lather of lotion. Her outfit was alluring in a casual way, a short dress with thin shoulder straps, like something she might sleep in. She shut the door and crossed her arms under her chest.

She wasn't wearing a bra and had nicer cleavage than he'd expected, and it took some of the wind out of his sails. Mist lingered around the open bathroom door. Yi-An had just taken a shower and had begun to settle in for the night. Her homey presence disarmed him.

"What happened at the expo center?" was the best opening he could come up with.

She blinked matter-of-factly. "Nothing. The bomb threat was a prank." Despite her neutral tone, her eyes were hard.

"That's all you have to say about that?"

She raised her chin. "What else should I say?"

She was playing dumb but her chest was heaving.

Carver took a step closer to her. "How about explaining why you're having me followed?"

Her lips twisted but she only stared.

"No comment all of a sudden? You've been tailing me since I landed at Taoyuan International."

She scoffed. "So what? I was keeping an eye on you, and you were using me to get to Mr. Lin."

"I didn't use you."

"No? What about your charade to deliver a schedule to my boss? Flirting with me to find out his location at the steakhouse?"

"It's not like that."

"I'm not an idiot, Vince. I know what you want."

"Why don't you tell me?" he challenged. He stepped into her and she backed away slightly.

She almost shivered as she looked up at him. He stood so close he could smell the fragrance of the shampoo she'd used. Her bare arms and neck looked so soft. Yi-An breathed hard, chest rising and falling.

Carver grabbed her shoulder. "Are you using me, Yi-An? What is it that *you* want?"

Her expression was defiant but excited. "I don't want anything."

He leaned close. "You sure about that?"

Her eyes faltered and he kissed her. She slid her arms around his barrel chest as he forced her against the door. They pressed into each other, kissing and clutching with hungry abandon. He slid the straps of her dress aside and they fell to her elbows. She pulled her arms through and he stepped back. With a little wiggle, her clothes slid down her legs. Yi-An stood shakily, wearing nothing but lace underwear, breasts looking every bit as delectable as the rest of her.

Carver removed his jacket. As he started on his buttons, she lunged and ripped his shirt open. She may have looked soft, but Yi-An was far from a delicate flower. When she went for his belt, he removed the SIG from his waist.

"Where'd you get that?" she asked.

"Where'd you get yours?"

He dropped it on the nightstand beside her pistol and removed the rest of his clothing. Then he grabbed her butt and lifted her into him. Her legs curled around him and her nails traced his chest.

"My," she said, breathless, "what do they feed you?"

Carver smiled and threw her on the bed.

* * *

Some time later they lay on top of the covers, her nestled over him, skin glistening in the cool air. Yi-An's head rested on his chest, and his arm traced up and down her back.

"I work so hard," she said, "to be treated as a professional, and look at what I've just done."

"I had a hand in it too," objected Carver.

"Be serious."

"Fine. Who cares what we've done?"

"You'll think less of me."

"Maybe I think more of you."

She turned to look into his eyes. "Do you?"

He thought for a moment. "I'd like to get to know you better," he answered truthfully.

Her cheek returned to his chest. "You want to take me to America."

"Lunch would be a good start."

She snickered.

The conversation was already getting away from him. Carver wasn't sure there was a need to get so serious all of a sudden. He knew, in part, this was a failing of his. He was a hard person to get close to.

"I'm sorry to say I won't be about the city tomorrow," she said. "Mr. Lin canceled his scheduled appearances."

"He's not going to the expo center to make up his big speech?"

She hiked a shoulder. "He's not addicted to the limelight like Mr. Lachlan. Chen-Han has humbler aspirations."

"It sounds like you admire him."

"Is there a reason not to?"

Carver didn't give his true opinion. Yi-An was his kind of woman in a lot of ways, but he didn't let that fact misguide him. They were playing for different teams.

"I don't know," he started. "He supposedly had this rock-solid agreement with CPS and now he's flirting with Asia Pacific Quartz."

Yi-An snorted. "Talking to them is a negotiating tactic."

"From the humble businessman?"

She shook her head even as it rested on him. "Dealing with Americans means speaking their language. You and I both know Mr. Lachlan is best persuaded by profit."

She had a point, but it didn't explain everything. "Then why all the secrecy?" he asked. "Asia Pacific wasn't on his schedule."

"It was a late adjustment."

"But why the need for one in the first place? Why the

last-second interest in Spruce Pine?"

Yi-An sighed. "I can only say that Mr. Lin is exceedingly thorough. If he has a concern, he won't proceed until he sees it addressed. Call it military precision."

"Military? Lin is a veteran?"

"All men his age are. The ROC Military Service Act makes it compulsory. He received national defense training." She lifted her head and scooted up so she could rest on the pillow beside him. "All this talk about my boss is putting me to sleep." She lifted the blanket over them.

Later on, in the middle of the night, Carver woke. The room was dark and Yi-An was sitting up on the edge of the bed. The steam of the shower was long gone and the air conditioner had chilled the room. Her arms had goose bumps. She must have been freezing.

He rolled toward her and she turned her head. "Is this real, Vince?"

Carver worked his eyes open and closed. He was too tired to answer that question so he rubbed her back.

"Do you ever wish you could be somebody else?" she asked. "Just clap your hands and have a different life?"

He sat up and embraced her. "Why would I want a different life?" he asked. And then, "Why would you?"

She sighed and leaned on his shoulder. He rubbed her arms and waist to warm her and kissed the back of her head. Then he pulled her close to him under the covers. She shivered and seemed so much smaller than before.

"Were you scared," she asked, "when those people bombed your car in Arizona?"

He continued rubbing her stomach and legs as they lay on their backs. "To be completely honest, there wasn't time to be. It just... It just happens and you react. That's how the world works."

She mirrored his hand movements, tracing his body in return, stopping suddenly as she brushed his upper thigh. She squeezed lightly before shutting her eyes, breathless.

"Take me, Vince. Take me away from here." Her legs drew open and she pulled herself onto him. "Be gentle, like you love me."

18

Carver flinched awake at the sound of his phone. It was 5:30 in the morning and Shaw was calling. He rubbed the sleep from his eyes and answered lightly. "What is it?"

"Where are you?"

Carver turned. Yi-An was nestled between two pillows under a mound of bedsheets. He stood and reached for his clothes. "I'm around. What's up?"

"Have you heard from Davis? He was supposed to relieve me thirty minutes ago."

"He's not in the hallway? I'll be right there."

"I haven't seen either of you all night. I thought you were into one of your things again."

"What's that supposed to mean?"

"I don't know, Vince. You tell me."

Carver grunted and ended the call. He would have liked a shower but he didn't have a fresh set of clothes anyway. He dressed, retrieved his gun, and sent one last look to Yi-An quietly breathing under the sheets before heading out.

Two of Lin's bodyguards eyed him in the hall. He ignored them and trudged to the elevator to go up a floor where Shaw waited for him.

"The prince returns."

"Can the sarcasm. When was the last time you saw Davis?"

"When I relieved him last night. I babysat at the spa and dinner and didn't get back until late. I figured you both turned in early. Where were you?"

"It's not important. I wasn't with Mike."

"He doesn't miss his shift changes."

"I know." Carver started for his room.

"I think it's about time you came clean with me, Vince."

Carver stopped and looked his friend in the eye. They were interrupted by an angry Sparroway stomping toward them.

"There you are! Where the fuck have you been?"

"Excuse me?" asked Carver with a bit of bite.

The security coordinator scoffed. "Don't give me that attitude. You're supposed to be this big hotshot, but you're never around."

Carver huffed. "I don't have time for this right now." He headed toward his room and they followed.

"Don't have time for it my ass!" he berated. "There was a real threat last night and you didn't check in. I expect you to answer me when I message you."

Sparroway had picked a real rotten time to grow a spine. Carver hastily withdrew the key card from his pocket and buzzed into his room. He waved Shaw inside and set his hand on the other man's chest to keep him from entering. "I'm sorry, Sparroway. My team was in place, but I should have gotten back to you. We done with this now?"

Shaw did his best stone-cold stare in the background.

The thick beard hid his expression at all times, which added to the intimidation. Sparroway searched for words, wholly flustered by Carver's complete agreement with him.

"Just get your team in order," he finally said. "You may be the golden child right now, but your fifteen minutes with Walter could be over at any moment. We need you in his ear because lord knows he doesn't listen to me."

Carver acknowledged the surprising insight with a nod. Sparroway was in over his head but he was no fool. "Take over in the hall for a bit. I need a powwow with my team."

When the door was shut, Shaw said, "The man's not wrong."

"You too?"

Carver blinked at the key card in his hand. He patted his pockets in confusion before pulling out his money clip and finding his key card where he had left it. He frowned.

"Vince, you hear what I'm saying, brother?"

"I hear you. I think we have a problem."

Carver went to the desk where the second key card to his room was still in its envelope. He pulled the SIG from his waist, set it on the table, and removed his jacket.

Shaw whistled. "Where'd you get that?"

"A friend." Carver put a finger to his lips and then signaled around the room before pointing to his ears. *They could be listening.* Then he unpacked his holster and slipped it over his shoulders. "I don't know where Davis is," he said loudly. "Maybe out exploring the city again. He's big on street food."

Shaw's beard furled with his frown. He understood the

gist of what Carver was doing but couldn't possibly comprehend why. Carver signaled him to follow and they returned to the hall. He banged on the next door down and dialed his phone.

"You think I didn't try that?" asked Shaw.

The ringtone from their friend's phone seeped through the door. Carver put his ear to it to make sure, but it was his. Carver once again produced the suspicious key card and whispered so Shaw could barely hear him.

"Last night I caught a man sneaking around fourteen. He took a fall down the stairwell, but not before I retrieved this from him. He'd used it to get into Lin's room."

"That's not yours?"

"It is now."

Carver scanned it and the door opened. They traded a concerned glance and Shaw put his hand on his holstered Glock.

They moved in. The bed was disheveled but empty. Carver swiveled to clear the bathroom and the door bumped into something. He shoved it open and found Davis lying against the door.

"Fuck!" he yelled.

The holster Davis used was strapped to the door handle. The other end was looped around his neck, supporting his weight as he slumped on the floor. Carver unhooked the strap and helped him to the floor.

"Goddammit," muttered Shaw.

He checked for a pulse but confirmed what he already knew. Davis was dead. They pulled away to stand over the body. It was a dehumanizing sight. Davis's pants and boxers were wrapped around his ankles and his hand was over his crotch.

"The room's been tossed," reported Shaw. "Open drawers and luggage. Davis was a neat freak."

Carver knelt down to put their friend's clothes back on.

"What are you doing?" cut in Shaw. "You can't mess with the body."

"This wasn't an accident," muttered Carver.

"Even more reason to leave him alone."

"I won't leave him like that."

Shaw grimaced before crouching down and helping him with the big man. Once Davis was presentable, they lowered their heads in silence to honor their fallen brother-in-arms. After a minute, Shaw rose and returned to the main room to look around. Carver lingered.

This was entirely his fault. Maybe he shouldn't have told Davis about the CIA, or maybe he didn't tell him early enough. Maybe his team was in over their heads, just like Sparroway, being promoted past their qualifying expertise from security contractors to spies.

It was a fleeting thought, driven by guilt and sorrow.

Carver was confident in his abilities. He'd performed similar work in Delta, with markedly less fancy accommodations, but similar dangers. Shaw too. He was a former SEAL and one tough nut. But maybe asking Davis to be a part of this had been too much.

War was a series of imperfect decisions that needed to be made quickly. Drilling yourself over the past was only helpful when taking lessons into the future. Even then, sometimes the only lesson to be gained was how random life could be. The difference between one soldier dying and another living was a fractional trajectory of a piece of metal speeding through the air faster than sound. Life and death can't be dictated or controlled. They just happen, and most of the time there's not even a good reason why.

One thing Carver could suss out: Chinese State Security had likely called in a bomb threat to pull Lin's security to their principal, to pull them away from the room. They infiltrated the hotel with a universal key. They had every opportunity to kill Davis. Carver sneered and left the bathroom.

"It must have happened before we turned in for the night," said Shaw. "Once I posted in the hallway, I'm telling you, no one came or went."

Carver nodded. This must have happened right after they'd talked. But why Davis and not him or Shaw? Carver again considered the ramifications of allowing Davis to be a party to the plot. Ultimately, he concluded he had done the right thing.

At the end of the day, they were warriors. This was the job, and it was what they were good at. He often blamed the intelligence agencies for being tight-lipped with their knowledge. Carver was familiar with the damning results. He was now guilty of the same mistake. He decided to let Shaw in on the details as soon as he could. But not when they could be listening.

"We have an active threat to Lachlan," was what he said

aloud. "There are parties or agencies involved, and they're not the dime-store mercs we ran into in Arizona."

Shaw bobbed his head knowingly. "So what are we gonna do about it?"

"We're going to protect the principal." Carver checked his watch. "You have a couple hours before Lachlan heads out for the last day of the SEMICON. That gives you time to shower and rest. You need to go in place of Davis."

He made no complaint about the double shift. "And you?"

"I'm gonna call the police and get some help. I'm also gonna do some digging. We're getting on a plane tonight and I want to know what we're flying into."

"Copy that."

"My room's empty. Let's go clear your room."

They strode down the hall, drew their weapons, and entered. Shaw's place was a bit of a mess, but that was normal. This meant Davis specifically was targeted. With so little time, Carver left Shaw to it. He found Sparroway in his room and told him there'd been an accident. He would stay at the hotel and Shaw would go to the expo center. It wasn't lost on Carver that Mr. Lin and company would also be staying in today.

The next several hours were a slog. The initial police response was prompt but it took some time for the detective to arrive. The security crew rubbernecked no matter how many times Sparroway attempted to get them in line. Carver had to answer the same set of questions three times under increasing scrutiny. He kept Shaw out of it so he'd be free to tail the principal, and for once it helped having an asshole with money around. While the detective intended to hold the entire floor for questioning, a few phone calls from Lachlan freed them up to leave.

The Taipei City detective treated the situation with appropriate gravity, though much of that was attributable to the swanky venue. He wouldn't commit to ruling the death a homicide and Carver didn't know that it mattered. They wheeled Davis out on a cart disguised with a tablecloth while a forensics team went to work.

While Carver waited in the hall, a bright-eyed police officer with an overlarge hat respectfully approached. "Mr. Carver?"

"Yeah?"

He handed over a card. "You have a guest in the Jade Lounge."

The card had the name Harriet Spokes and the stamp of the American embassy. By the time he had formulated the question, the young officer was gone.

Carver went down to the same lounge he'd ended the previous night in. It was sunny and welcoming with daylight streaming through the windows, and the tables were set for afternoon tea. CIA officers Lanelle Williams and Arthur Gunn sat in the corner with three placements and a choice selection of colorful cakes.

"The embassy, huh?" Carver dropped the business card with the alias on the table. He scanned the area and noted that no one was interested in them. Then he sat.

"We heard through official channels," said Williams.

"We came as quick as we could. I'm sorry."

"What did you tell him?" asked Gunn.

Carver blinked coolly. "Excuse me? My guy is dead and you ask what I told him?"

"It's a worthwhile question," tempered Williams. "If he knew something he could have talked."

Carver shook a head full of steam. "I did what you told me," he lied. "I didn't say anything."

"Why did you call the police?" she returned.

His voice echoed in the small tea room. "Because this shouldn't be covered up." After a moment of them shifting uncomfortably in their chairs, Carver leaned forward and lowered his voice. "Did you do this?"

Gunn snorted. "What are you talking about?"

"I'm asking if you had a hand in this."

"Why would we? My God, who do you take us for? You need to get your head together, Vince. Focus."

Carver leaned back with a huff. "I just... Seeing him like that... I found him with his pants around his ankles."

"Auto-erotic asphyxiation," extrapolated Williams. "Standard playbook. You want to discredit someone, create some distance around them, you make sure they die in a compromised fashion. It embarrasses people. Gets them asking the wrong questions, or avoiding the subject entirely."

"Wait, what are we talking about here?" asked Gunn.

"The MSS could be responsible."

"That's a reach." His face displayed blatant skepticism.

"It's a distinct possibility, Arthur."

"Or maybe the guy was a pervert. Look, Vince, I'm sorry here, but the idea of state involvement at this level is ludicrous."

"I killed two men," he growled, startling them both. "One at the night market, another last night sneaking around the hotel."

Gunn's face twisted into panic. "You killed someone else?!?"

"For all we know it was the same guy who offed Davis. But he wasn't alone."

Contemplative silence followed until Williams asked, "Do you want to call this off?"

"No way. If these bastards think they can scare me away, they need to think again." Carver opened his jacket to emphasize the SIG.

Williams sighed. "Please... *please* don't shoot anyone else unless you absolutely have to."

Gunn sat up straight. "You gave him a pistol? What exactly do you have him doing over here?"

"We have enemy operatives in the field."

"We don't know that."

"I was followed, Arthur! For all we know Vince could have saved my life. Or saved the operation."

"You need to run these decisions by me."

"No, I don't. Arming the asset is my discretion. What happened with his team member only reinforces my decision."

Carver didn't appreciate them talking about him like a commodity, but he let them have their heart to heart. He gulped down some tea but wasn't in the mood for sweets.

"Hold on, hold on. I think we're getting ahead of ourselves," asserted Gunn. "We can't afford all these assumptions without evidence. What do we know for sure?"

"We know Lin's double dealing with Asia Pacific," said Williams.

"We need something untoward. A smoking gun."

Carver figured he had let them go at it long enough. He reached into his jacket pocket and produced the USB drive. He handed it over and told them what he'd gleaned about the bomb materials.

"I think they're exerting pressure on Lin," he explained. "And I'm not so sure Lin isn't fighting back. He canceled his expo visit today and detoured the whole procession to North Carolina, where he's presumably safer."

The CIA officers deliberated a moment. "I'm not sure I like this focus on Spruce Pine," concluded Gunn.

"Why not? It's a last-second audible. It's a hold-up of the official deal. Any deviation from normal right now needs to be scrutinized. The key to this thing is in Spruce Pine."

Williams frowned. "How so? A data transfer would be easier with Asia Pacific on location. That means here and now."

"I don't know. But the MSS is interested in Spruce Pine. I saw it on the guy's face."

"Whose face?" asked Arthur.

A shrug. "I don't know his name."

He scoffed sharply in reply. "This is what I'm talking about. I don't know what stories you two have been telling each other, but the thought that the CCP has assassins on the ground in Taipei is pure fiction."

"We won't know until we check them out."

Any sympathy Williams held for Carver's plight immediately dried up. "Vince..."

"What? The MSS is in town. We need to get on top of this yesterday."

"Negative," said Gunn, giving voice to her objection. "We aren't authorized to engage them. There are acceptable ways to play this game."

"Game?" growled Carver. "What happens when they break the rules?"

"Vince," he said, "you're not thinking right. You were the one who crossed the line first. Whoever it is you were following, you killed two men. It's not beyond plausibility that Davis was payback."

Carver bit down hard because it was the straight truth. The likeliest of all the scenarios he'd run through.

Williams sighed. "Maybe we need to stand down." Gunn furrowed his brow but looked open to the idea.

"We're making progress," Carver urged. "At least check out the data."

"Of course we will," said Gunn. "But maybe the best thing is getting on that plane and returning stateside."

"This operation isn't over."

The two intelligence officers shared a furtive glance.

"What is it?" asked Carver. "What are you not telling me?"

Williams chewed her lip. "The risk has escalated beyond

acceptable levels."

"All the more reason to take the fight to them. Don't bail on me now, guys. I can do this."

"You think we're the ones in charge?" chided Gunn. "This decision isn't yours *or* ours. While the two of us have operational flexibility, the death of an American civilian changes the math. It might look like I'm calling the shots here, but I do what I'm told just like everybody else."

Carver winced. It hurt him to say it but it was all he had left. "Davis hasn't been ruled a homicide yet. If you can't squeeze another day of operational flexibility out of that, you're useless." He stood to leave and they jumped to their feet in panic.

"Settle down, Vince," urged Gunn. "I know that look. Don't try to go after anyone on your own."

"I thought you had my back?" he replied.

"We do," assured Williams. "But no going cowboy on us. You're here for a simple reason. To watch Lachlan."

"And if he's not the one selling the data?"

Gunn's expression was annoyed. "Let us be the judge of that. The data's coming from him. That's where our eyes need to be."

Carver snorted and shook his head. "You're serious? After all this, you want me to babysit."

"It's not babysitting, it's doing your job. Protect your client. Hell, shouldn't you be convincing Lachlan to secure his data in your company's vault? Marino said you were the best at this work. Act like it."

"I'm not going back to work, business as usual,"

protested Carver.

"What's the problem?" asked Williams. "You stay out of harm's way. Everyone else gets through this."

Carver worked his jaw. It was just like the CIA to make a whole lot of plans to do a whole lot of nothing. "Screw this." He turned to go.

"Don't do anything stupid," ordered Williams. "Sometimes running is the tactical option."

"I'm not running."

"It wouldn't be the first time."

He stared daggers back at her.

"Don't try to intimidate me, Vince. It's who you are. Your childhood friend died drag racing and you ran off to the army. Your Delta buddy got killed and you quit the military. Maybe it's time you concede this one too."

"That's low, Lanelle."

She hiked a shoulder. "It's the truth. Think about the upside. You walk right now, a new contract with Walter Lachlan goes with you. Your company is set."

The comment burned Carver's ego. "So that's it, then," he chortled ruefully. "After all this, you still think of me as a mercenary. A hired gun doing this for profit."

"I didn't say that."

"You've called me a mercenary before. Instead of being so patronizing all the time, you should get off your high horse and wonder who bothered hiring this mercenary in the first place."

She huffed and readied a reply, but Carver was already storming to the exit.

19

The scars on Carver's left arm burned as he rode to the fifteenth story. Betrayal had a habit of making him hyperaware of the wound. It was a psychological reminder that deception and lies had physical consequences. Unlike Davis, Carver was lucky it was only a reminder.

If the CIA expected Carver to be a good boy and quietly sit on Lachlan, they didn't deserve to be called an intelligence agency. Delta operatives didn't color in the lines. They were one-man teams who drew their own pictures. They were trained to do whatever it took to complete their mission. That was why Williams and Gunn had recruited him in the first place. Carver would see this through even if they wouldn't. It was time to assume operational initiative.

Now, more than ever, he wished he had taken Shaw aside and read him in, but it had been impossible at the time. It was good enough to know that he and Lachlan were in the public eye at the SEMICON. If Carver's hunch was correct, they were safer there than at the hotel.

The action was on Lin, not Lachlan.

There was no more time for business banter and cocktail

dalliances. Waiting and watching would prove too little too late. Carver had a date with a business jet in eight hours and he wasn't boarding that flight without hard evidence.

He showered and changed into a fresh set of clothes. Instead of a suit he opted for the more tactical beige button-up and pants, including his ballistic vest. Downstairs, he picked up a bottle of midlist whiskey and took it to fourteen. Lin's wing was crowded with security who stiffened at his presence.

"It's okay," he said, holding up both hands with the bottle as a peace offering. He zeroed in on the man who had warned him off the night before and approached.

"I talked things over with Ms. Su last night," he explained, "and I'm embarrassed to admit I acted like an ass to your team. From one security officer to another, I wanted to say no hard feelings."

The man blinked stupidly but grabbed the bottle and bowed his head in thanks. The others watched with a few nods. Not only was the hallway full, but there were guards posted outside Lin's door as well as another one. Carver wondered who stayed there. Yi-An's door was unguarded.

"We were told," said the security guard with the bottle, conciliatory today, "not to allow anyone to disturb Mr. Lin this morning."

"That's fine," Carver replied. "I just wanted to give you the bottle. Just..." He frowned as he backed away. "I'm probably not supposed to say anything, but somebody was prowling around Mr. Lachlan's floor last night. If I were you I'd keep an eye on the elevator and the stairwell. You never know."

They looked at one another as if already aware of the threat. As Carver left, the men discussed and shuffled to cover those positions. It didn't draw them all away from Lin's door, but a few was better than none.

Carver returned to his room and dialed food service. He ordered lunches and appetizers for ten men and asked for empty glasses. He dictated a note with the meal that said, "Compliments of Mr. Lachlan on a job well done."

After a short wait he headed down the empty wing on the top floor opposite the guards at Lachlan's presidential suite. Not coincidentally, it was the room directly above Lin's.

He buzzed inside using the universal key card and checked the balcony. It was large and overlooked the one below it. Carver then stripped down three beds. He tied the thin sheets into a rope and secured them to the outside railing.

After he was sure the guards would be in the middle of their meal, he lowered the improvised rope and rappelled down the sheer wall of the hotel. While he wasn't above the floor of Lin's balcony, swinging in after an outward jump would not be difficult. As he readied the hop, the glass door slid open and Mr. Lin strolled outside with his eyes on the rope.

Carver jumped away from the wall, scaled his arms down the bedsheet, and pivoted right into the businessman on the downward swing. Mr. Lin's cry was cut short with a knee to his stomach. He rolled on the floor and gasped for air.

"I need you to be quiet," said Carver, drawing his gun and placing it between two very wide eyes. "Quiet, okay?"

Lin mustered some courage and nodded. "What do you want?"

"Just a chat." He patted the businessman down for weapons but didn't find any. Carver backed off so he could sit up.

"I... I have an armed security team outside my door, as I'm sure you're aware."

"I am. Do you think they're faster than my bullet?"

Lin straightened his glasses. "I get your point, Mr. Carver."

Carver stood over the man and lowered the pistol slightly. "Do you know why I'm here?"

"It's easy to guess. You're Lachlan's thug, threatening me for dealing with Asia Pacific."

"Nice try. It's because you and I both know who runs Asia Pacific Quartz."

Lin's features froze. The jig was up and he knew it. He spoke with a deflated sigh. "You want to profit out of this too..."

"Don't project your sins onto me, Chen-Han. I'm here to make sure the sale doesn't take place."

He snorted. "What sale? If you know who Asia Pacific is, you know they're not wining and dining me."

"The red at the steakhouse looked good."

"It's a figure of speech, Mr. Carver. The only thing I'm getting out of the arrangement is the life of me and my family."

Carver's eyes narrowed. "Explain."

"My son." He stood, some of his forty-odd years showing after the tumble. "Come in. Let me show you."

Carver nodded him to take the lead and they went inside. Three suitcases were lined up beside the front door. "Going somewhere?"

"I'm flying out momentarily."

Carver put the gun to his lips and shushed the man. "Keep it down. Remember, you scream for help, there's nobody left to save by the time they get the door open."

"I'm a beaten man already. I'm not screaming for anything." He trudged to the nightstand and reached for a wallet.

"Stop," instructed Carver. He motioned with the gun. "Back away." He switched places with Lin and grabbed the wallet. "What am I looking for?"

"Just photographs."

Carver found a few. An old photo of a newborn son. Another with his wife and a familiar grown man. "Your assistant is your son?"

"He's the heir to Taipei Semiconductors, following in his father's footsteps. With the love of my life gone, he is my one pride and joy."

"Does he know about your deal with Asia Pacific?"

Mr. Lin adamantly shook his head. "He will never know."

"Then why do it?"

"Because if I don't, the CCP will have him killed. They said his family would find him naked with a dead prostitute.

They would paint it a murder suicide." The stoic mask broke slightly and he sat on the bed. "It would ruin his reputation and his legacy. And only after that..." He paused, unable to fight the emotion off any longer. "They said after that, if I wasn't strong enough to kill myself, they would arrange my suicide for me." He pulled off his glasses and covered his eyes.

Carver bit down. The compromising death mirrored what had happened to Davis. Lin protecting his son also explained the security guards outside the other door. Father and son were sticking close in the face of danger.

"I caught a man going through your room yesterday."

He looked up at Carver with wet eyes. "Here?"

"You left it unprotected when you called your men away. He had a thumb drive of data from your computer."

Lin wiped wide eyes. "How do you know about that?"

"Because we had a falling out."

"Who are you?"

"Someone in a position to help, but only if you help me. I took the thumb drive from him."

Lin swallowed.

"I found the invoices for the bomb materials."

He nodded eagerly. "Yes! That is *their* plan!"

"A bomb threat on the SEMICON?"

"No, the CCP doesn't care about the conference. They've been extorting me for the access codes to the fabs in America. They're collecting details on everything... layouts, procedures..."

"What does this have to do with a data sale?"

"There is no sale. They've been hoarding proprietary information—whatever I could get them. But their goal isn't theft, it's sabotage. The CCP plans to bomb the Spruce Pine facilities in order to cripple your country's chip production capabilities."

Carver tightened the grip on his pistol. Chen-Han Lin wasn't a mastermind. He was just the guy providing access under extreme duress. This completely changed the playbook.

So much for Chinese agents not being active within the US.

The fact also made Carver re-examine what he was doing in Lin's room in the first place. To Carver, "live by the sword, die by the sword" wasn't just the cautionary warning most take it for today. It was a guideline, a rule to be followed. People are either warriors or they aren't, and only those who live by the sword deserve the risk of dying by it. Civilians living outside this life, those whose biggest worries were family and dating and what to get for dinner on a given night, they hadn't made the same pact. They don't expect a violent end because they don't participate in violent dealings.

Carver thought back to the Spruce Pine presentation given by Lachlan's assistant, Panesh. "I don't get it. What good would bombs do in a quartz quarry? It's just a bunch of rocks."

"It's far more than that," assured Lin. "There are mining operations, sorting and cleaning facilities, and fabs to form the material into wafers. These get sent out to more sophisticated plants all over the world. China intends to disrupt and take over that supply chain."

Carver holstered his pistol. "Just like that?"

"A temporary halt is all they need to gain significant inroads to the market. Look at our current reality. Global production lines are stalled as they wait for chips. Ford lost half a billion last quarter due to semiconductor shortages. These kinds of delays are unsustainable. Further problems in the supply chain would ripple throughout the industry. As starved as the world is right now for semiconductors, businesses will have no choice but to adapt to the quartz they can get. The world will be forced to settle for a lower-quality Chinese product. And once manufacturing goes that route, it will never return to the more expensive source material. Companies cut costs, they don't grow them. China gets their foot in the door permanently and jump-starts their domestic value."

"At the expense of ours."

He nodded grimly.

"What about your partnership with Lachlan? The new construction in Arizona?"

"Building a state-of-the-art fab takes two and a half years at best. That's a long time for an upstart to establish themselves in a flailing market."

Williams had told him the same the day they first met. The US had failed to see the threat of Chinese dominance until it was too late. They were now playing a desperate game of catch-up.

A knock jarred him from his thoughts. "Room service."

Carver drew his gun again. "What is this?"

Lin raised his hands. "I ordered before you broke in."

"Put them off."

He nodded and called out, "One minute please!"

Carver hurried to the door and checked the peephole. A waiter with hotel attire stood beside a cart. Lin's security staff lingered by the door. Carver went back to the bed.

"What's the next step?" he asked.

"I travel to Spruce Pine as planned. If I don't they'll kill my son."

"What about the bombs?"

"What about them?"

"Where are they?"

Lin sighed. "The logistics are handled on their end, Mr. Carver. I don't know who has the bombs or who is handling the operation. I don't even know their exact target. My task was to give them access to Spruce Pine, and I've done that."

Heavier knocks this time. "Mr. Lin," called one of the security officers. "Your lunch is here."

He watched Carver flatly. "I can't hold them off forever. I run a tight schedule and I have a flight window to make. They will eventually come in."

"You have to know something," Carver insisted.

The man affixed his glasses to his face. "I was informed about what happened to your team member. I understand why you're so angry now. Please don't put my son in those same crosshairs."

"The MSS operatives," he hissed. "How many are there?"

Lin watched him with a curious expression. "A five-man fireteam."

"Mr. Lin," they called, pounding on the door.

"Coming!" He stood. "May I?"

"The balding man with the pot belly. Who is he?"

"Zhen Sheng, a retired PLA captain. He's the one who will order the hit on my son if I'm seen talking to you. The one who made the call to kill your friend."

"You know that for a fact?" Carver snarled.

"No," he said calmly. "But it stands to reason. He's the one in charge."

"Mr. Lin," called the guard. "We're coming in."

The door lock clicked and Carver sprung for the balcony. Two security guards rushed in, eyeing the room and approaching their boss. Carver stood by the outside door holding his SIG ready.

"Are you okay, sir?" they asked.

Mr. Lin drew the curtain shut. "It's nothing," he said. "I just needed some air. Please, show room service in."

The guards retreated and the server wheeled Lin's food in. Carver holstered his weapon, grabbed the hanging bedsheet, and climbed to the upper balcony.

20

The RAV4 slowed through the streets of the warehouse district. Carver burned with anger at the thought of what had happened to Davis. At the idea of men threatening and killing for political and national leverage. All behind the curtain of private industry.

War was never pretty, but it used to have the sportsmanship to admit what it was.

Carver parked a block from the front for Asia Pacific operations. He checked the SIG and the fit of the vest under his shirt. He stood on the sidewalk a minute just listening, brown shooting lenses cutting through the sharp sunlight. The lack of activity was eerie but, as far as safe houses went, the MSS had chosen wisely.

He began his march toward the building, and a sedan screeched down the street and cut into the curb ahead of him. Gunn jumped out of the driver door and raced to Carver.

"What do you think you're doing?" he snapped.

Carver numbly smoldered. "You're following me?"

"It's for your protection, asshole, and I'll have you know that ends if you go in there."

"I've got my own six."

"You don't understand. Self defense is one thing... You're not cleared for wet work."

"I don't remember asking permission."

His head looked about ready to burst. "This is an unacceptable escalation."

Carver snorted. "Don't talk to me about escalation. I didn't even have a gun the first time they tried to kill me. And besides, this has broader implications than a simple data breach. This is military statecraft. They're attempting to bomb the United States."

"What?!? You've gone off the deep end."

Carver placed a finger on Gunn's chest. "Your opinion is your prerogative. You'll change it when you analyze the documents on the drive I gave you." He stepped around Gunn and continued down the street.

"This isn't how intelligence works, Vince. We have whole teams who analyze the data. Then leadership calls the shots."

Carver kept walking and Gunn hurried after him.

"You're no longer part of this operation," he said. "You did your country a service. Your part's done."

Carver didn't stop or respond.

"Damn it, Vince, are you listening to me?" Gunn ran to put his body in the way. Their scowls locked on each other. "I'm gonna need that pistol back," he said. "That's an order."

Carver's face was a mask. "Try and take it."

Gunn stumbled back a step in shock. His brow furrowed

in indecision, and his hand inched toward his waist.

"Arthur, if you draw on me I can't be responsible for what happens."

He froze and his jaw sagged. "Jesus. I'm the CIA."

"And I'm an American patriot. Two guesses which I put more stock in."

For two seconds Gunn stood poised like a sheriff in a high-noon standoff. But he was an operations officer. He wasn't trained in forward action, and any recent shooting was against a paper target. His hand lowered and his shoulders hung limply.

"You're here because it's your job, Gunn. I get that. I'm doing this because it's the right thing."

"You're doing this for revenge."

"Sometimes the two things align."

Carver drew his gun to cut off further argument and jogged across the street. The warehouse yard had no exterior personnel. There were two possibilities as to what waited for him inside. There could be a legitimate operation, real employees going about their workday with the MSS embedded in an office, or it was only them. Judging from the lack of activity, Carver was guessing the latter.

Going in hot was the only option. Not only was the interior unmapped, but any Chinese operatives would recognize him on sight by now. He hoped Lin was right about there only being three intelligence agents left. The CIA had only provided him with ten-round magazines, and he only had two.

Carver stopped at the wall and peeked through the motorized gate. The car Zhen Sheng had ridden from the steakhouse was parked. Just behind were three concrete steps to a front door. A camera perched above pointed at the main gate.

He reversed along the wall and around the corner where he dragged a plastic garbage bin into position. He climbed up, took a calming breath, and vaulted over the wall. No visible cameras pointed at him, but speed was a safer bet than confidence. Carver sprinted to the wall of the warehouse, traced along it, and hefted himself between the metal bars of the porch. The door was unlocked so he stepped in and set it softly back into position.

The small foyer that greeted him had a central desk that hadn't seen use in a while. A sign of Chinese characters presented some defunct brand. He stepped lightly ahead, leading with the SIG.

A door to the back hallway was propped open. That's twice these guys didn't take security seriously. Carver peeked in and out. No one. He advanced down the hall, past empty offices, until he heard clicking ahead. Carver stopped at the next open door and risked a peek. A man stood over a keyboard clacking the keys and muttering over technical difficulties. He faced the other way.

Carver confirmed the hall was still clear and quietly stepped into the room. His left hand fell away from the pistol and to the combat knife at his waist. He drew it silently and the man stiffened. It was one of the bodyguards from the steakhouse.

The MSS operative spun around and batted Carver's arms back. Carver hopped away from a strike before lunging with the blade. He sliced into the man's neck, but he twisted away from what would have been a lethal blow. The man shouted a cry of pain and warning before Carver smacked his head with the butt of the pistol. He drooped to his knees in a daze and Carver finished opening up his neck.

He spun and re-sheathed the knife, readying the pistol for action. That kill hadn't gone as quietly as it should have and, lax security or not, the MSS operatives would be aware of a threat. Boots pounded down the hall. Carver backed to the old desk and overturned it as a man called out. A blind pistol reached around the doorway and fired as Carver took cover.

The man attempted to advance inside with active suppression, but Carver slid out from the bottom of the desk and returned fire. Bullets pounded the room and the man retreated into the hall.

Carver waited with a bead on the doorway. Then he swiveled his aim to the wall beside it and released a burst of rounds. The grouping punched through the drywall in a small spread. The man grunted and fell to the floor. Carver stood and walked sideways in the office until he had eyes on the downed operative. He fired a single round into his head and switched out the mag for the spare.

Carver slowed his breathing and listened. Bullets pounded the wall in the same place he'd fired through. He dropped to the floor and rolled away as the barrage went over his head. When the enemy mag was expended, he bear-walked on all fours to the doorway, stuck his body out, and fired down the hall.

Zhen Sheng recoiled and dropped a pistol and magazine mid reload. He disappeared into the back room and shut the heavy wooden door. Carver stood and put two rounds into it, but he wasn't sure they were making it through. He ran forward and jumped into the door with his boot. The frame smashed apart and he landed inside as Zhen Sheng reached for a revolver lying on the desk.

Carver fired once and split the varnished surface of the desk. Zhen flinched and froze in place. Slowly, with hands raised, he turned around.

"Some of you are smart at least," said Carver.

The office was empty and didn't lead anywhere else. Carver had passed a door to the rear yard in the hallway. Here, he checked through the window and didn't see anyone outside. Lin's intel had been spot on.

Zhen groaned through clenched teeth. His left forearm was bleeding.

"That arm might have just saved your life," said Carver. "At least for another minute. Get on your knees."

The balding man stared with cold eyes. "No."

Carver was silent a moment. "You think you can reach that revolver before I shoot you?"

"No. It's an ornamental gun. It was my father's. Part of the old guard."

"Then get on your knees."

Zhen worked his jaw before releasing a sigh. "If I'm going to die, Mr. Carver, it will be on my feet."

Carver didn't react. They were both men of action. Warriors. They'd each seen death a hundred times and mulled over their own a hundred more. Neither of them dreamt of dying on their knees.

"You're very capable," congratulated the Chinese operative. "We, of course, knew of your team's military history."

"Then you should have recruited more men for the job in Arizona."

Zhen canted his head in amusement. "Dear boy, you don't think I orchestrated that mess."

"Who did?"

"How would I know? Is this really what you incited an international incident over?"

"Where are the bombs?"

His eyes twitched. "What bombs?"

"Don't play dumb with me."

"There's a difference between dumb and uninformed, even in the intelligence business. Why don't you tell me what you're referring to?"

Carver sneered at the man's self-assured demeanor. "Lin told me about the bombs. I saw the invoices."

Zhen Sheng's eyes sparkled. "I knew the bastard was up to something. He was too cooperative. And then the sudden need to visit Spruce Pine." He snorted. "I sent an operative to peek at his computer, but we both know how that turned out."

Carver's scars burned. Someone was playing him. "Your only chance of getting out of here alive is cooperating."

Zhen frowned. "Allow me a counter offer. The CCP is always in the market for information, Mr. Carver. You suddenly find yourself in a most profitable position. Put the gun down. Let's talk about your future at Dynamic Security Solutions and taking on Walter Lachlan's secrets."

Carver's gaze flitted to the revolver on the desk before returning to Zhen. "What does DSS have to do with anything?"

"It's all about positioning," he explained. "Your company is poised to gain Walter Lachlan's full trust. You're in the best position to secure his data. Just do what you're supposed to do and we both profit. I can make you a very rich man."

"And a traitor to boot."

He scoffed. "What is the meaning of that word, really? Every individual on this globe maneuvers for their own benefit. Even in so-called democracies, the individual doesn't vote for the betterment of their country but for themselves. The world is driven by personal interest. Do you think your government is above that?"

Carver grimaced at the thought of the CIA sitting on their hands outside. "There's intelligence for the sake of protection and intelligence for the sake of greed."

"Nonsense. Intelligence is practical knowledge that facilitates decision-making and reduces uncertainty intrinsic to policy-making and research. It is entirely for personal interest." His words sounded right out of a textbook.

"Where are the bombs?" Carver demanded.

"You're not listening. My business is intelligence, not

bombs."

"Bullshit. What are you doing in Taipei?"

"I'm always in Taipei. It is my assignment. It is my country, still in denial."

"It's not yours."

He chortled. "Oh, but it is. Even now. Taiwan is a honeypot. All good operatives know this."

Carver shook his head. "You were following the CIA at the night market. You called in a hoax bomb threat. You broke into Lin's room."

He spread his hands and flinched when Carver stiffened his aim. Zhen released a breath and said, "We were just keeping him honest."

"And what about Michael Davis? What did he do to you?"

Zhen raised an indignant chin. "Your asset was caught on a traffic camera speeding away from the night market where he killed my operative unprovoked."

Carver grimaced and Zhen's eyes lit up.

"So we were mistaken then?" He lost a bit of pomp. "I should have known it was you. Either way, his death was necessary for the killing of my man. It's fair-trade spycraft. Our accounts were settled, one asset for another, until you went and persevered with this madness."

"It's not madness. And he wasn't an asset, he was my friend." Carver's finger tightened on the trigger.

Zhen glanced at the nearby revolver. "Whatever you're thinking of doing, don't. You see me as an enemy, but I work with the CIA every day."

Carver was incredulous. "What are you talking about? More fair-trade spycraft? You killed Davis and he didn't even know about you."

The old man sighed with not ungenuine sympathy. "I see. I admit, the circumstances are regrettable, but unfortunately Davis—"

Carver pulled the trigger and Zhen's neck erupted. His mouth gaped in shock as his hands attempted to plug the spurting fluid. He took a step toward the revolver but his body gave out and he collapsed on the desk, leaking blood on his father's weapon. Carver put another bullet into his head.

He performed a brief search of the room and the property, but he didn't have the time or authority to stick around. Carver strode through the yard and jumped the metal gate. As he returned across the street, Gunn waited with hands on his hips, conversing with Williams, whose car was now pulled up behind his.

"What did you do?" he said in awestruck defeat.

"I don't know what you're talking about," said Carver.

"You could be arrested for this..."

"They were conducting an illegal operation and murdered my man."

"You can't take diplomacy into your own hands."

"I just did. Besides, there won't be any fallout. I have a feeling the public will never hear a word about any of this. You guys are good at making problems disappear."

"What is this place?" asked Williams. "How did you find it?"

"Because they weren't serious about security."

Her face hardened. "That's it, Vince. You're done."

"Fine by me. I'm going to North Carolina anyway."

"I should have known," she countered. "You don't run from a fight until *after* you've made a mess of things."

"I'm not running. I have a job to do. There are bombs headed there."

Gunn idly shook his head in shock. "What bombs... ?"

"Lin's targeting Spruce Pine. The goal isn't depletion, it's disruption. The CCP just needs a foot in the door. Check the accounts on the drive I gave you."

"We've been aware of a possible threat vector," tempered Williams, "but we've been concerned with a virus. Chinese operatives wouldn't physically attack US soil."

"Someone is," stated Carver. "I have a plane to catch."

"Vince," she called. "Your weapon."

He handed her the SIG and the empties. Then he hopped into his rental and left them to whatever cleanup they deemed necessary.

21

Sparroway flagged the RAV4 down at the airport. Carver parked and hefted his duffel bag over his shoulder.

"You tend to be late a lot, don't you?" noted the interim coordinator.

"It's been a day."

Sparroway sighed. "Yeah, I can understand that. Sorry about Davis. My team will finish coordinating with police and follow up with you the next day. Rental?"

Carver handed over the keys and shook Sparroway's hand. Then he climbed the steps of the waiting Bombardier Global. The flight crew was in the middle of prepping for takeoff. A stewardess and two of Sparroway's staff were in the cabin. Lachlan, Panesh, and Shaw sat around a rear lounge table sharing drinks.

Their discussion paused at his entrance until Panesh asked about cloud encryption. Carver found a seat to set his bag on. Shaw was, hilariously enough, pitching them on the DSS data vault. Listening to his roughneck attempt to explain packet security was comedy gold.

In truth, some things would be easier if Lachlan relented and used their data solutions, but the process wouldn't be without headaches. The man was a control freak, perhaps overconfident in his own security and technology but confident nonetheless. Convincing a billionaire they didn't know the way of things was an uphill battle.

Lachlan wasn't a blind man. The need for an operations specialist had been cemented after the fiasco in Arizona. But that was an arena where it was easy to admit being out of his depth. Data security—convincing a techie to use someone else's tech—was a much tougher sell.

"You don't mind if I smoke, do you?" asked Lachlan, trimming a cigar and reaching for an ornamental cigar lighter on the table. "Of course you don't."

Carver joined them at the table.

"Casual Friday?" snorted Shaw. Carver wore the beige tactical outfit minus the ballistic vest while Shaw was still stuck in the monkey suit.

"No, I like it," noted Lachlan. "It makes you look military. You should wear what you want in Spruce Pine, gentlemen. I don't need to impress anybody."

It was a welcome invitation. It would be a return to their Arizona outfits when they weren't directly on close protection.

"I'm sorry we had to continue business today," pivoted Lachlan, "after what happened."

Carver shook his head and accepted a whiskey from the stewardess. "It's all right. The security team's not supposed to distract from your work."

"But this wasn't just any distraction..." Lachlan took a few introspective puffs to get his cigar going. "If you don't mind me asking, what happened exactly?"

"I don't mind, Walter, but I don't have answers."

"It's just... suicide doesn't ring true for me. Michael shadowed me for a couple of days and he was more upbeat than the two of you."

"Let's just say, as your ranking security officer, I'm glad to be returning stateside."

He squeezed the cigar in a frown. Carver didn't especially want to talk about Davis but it couldn't be avoided. Lachlan was paying for top-notch support and he deserved answers. Luckily, the billionaire's gears were churning in another direction. "Is it true? Chen-Han's data was breached?"

At this point it was impossible to know what stories had passed through the grapevine. Getting some things out in the open would be welcome. "I don't know that he actually lost anything," said Carver, "but people were rummaging through his computer."

Lachlan shook his head as he took a pull on the cigar. The flight crew sealed the cabin door and the smoke hovered over the conversation. "It's amazing to me some of the spycraft that goes on. It's why, even in partnership, we can't share everything with the Taiwanese."

Carver thought about Zhen's honeypot comment. China was so close. It was almost impossible to curb their access. It likely explained the shift of production to Arizona.

"You've been selling him on the data vault?" Carver asked Shaw.

He stroked his beard. "I've been outlining our three-sixty

security solutions. Lord knows I'm not the guy to ask, but setting up a meet with Mark and the eggheads next week would be wise due diligence."

Carver chuckled. Marino had been in his ear all right.

"What do you think, Vince?" asked Lachlan. "You've been strangely quiet about your services."

"That's because my services are kinetic. Anything Nick or I say about computers is suspect at best."

He laughed. "That kind of honesty is why I'm interested in your opinion. Seriously, what's your take?"

"My uninformed opinion?" Lachlan nodded and Carver chewed his lip. "I think you know best what your data is worth and who wants it. More than I do. Shaw is exactly right about due diligence..."

"But?"

Carver sipped his drink and met the man's eyes. "But your industry has national security implications. You need to weigh ultimate security with convenience, and err on the side of caution. What are your concerns?"

"Storing my secrets offsite on a network I don't control," he said plainly.

Carver nodded. "Who's to say you're not right?"

"Not anyone," exclaimed Lachlan, leaning forward and extinguishing his cigar in a mid-century ash tray. He stood and said, "Enjoy the flight, gentlemen. I have some calls to make. Panesh, a moment?" He retired to the back suite and Panesh hurried to follow.

Shaw stared at Carver hard. "What the hell?" he whispered. "That sale was halfway done."

Carver hiked a shoulder. "The least of our concerns right now." He glanced at the nearby bodyguards who had only a passing interest in what they were doing. Carver ripped the top page off a nearby notepad, grabbed a pen, and began writing something. He slid the note across the table and Shaw leaned in to read.

It said, "Don't talk. Might be listening."

Shaw's eyes locked on his and he returned a slight nod. Carver pulled back the paper and wrote more.

"CIA looking into Lachlan/Lin data theft. MSS killed Davis."

His friend angered at the hard truth in ballpoint. Carver flipped the page over to write on the back.

"Paid them back in kind. Uncovered bomb plot in NC. No bombs yet."

Shaw picked up the note this time to read it again. His disbelief was evident, but it was more about the situation they found themselves in than any distrust of Carver. He handed the note back with a questioning look and Carver simply shrugged. He didn't have the answers, but at least they were discussing the right questions.

The door to Lachlan's suite opened and Panesh exited. Carver took the cigar lighter to his note as Panesh collected his drink from the table. He sat a few yards away in his own seat and opened a laptop. Carver dropped the blackened remains of the paper to smolder in the ashtray.

"Hey, Panesh," he said idly, "what can we expect in Spruce Pine?"

"You saw the presentation," he said, attention still on his

screen.

"I mean along the lines of the actual facilities."

The executive assistant broke away from his computer, removed his glasses, rubbed his eyes, and replaced them. "State of the art. You didn't tour the interior of the Arizona facilities so you haven't seen anything yet. The fabrication plants are called fabs. They're highly susceptible to contamination. The factory floor is sterile, thousands of times cleaner than an operating theater. Even normal light can damage the chemicals. Most of the work is performed by vacuum-sealed robots and workers in containment suits."

"What about security?" asked Shaw.

He canted his head. "The mine and facilities have enormous value. The grounds are replete with security guards and gates. Authorized personnel only. Mr. Lachlan had to pull some serious strings to gain access."

Carver nodded along, appearing bored and interested at the same time, like he needed to ask these questions but they weren't especially momentous. "And how important is Spruce Pine? Strategically?"

Panesh smirked. "Are you serious?"

"Humor me."

He spent a moment of thought and shrugged. "Spruce Pine isn't just strategic to the global economy, it's vital."

"I wonder what would happen if something went wrong," mused Shaw. "If there was some kind of industrial accident."

"We don't need to wonder," answered Panesh. "It happened. In 2008, a quartz facility was damaged in a fire.

The blaze cut off the supply of the world's high-purity quartz overnight. It caused a global squeeze. Without the constant production of glass crucibles, the entire semiconductor industry would break down."

Carver's eyebrows inched up his forehead. "That sounds catastrophic."

"Believe me, it is. There are one or two deposits in North Carolina providing HPQ but nobody realizes this. They just think it's silica, it's sand, and that it's abundant. But at this level of purity, the truth is far, far different."

Carver killed the last of his whiskey and frowned with Shaw. If an accidental fire could have such a ripple effect, he could only imagine what a few strategically placed explosives might do.

22

There was plenty of time to sleep on the overnight flight. Carver used the in-flight phone to coordinate with Mark Marino and Juliette Morgan. A large part of the discussion centered on Davis and getting his affairs in order. Their friend left behind a wife and a young daughter. Mark was beside himself.

The evening turned to day and they landed for an early dinner in San Jose before switching to the more compact Gulfstream Lachlan used for domestic travel.

Spruce Pine was an idyllic town in the Appalachian Mountains, and their night arrival only added to the terrain's mystique. It was a scenic wooded area, located between Asheville and Charlotte but north of the Blue Ridge Parkway, in the secluded Toe River Valley. The mining town was home to countless rock hounds but veering into a new tourist economy. Perhaps it was no coincidence it was home to more UFO sightings than anywhere else in North Carolina.

Lachlan had wanted to rent a 400-acre retreat on the North Toe River but it was occupied. For security purposes, Carver recommended a run-of-the-mill roadside motel with a single approach point. The billionaire surprisingly agreed, earning Carver's respect. It wasn't often a man of many creature comforts reduced himself to two-star Middle Americana.

They checked in after midnight, though most had had their fill of sleep by then. Once Lachlan and Panesh retired to their rooms and security was in place, Carver grabbed Shaw and led him along the motel's outdoor walkway. The brick building was shaped like a U around the parking lot. Their rental fleet served as a barrier to the rooms, and the view of the street was unobstructed. In the quiet of night, Carver rapped lightly on the second-to-last door. It opened and a woman with brown hair and piercing green eyes beckoned them in.

"Fancy seeing you here," said a surprised Shaw.

"You guys took your time."

"Oysters in Frisco," he said in explanation.

Juliette Morgan was acting in the capacity of their security advance party. Not only had she arrived early and cleared the motel, but she brought goodies with her. Several firearms were strewn out on the bed for them. Carver picked up his Tavor X95.

"It's about time," exclaimed Shaw, hefting his M4. Beside it was his favorite range gun, a Mk 11. A pair of kitted-out P320s rounded out the arsenal.

"So what's going on?" asked Morgan.

And finally, sure that they had complete and utter privacy, Carver told his team the full story.

"But I want this to go down like business as usual," he

concluded. "Neither of you will be in harm's away until an active threat is identified."

"Yeah right," scoffed Shaw.

"I'm serious. We need to play things cool. Juliette, you'll be on recon. I want eyes on wherever Lin's staying. Nick, you'll shadow Lachlan. We don't know his level of involvement, and now that we're back stateside he might be in danger again. We'll maintain radio discipline and do this by the book."

Shaw shrugged and said, "Until the shit hits."

"Until the shit hits," Carver agreed.

He gave Shaw some downtime and took the first watch of the night. One of Lachlan's men sat in a running vehicle, its headlamps fighting a losing battle against the impenetrable darkness down the street. Carver idly patrolled the lot, getting a feel for the crisp Carolina air. A call from Williams came in, and he realized he had a missed one from her earlier in the evening.

"I'm surprised you're still talking to me," he answered.

"The supply invoices for the bomb materials were authentic," she reported. "I also uncovered proof of Chen-Han Lin taking payments from Asia Pacific. These are buy offs, not threats. Maybe you were right that Lachlan's not involved in this."

Carver gritted his teeth. "I'm not taking anything for granted. Does that mean you're working the case?"

"Negative. I was sidelined for failing to control an asset. Arthur's coming in. He wants to help."

"Why start now?"

"Just stay out of his way, Vince. This is over your head."

"That's funny," he chuckled. "I was about to say the same thing to you." He hung up and she didn't call back.

Carver wasn't sure what to make of Williams. Of the two CIA contacts, she was the less agreeable. In a strange way that worked in her favor. She didn't try too hard to appease him like Gunn did. There's something to be said for a straight shooter, even if they're shooting at you.

The next morning the crew lined up on the asphalt outside the motel door. Two Range Rovers, each driven by a close protection officer from CPS. Shaw and Lachlan would ride in the lead vehicle and Carver would tail in back. As they waited for the billionaire to finish a phone call, Carver straightened and slid a dollar bill into an especially belligerent soda machine.

"It doesn't take," muttered Gunn. "You need quarters."

Carver noted the man from the corner of his eye and did his best to look unimpressed. He smoothed the rejected dollar bill and tried again. "Heard you were in town."

"And I heard you were running your own op," he returned.

Carver didn't like the CIA poking so closely into his business, but he didn't show it. "I'm not doing anything illegal, Arthur." The machine whirred loudly as the bill slid out again. Carver removed it and checked the corners.

"You know," said Gunn, "you could do with some relaxation techniques. I'm not here to bust your balls."

"If you have viable information, let me in on it. Otherwise why are we talking?" Carver lined up the bill perfectly and slowly fed it into the slot.

"Come on, Vince. Mistakes aside, I'm here to help."

"You fired me, remember? I'm not your asset anymore." The bill sucked into the machine and stayed put. Carver smiled at the CIA officer. "You see, Gunn? In this life there are winners and there are losers." He pressed the button for the soda with the most caffeine. The internals of the machine hummed as it dispensed the selection, except no can came out of the bottom. Carver checked the bay door and tried pushing other soda buttons, but the machine had eaten his money.

"Winners and losers, huh?" teased Gunn.

Carver grumbled and noted Lachlan loading into the car. "I have to go. One of us has a real job."

"Oh yeah? What's that?"

"Simple. I'm just private security protecting a client." He moved to the follow vehicle.

"Sure you are," muttered Gunn, staying in the shadow of the awning with his hands in his pockets.

"I'll drive," Carver told Lachlan's guard. The man handed over the keys and got in the passenger seat.

Spruce Pine was small and they were outside town in a minute. They drove another fifteen through the small hills and valleys that made Appalachia famous. The roads turned to dirt and grew steep as they ventured into dense woods with only one way in or out. Sheer walls of bare white rock overshadowed the wooded canopy until the forest cleared and they encountered an expanse of gaping pits of white feldspar.

The quartz operations were absolutely massive. Mack trucks with tires twice Carver's height were themselves dwarfed within the deep pit. White roads weaved and wound through the vast mazelike quarry. They drove past the heavy machinery of chemical plants with industrial lakes. Finally they pulled alongside a rented Ford parked beside a security vehicle at an overlook. Mr. Lin and Yi-An stepped out to greet the new arrivals.

"The view astounds me every time I see it," said Lin. After shaking hands with Lachlan and Panesh, his gaze lingered on Carver. "I see Walter extended your services into the back country."

"Yup," he said matter-of-factly. "I didn't see you back at the motel."

"I rented a quaint little bed and breakfast on Pine Avenue. It's painted a sickly yellow but I suppose it has its charm. I trust everything is well with your accommodations?"

"Nothing to worry about," said Carver. He glanced toward the vehicle. "How's your son?"

Lin's lips tightened. "Unfortunately, he has taken ill. Long flights don't agree with him. But he's well guarded under lock and key."

"I don't think you need to worry anymore." Carver offered his hand. "All our problems are taken care of."

Lin paused for a beat, unsure what to make of the statement. He smiled graciously and shook Carver's hand. "Thank you, my friend. It looks like Walter was wise to employ you."

Yi-An curiously watched the exchange. She was still in the dark about him breaking into her principal's suite the day before. As for Lin, Carver figured he was more likely to make a mistake if he wasn't suspicious.

"Gentlemen," said their host, a blond man in shorts and a vest. "If I can have your attention, we'll begin our tour."

As the guide described the thick veins of quartz in the ground, kicking at the exposed rock as a visual aid, Carver texted Morgan the details of Lin's bed and breakfast. It was worth keeping an eye on his son.

While Lin was cordial with the proceedings, Lachlan grew anxious and irate, questioning the need for such theatrics. He argued that if Lin wanted to ensure the technical specifications and production output of the fabs, they were wasting their time outdoors. The guide offered to advance the tour to the beneficiation plants where the quartz was cleaned and prepped. It was only then that Lin relented and agreed to skip straight to the final step in the process, the fabrication plant. A relieved Lachlan returned to his vehicle and the party drove on to the facilities outside the quarry.

"Your guns have to remain in the trucks, sir," said their host on arrival.

"No chance," said Carver.

"It's not a request. The fabs are clean rooms. Environmental control is critical to the success of semiconductor wafer fabrication. Even the air is scrubbed. We can't allow the slightest of pollutants inside. We even ask you to limit your security staff past the main room."

Before Carver could object, Lachlan butted in. "It is what it is, Vince. I've been here many times and we can't do anything about it. Trust me, I'm safer inside that fab than I am anywhere else in this town. Let's just get this over with, shall we?"

They had no choice but to comply. They kept their sidearms holstered and locked up the long guns. One of Lachlan's men stayed with the vehicles. Carver peeked into Lin's empty vehicle for any visible packages or bombs. Not only did he not see anything, but they left the car unguarded and unlocked. He followed Lin, Yi-An, and her sole PPO inside. They were checked by the armed onsite security staff and made to give up their pistols.

Yi-An smirked.

"Aren't you a little light on the protective detail?" he asked her offhandedly.

She shrugged. "It's like Mr. Lachlan says: these fabs are ultra secure. After what happened in Arizona, Mr. Lin wanted the bulk of his crew watching his son."

It would have been easier not to split his party, both from a security standpoint but also from a recon one too.

The environment inside the airlock was heavily controlled. The constant hum of air vents reminded that the air was scrubbed. As they donned plastic bunny suits over their clothes, their host explained that fabs were like icebergs. As much as they saw on the surface, there was more below. The pumps, the machinery, the large computer systems, they were all underground.

They entered the next room into a world of stifling

yellow light. The narrow wavelength was necessary to protect the photosensitive product from harmful white and ultraviolet light. Mirrorlike cabinets lined the walls on either side of the grated floor. Long tracks of machinery hung overhead. There were too many moving parts to keep track of, lights blinking, readout screens, and only the occasional human being. It was explained how the fab operated twenty-four hours a day, seven days a week. The plant was fully automated and technicians within were only required for limited preventive maintenance.

Lachlan seemed intent on storming forward as quickly as possible, as if there were some end point where he could declare victory. Lin hemmed and hawed and asked multiple questions about each stage of the fabrication process. While the surroundings were straight out of a futuristic techno thriller, the information being conveyed was ultimately boring. The tour guide discussed the process of preparing quartz ore. Spruce Pine was a bottom-to-top operation. They not only mined the quartz but they crushed it, sized it, and cleaned it to ensure its high-purity status before being shipped to a host of fabs across the world and country, including this one.

"It's an extensive quality-control process," explained the host. "Sand purification requires washing, desliming, scrubbing, magnetic separation, flotation, acid leaching—"

"Does that happen underground?" interrupted Carver.

"No, the sand goes through the beneficiation plants we passed at the quarry."

Lin, who had seemed to be dwelling on every subtopic

until now, indicated that he wanted to move forward. It was strange behavior for someone who had otherwise appeared to be stalling.

Carver's phone buzzed in his pocket, but he wasn't able to answer it through the suit. He excused himself and was led back to the main room, where he took off the bunny suit and checked the message.

Morgan had found the bed and breakfast. She confirmed that Lin had booked it, but it was currently empty.

The plot fell into place. Lin wasn't interested in Spruce Pine technical specs. He was going through the motions, stalling and providing a high-security distraction while the real play occurred elsewhere.

Carver texted his team, discarded his suit, and recovered his firearm on the way outside. He jumped in the rear vehicle without explanation to Lachlan's other man and he drove off toward the quarry.

Lin was attempting a well-executed and classic switcheroo. High tech was fancy, but low tech made the world go round. The bombs weren't going to the state-of-the-art fabs. As damaging as that would be, security was too high and there were a slew of them strategically placed throughout the country.

But...

The beneficiation plants, where the ore was cleaned and prepped before being shipped out for fabrication, these were in lower supply yet just as vital a step in the Spruce Pine supply chain. The goal wasn't depletion, it was disruption, and the stage between mining and fabricating was a perfect homegrown bottleneck to the entire US operation.

From a security standpoint, the beneficiation plants were much more vulnerable. The majority of on-site guards enforcing access control were stationed at the fabs, leaving the grimy factories to the scores of relatively unrestricted workers.

It was smart, and Carver was late.

The Range Rover raced back into the quarry, X95 on the passenger seat, tires kicking up a cloud of white feldspar in its wake.

23

Carver took the SUV downhill toward a series of warehouses on the waterline of a man-made lake. Tubes interconnected with a series of vats among scaffolding. A spiderweb of pipes covered the dirt in the underbelly of the facility. The Range Rover skidded to a stop next to the same model Ford SUV Lin had rented.

His son was already inside.

Carver checked his weapon and the fit of his vest while scanning the perimeter. A couple of workers attended a piece of machinery across the lake but the area was otherwise empty. After strapping the Tavor over his shoulder, he sprinted toward a door located on the upper slope of the warehouse.

Heavy pounding and grinding drowned out all local noise. Industrial machines painted bright green, yellow, and blue stood like titans on a terraced floor that sloped down toward the lake. Nearby, behemoths shook back and forth as they screened and classified the ore.

A network of stairs and scaffolding crossed overhead, with the occasional worker going about their day. There were no clean suits or security checkpoints, just industrial machinery and plant workers. Carver stood in the thick of the operation without attracting attention.

He raised the rifle and advanced through the space, weaving in and out between machines. He slipped behind a large centrifugal chamber as a worker strolled past. Carver searched the factory floor for anything that looked important, but it was close to finding a needle in a needle stack. They all looked the same. He had no idea what many of the machines did, much less which were the biggest bottlenecks. He decided to look for central connecting hubs and advanced past stacks of large spiral tubing.

Two men in gray jumpsuits downslope of him set a package at the base of an active assembly line. While workers oversaw the incoming ore from a distance, this section of floor was empty. Their outfits were similar enough to not draw suspicion, but Carver recognized their faces. One was the man that had followed him from Taoyuan International. The other had picked him up after their street encounter. Carver now realized that, due to the draft, each man would have just enough limited military experience to be dangerous.

The noise was too intense to hear what they said so he watched as the two men turned on the device and lugged a canvas bag elsewhere. Carver ensured the area was clear before ducking his head and running over.

It was Semtex, which matched the invoices. Carver hadn't seen the stuff since his off-books military days. Luckily, the setup was straightforward. The detonator was hooked to a cell phone, set to blow whenever its number was dialed. There were no visible countermeasures.

Although Carver was a little out of his depth, he couldn't afford to sit on his hands. And since it was too loud to communicate over a phone or radio, and messaging would be too slow, he decided to take it upon himself to disarm what was surely one of several bombs. In this case, rather than fudge with the wire job or remove the device, Carver simply turned the connected cell phone off. He removed the battery so it couldn't be reactivated and bent it in half.

Carver flinched as a gunshot split through the cacophony. It hadn't been fired his way, but it was near enough. He tucked his rifle and advanced. Two workers fled past him in panic. Carver hurried to the edge of an industrial slurry pump feeding an upraised pool of gray sludge. On the far side of the pool, another gunman helped Lin's son apply another device to the side of a multi-deck shaking-table pipeline.

Someone called out and the men turned to the main walkway. Yi-An approached with a pistol in her hand. The damned woman had followed him out of the fab. No longer in the bunny suit or slacks, she wore a black tactical jacket and pants with a black cap and her hair tied behind. She was suspiciously well-suited to the look.

Yi-An berated them as she approached, and they matched her tone in response. Carver could barely hear the argument and knew it didn't matter. He snuck around the machine to get a closer look and almost tripped over a dead worker. A bullet had penetrated his heart.

Lin Jr. shoved the canvas bag aside and stepped toward

Yi-An while his compatriot retreated behind the gargantuan machine. The raised slurry pool was waist height, so Carver had decent cover as he advanced along it in a crouch. As Yi-An conversed with the heir to Taipei Semiconductors, the guard he was with circled around the machine.

"Behind you!" Carver yelled.

They turned uncertainly, having trouble locating the sound. Then Yi-An's own underling clamped an arm around her neck and squeezed. Carver pulled up the weapon but was unable to get a clear bead on her attacker. He considered Lin Jr. as the next best target, but before he could fire a gray suit popped out from an industrial-sized grinder thirty feet down. Carver pivoted his arm and fired a barrage.

The ball mill resembled a giant roller with meat hammer spikes as big as a person's head. Sparks glittered off the machine, and everyone flinched as gunfire split the mechanical floor. The man fired a pistol for suppression but he was outgunned and outclassed. Carver patiently corrected his shot and fired another burst. The man jerked at the multiple contact points before noodling right into the rolling grinder. He was pulled downward and crushed without even time to scream.

Lin's son was gone but Yi-An still kicked and clawed at the man behind her. Carver broke out of cover and rushed at them. Yi-An's struggle slowed and she went limp. The man spun her around as Carver descended with the butt of his Tavor. It hit his head and Yi-An dropped to the floor.

The man grabbed the rifle with both hands and shoved

back against him. Carver drew his pistol but ducked as he came under fire from across the pool. It was his old follow man.

Carver spun the guy holding his rifle around to set his back against the edge of the slurry pool. He placed the SIG over the man's shoulder and fired. The deafening noise at the man's ear was painful. He struggled, making hitting any target impossible. As Carver fought with his aim, he checked his back to make sure Lin's son wasn't sneaking up on him.

Locked in tense combat, the man surprised him by grabbing his pistol and slamming it into the metal rim of the slurry pool. After the third strike, Carver winced and dropped it into the sludge. Now unsuppressed, the follow man across the pool once again opened fire. The close guy yelled at him. Carver just held him up as a body shield.

Lucky for him they were bad shots. Their struggle over the rifle continued. Carver put his hand in the man's groin and lifted, upending and dunking him into the slurry. The man panicked and released the rifle, allowing Carver's other hand to grip the guy's submerged neck. Incoming pistol fire continued as Carver ducked and held the man under until he stopped flailing.

Carver put his back to the pool and fell to his haunches where the rounds couldn't find him. Beside him, Yi-An blinked away her daze.

"Stay down," said Carver.

Her brow furrowed and she said, "What?"

"Stay down!" he shouted. He grabbed her leg and pulled

her toward him.

She recollected her wits and pointed her pistol at him.

"Get over yourself," Carver snapped. "Lin's planting bombs. He wants to damage the supply bottleneck of high-purity quartz."

Her eyes smoldered in defiance but not disbelief, and she withdrew the pointed weapon. Yi-An had followed him here for a reason. Perhaps her suspicions had been on him. The fact that they were both being shot at now proved they weren't in on it.

Carver crawled to the explosive device. It had been placed but abandoned before being activated. He pulled the phone's battery anyway and tossed it over his head into the slurry.

"How many bombs do they have?" he asked.

"How should I know?"

He frowned. The canvas bag was gone. Lin had removed one device and taken it with him. He guessed it could fit two bombs. "How many canvas bags did Lin's son have?"

"He had two of those. They were supposed to be for scale models."

"That puts us at three or four devices. I've disabled two."

Carver peeked around the shaking table where Lin Jr. had escaped to. Bullets ricocheted off the cement floor and he withdrew.

"They have us pinned down." He pointed. "There and over there."

She checked her weapon. "I'll cover you."

He narrowed his eyes. "You know what you're doing?"

"You'd better hope so."

She twirled around the opposite end of the machine and opened fire. Carver charged toward the next machine. A flash of movement caught his eye and he fired at it. The man retreated and Carver pressed after him to flank. Two bullets whizzed by him. He pointed the rifle and fired a spray that sent the man retreating. Once flushed out, gunshots cracked and he crumpled. Yi-An had been poised in wait. She nodded at Carver as she reloaded her mag.

He did the same and eyed the factory. The dead guy was the follow man's friend. He didn't have a bag and there were no bombs in sight. That put Lin's son and the follow man as the remaining known combatants.

He hadn't seen which direction Lin's son went. If the other guy had been across the slurry pool, there was a good chance his second bomb was over there. Carver signaled Yi-An that he was heading that way. He made sure no guns were peeking out at him and made his way over.

The other side of the pool was populated with large crushing machines, hammer mills and roller mills, all whirring threateningly. It was impossible to know where the follow man was now so Carver advanced cautiously. The rifle thoroughly swept over all threat vectors. As he cleared an especially loud cylindrical crusher, the man lunged out with a knife.

Carver batted the weak stab aside. The man's holstered pistol was empty. He spun around for another swipe and Carver caught the arm. He bent it backwards until it cracked, then he kneed the man's stomach. The pitiful attacks hadn't even come close. He pointed the rifle at the man whimpering on the floor.

"You're not MSS," Carver said, voice getting lost in the machinery. He spotted the device he was looking for on a neighboring machine. Loudly, he asked, "Where's Lin taking the fourth bomb?"

The man's eyes widened and flitted downslope. As Carver looked past, the man pounced on him. Two bullets exploding from the rifle and burst through his chest. Carver sidestepped and the follow man continued the arc of his final attack before crashing lifelessly to the floor.

Carver disarmed the third bomb and hurried through the plant. After one last ledge, the floor gave out to gravelly dirt. There was no back wall, and massive pipes sloped down into the exposed lake. He descended through the tangle of pipes and wires, clearing every obstacle. He checked what appeared to be a large relay junction but didn't see the bomb. Near the bottom of the lake, he turned and saw legs scampering away.

He didn't have a shot so gave chase, first over the piping and then outside over the wet sand. The sunlight was blinding but he could make out Lin's son running up the slope back toward his vehicle. Carver chased him uphill. Lin's son used the key fob to unlock the car and Carver emptied his magazine into the vehicle, breaking glass, punching through fiberglass and fabric, and popping tires.

Lin's son frantically spun around as Carver changed the mag. "Don't shoot!" he cried, wild eyed, hand on a cell phone. "I'll—"

Carver double-tapped the X95 and Lin Jr.'s head exploded. He fell backward and dropped the device without incident.

24

Lin's SUV skipped down the rocks and swerved to a stop. He exited in a deranged state at the sight of his son, scampering over and collapsing to his knees in grief.

Carver's rifle swiveled to Lin's PPO as he reached for his weapon. "Drop it," he warned.

The man froze. As much as Carver wanted to put him down, this wasn't a battlefield. For all he knew, this sap was just as in the dark as Yi-An had been.

"Remove the pistol slowly. Toss it my way. If you shoot, I shoot. Understand?"

The man nodded and did as instructed. Carver recovered the pistol and set it in his empty holster.

"My son!" cried Chen-Han. "What have you done to my boy?"

"You're the one that got him killed," returned Carver, pacing to the broken man. "The second you got him tied up in a plot to attack the United States."

"We did this *for* the United States... For Taiwan..."

"Playing right into the CCP's hands?"

"No," he growled, tears streaking down his cheeks. "This was always an attack *against* the CCP."

Carver bit down as he worked it out. "This was a false flag. You wanted the United States to think the MSS attacked US soil."

"China knows the consequences of crossing the line. Retaliation would be devastating, so they operate in a manner that prevents the world from declaring war on them."

He gazed longingly at his dead son, choked up, and sneered. "But make no mistake. The CCP is at war with us both. It's just a different kind of war. Nuclear proliferation put an end to world wars. Proxy wars are only fought in failed states. Even your cold war with Russia is a relic of the past. Globalization is here. Societies are interconnected. Today's battlefields are economic, and their weapons are policy."

"So you're the good guy."

"The CCP operates with ill intent, Mr. Carver. They see the world as their enemy and act accordingly. They will do anything and everything up to the red line of war. My intent was to force them across that line. For once. So the world would take notice."

"We would've known it was you."

"What does it matter? The MSS has their hooks in me. There is enough of a paper trail to prove I'm their lapdog. The CCP would never have been able to escape the implication."

Carver grimaced. "You're talking about the deaths of US citizens. Lives and livelihoods destroyed."

"It is not your citizens who will suffer militarily when US

soft power in Asia degrades. Taiwan's reckoning is closer than you think. The MSS has infiltrated our economy. They've been bending me over for years." Lin shook a forlorn head. "I swore I wouldn't leave my son to that. I did this for him... I did this for my country..."

Carver scoffed. "You're just a patriot who decided to be a terrorist, is that right?"

"It was the only way to provoke the United States to return fire against an adversary that has been gunning for them for decades. Your rich despots don't care for the future of your people, only for their profit."

He reached into his jacket and Carver swung his rifle. "Stop moving!"

Lin slowly withdrew his cell phone.

"Drop it!"

Lin's eyes went someplace far away, and he almost smiled.

"Drop it!" Carver repeated. "I will shoot you just like I shot your son."

Chen-Han sighed. "Maybe it's what I deserve. A parent should never live in a world without their offspring. The least I can do is attempt to make his death meaningful."

Carver cursed, keeping the rifle primed. He would have no choice but to pull the trigger if Lin attempted to make a call.

"Stand down," called Yi-An. She trudged up the slope, pistol on her boss. She dropped a battery on the ground beside him. "I disarmed the last device."

Lin's brow furrowed. He hurriedly unlocked his phone

and she slammed the butt of her pistol into his nose. He dropped the phone and curled up on the floor, bleeding. Yi-An rolled him to his stomach, put her knee in his back, and zip-tied his hands as Carver covered her.

When she was done he nodded at the PPO. "He clean?"

She had an exchange with him in Mandarin, and he answered her questions promptly. She turned to Carver. "He didn't know anything. I believe him." She holstered her weapon and stood with a grunt. "Even I had no idea. I let it happen right under my nose..."

"Don't feel bad. They probably realized you were an agent of the NSB."

She turned sharply to him in shock before submitting a grin. "Most people don't know Taiwan has a CIA. Except, of course, for other intelligence officers."

"You got the wrong guy," said Carver. "The Agency put me up to it, but I'm just private security. I swear. Not that I didn't have a few run-ins with the MSS."

She chewed her lip as she considered him. "You're a puzzling man, Vince."

"I don't see it that way. I've shown you every part of me..."

She snickered and looked equal parts dumbfounded and relieved. "We were aware the Arizona plot originated in your country. It looked like an inside job, so I was keeping an eye on you."

"The man you used ended up being loyal to Lin. None of your staff were fellow agents?"

"It's like you said. Security is private these days."

"I guess it is."

Lachlan's vehicle pulled off the road and parked higher up. Shaw was the first one out, leading with his rifle.

"It's clear," called Carver.

Shaw lowered the M4 and waved for Lachlan and the PPOs to disembark.

Yi-An sighed at her boss, weeping in the dirt. "He's right, you know. The CCP will keep pushing, right up to that line."

"Zhen Sheng was confident of that fact too." Her look indicated she recognized the name. Carver shrugged. "He's not so confident anymore."

"I can't believe this," muttered Shaw, joining them after a side-eye at a prostrate Lin. "You had all the fun without me. *Again.*"

"Sorry, brother. It couldn't be helped."

Carver texted Williams about what happened. She would have Gunn and the CIA in the area in short order. Yi-An and Shaw loaded the prisoner into the back seat of his own car.

Carver wandered up and met Lachlan on the slope. "I'm happy to say, Walter, that there shouldn't be any more holdups to your semiconductor deal. There's gonna be a shakeup at Taipei Semiconductors." He glanced back at Yi-An on the phone, likely with her superiors. "But I have a feeling they'll be in good hands."

"Holy hell," he replied. "You're CIA, aren't you? I should have known. You were always working something right beneath everyone else." He frowned in thought. "That means Michael died on a mission for me."

"Not for you, Walter. For national security."

He nodded. "Regardless, give me the contact information for his family. I'll see that they'll never want for anything again."

"I appreciate that."

The billionaire appraised Carver a moment. "You too, Vince. I like your style. Come work for me and get a piece of the pie for yourself."

For a few seconds, Carver truly considered the offer. "I've been thinking lately... Pie's great and all, but I'm a meat man myself, and it's about time I got back in on the main course."

"What's that supposed to mean?"

"I'll let you know when I figure it out. Have a nice life, Walter."

Carver strapped the Tavor over his back and strolled up the hill to greet incoming security. Lachlan gazed at him in silent admiration.

25

It was evening by the time CIA Officer Gunn left the quarry. Since the area was so remote, Carver hadn't waited on the backroads where he'd easily be spotted. Instead he parked a brand-new rental car on the only street leading back to Spruce Pine. When Gunn passed, Carver shifted to drive and followed.

He was led, unsurprisingly, to a brickwork brewery in town. Gunn entered alone and probably ate alone, but that was of no consequence. Carver picked up fast food and waited and watched. A couple of hours and a few drinks later, Gunn stumbled back to his car and drove home. Carver passed the house and judged it empty. Based on the location it was probably a rental rather than a safe house.

Carver parked, headed up the stoop, and knocked. Gunn wasn't entirely dismayed to see him and let him in.

"All four bombs were fully deactivated and removed," he relayed. "We didn't find any other devices or signs of sabotage, and the local authorities were pretty thorough. We even went through the fab you toured just in case."

"And Lin?" asked Carver.

"He's not talking yet. Your little NSB friend wants him,

but we have jurisdiction. It's likely we'll hold him for a week, get what he has to give, and send him back east in a trade for oversight into the new management of Taipei Semiconductors."

"The CIA doesn't do anything for free, do they?"

He chuckled. "It's fair-trade spycraft, my friend."

Carver bit down and stepped through the dimly lit interior. It was a lonely place. The living room was lit by a muted TV showing sports highlights. Neither man sat. They watched the screen without looking at each other.

"Lin wasn't exactly wrong about China," said Carver.

Gunn released a long sigh. "No, he was not. They engage in gray-zone battles for power meant to fall short of inciting all-out war. And since ousting our Beijing agents last decade, their intelligence operations, cyberattacks, and global drives for influence have only intensified. But that's why we do this job. And I have to admit, Vince, you did good work out there."

Carver didn't look at him. "Thanks."

"You ever think about joining the Agency?"

"Maybe, but I'd have to do it on my terms. Otherwise I might feel like I was being used."

He snorted. "Welcome to intelligence, kid. Anyway, consider it an open offer. For now you should celebrate. You made some overeager missteps, but I'm willing to look the other way considering the service you provided your country. You wrapped this up nicely."

Carver faced the officer again. "Aren't you forgetting the reason you approached me in the first place? We prevented a bomb plot, but we never uncovered the data deal."

"Right." His cheeks went taut. "I don't think we're going to get a Hollywood ending here. Unless you still believe Walter Lachlan is in on this thing?"

Carver wordlessly shook his head.

"Chen-Han Lin is in custody and his son is dead," stated Gunn. "The MSS, in light of significant losses, has backed away from any data recovery attempt. That's probably the best we're gonna get."

"You might be right, Arthur, but it begs the question. Lin was selling secrets to the CCP for years. He admitted that but denied this one. His big plot was about bombs, a much worse admission. Yet Zhen Sheng and the MSS expected a data bounty either way."

Gunn frowned as he mulled the statement over.

Carver gave him a moment before adding, "It's a shame Williams didn't come out for this win."

He hiked a shoulder. "Eh, let's call a spade a spade. She fucked up. But she'll bounce back. Do me a favor and don't worry on her account."

"I'm not anymore. It was touch and go for a while there. She didn't know the MSS was in town, or that she was being followed, or even the location of that warehouse I raided. By the way... How did you recognize that place?"

"What?"

"Even if you had followed me from the hotel, you knew exactly who was inside that building. You told me not to go in."

Gunn rolled his eyes. "Vince, it's not uncommon for

agencies like ours to collect intelligence on each other."

"But Williams didn't know. Let's call a spade a spade, right? You were working with Zhen Sheng. He told me himself."

Carver's final point was a lie, but it was one that struck home. Gunn tensed and swallowed. "Sheng was the acting security chief of Taipei and I'm the Agency's point man in the China Mission Center. Of course I had a relationship with him. I've been to dinner with the guy. He's taken me to his favorite acupuncturist."

"So you and Zhen had a relationship, and neither of you knew about the bombs."

"Look, that's what I'm trying to tell you. No one knew about the bombs. I wasn't even supposed to travel to Taiwan in the first place, but after you killed their guy I had to fly out and smooth things over. I'm on your side here. I came to help."

"You keep saying that, but I think you're only jetting around to cover your ass." Carver stepped toward the CIA officer with disgust painted on his face. "If these bombs had gone off under your nose while you were busy with a dirty deal... well... I can only imagine the size of the microscope that would suddenly be focused on your affairs..."

Gunn sneered in retaliation. "And what the hell's that supposed to mean?"

"Don't play stupid, Arthur. It's not a good look. You were the one orchestrating the data theft for Zhen."

He fired back with a blistering scoff. "Are you crazy?!? I'm the one who recruited you to get to the bottom of it!

Don't believe the word of an enemy MSS officer."

"Come on, it's not just his word. It's everything that happened. The MSS was following Williams but not you. How would they know to track her?"

"There are a hundred ways they could've known."

"One of them is that you told them to follow her. Not to hurt her, but to keep tabs on her."

"That's ridiculous!" he shouted, but his denials sounded more and more forced, and his bald head was sweating under the pressure.

Carver kept pressing. "Taiwan's NSB is of the opinion that the Euro mercs who attacked my team in Arizona were an inside job." Carver stepped closer as a vein on Gunn's head readied to pop. "They said the orders came from inside the US. They weren't sent by Lin, or by Zhen, but by you."

"They weren't supposed to kill anyone," he screamed, red-faced. "They were just supposed to scare Lachlan, okay?" The two stared at each other for a heated moment, and Gunn lowered his voice. "The CIA does things, Vince. Some operations succeed, some operations fail. You're not supposed to hear about them, and if you do you don't question them."

"At least we're finally getting to the truth."

"Well, bravo to you. You finally learned the CIA keeps secrets. It's how business is done."

Carver suppressed a chuckle. "It's good that you're a businessman, Arthur, because we can finally talk business."

"What is this, a shakedown?" Gunn was trembling and sweating and irate. It all fed into his bravado and he pushed

Carver's chest to back him away. "You want to make some kind of deal, Vince? Let me tell you the best you're gonna get. You keep your mouth shut about any perceived infractions on the part of the Central Intelligence Agency. For reasons of national security. You do that and I don't arrest you for murder and spirit you off to a black site. You wanna fight this? Fight me? You better count your blessings I don't declare you a traitor and trade you to the MSS. Then you can try and do business with them."

Carver patiently waited out the tirade. Even after Gunn was finished, Carver only stared for a moment. He shouldn't have been surprised by the threat, but it only hardened his resolve.

"That's not the bit of business I'm talking about," he finally said. "Don't forget I got Zhen to squeal before he died. You were working with him the whole time, including that ugly bit of fair-trade spycraft at the Mandarin Oriental."

Gunn grimaced at the accusation, but his anger would no longer allow him to back down.

"You greenlit Davis," accused Carver.

Officer Gunn hissed. "It was the only way to keep the peace! You killed a Chinese intelligence agent, Vince. There was always going to be retribution. Hell, I did you a favor. It was either Davis or you."

"Then it should've been me! But don't pretend you protected me out of the kindness of your heart. I was your little tool on your own private mission. You wanted me to keep working your angle, to keep you looking honest. You set me up to fail so you could trick the CIA into looking the wrong way while you exacted your payday. That means, after everything is said and done, you had Michael Davis killed for money."

They stared hard at each other, Gunn with red-faced indignation, Carver with an insatiable thirst for justice.

This was the gray that Carver operated in. His warrior code didn't only apply to those pulling the triggers. Sitting behind a desk didn't make you innocent. If you were guilty of ordering the deaths of others from the safety of a private office, well, you might find that safety from people like Carver was an illusion.

The Delta operative's fingers inched to the knife at his belt. "What you did is unforgivable."

Gunn's eyes went wide. "That's... You're... I'm CIA for chrissakes!"

"You're taking an early retirement."

Gunn backtracked and pulled the pistol from his holster. It was faster than Carver had expected, but he was ready all the same. He grabbed the gun and Arthur's forearm and flipped them up in a blink as it fired. The round entered the bottom of Gunn's jaw and exploded out of the top of his bald head.

The CIA officer sprawled backward on the floor, eyes wide open, brow still clenched in rage. The pistol remained in his hand. Carver wiped down the sections he had touched and casually retreated to his car.

26

A couple of days later, Carver was back in San Jose and quietly at work in the comfort of his beige leather Eames office chair. His sleep schedule was still upside down and he had arrived before 5 am to get certain affairs in order. The lack of distractions enabled all-too-painful clarity.

Williams called. "Hello, Vince. I'm in North Carolina right now. I'm not sure what happened over here, but I'm standing over the body of Officer Gunn."

"I can't say that surprises me," he replied.

She waited a beat. "Why don't I like the sound of that?"

"Arthur was compromised. He had some cross dealings with the MSS and it got him killed."

"Chinese operatives don't do wet work on US soil, Vince."

"Spin it any way you want. If you do a little digging, you're gonna find he was neck deep in the data theft."

He could practically hear her thinking through the phone. "I've... I've had some doubts, but he was trying to uncover the plot."

"Was he?" posed Carver. "He said he took orders just like everybody else. Did the operation originate with him?"

"No, actually. After the SIGINT came through, it would have been assigned out. Arthur had seniority with China. He could have volunteered."

"So he took over the investigation to make sure it didn't go anywhere. The data theft was always happening stateside. He sent us off to Taipei where we'd be in the dark while he tried to maneuver things to his favor. That's, of course, if you weren't in on it too."

Her voice went dead. "Don't ever insinuate something like that again. I wasn't a part of this. I didn't even want to read you in to begin with." She huffed to pacify her anger. "Who knows? You may be right. Which might explain why Arthur appears to have been killed by his own hand."

Carver shrugged. "It's the same justice Michael Davis got. At least Arthur had his pants on. He did still have his pants on, right?"

"Yes," she sighed. "I'm good at what I do and I trusted him... but I can see signs he might have been a part of this. I worry he was having me followed... Maybe all the lies finally caught up to him..."

"For what it's worth, Lanelle, I'm sorry. Being played is never fun. But don't worry, you can make it up to me."

"You're kidding," she said, unamused.

"The CIA has a mechanism to seize and divvy up private assets, right? I'm assuming if I scratch your back, give you a win, you can set me up. I'm not asking for government money, I just don't want to be ruined in the private sector for doing my part."

"Why don't you tell me what you have," she said slyly.

"Intel," Carver answered. "You recruited me for a mission, remember?"

* * *

An hour or so later, the workplace began to stir with the usual morning activity. Mark Marino strolled into his office and Carver entered just as he sat down. Residual frustration blew from Mark's cheeks.

"I'm angry with you, Vince. I mean, hooray for stopping the bombs and all, but then you go and break out of the Lachlan contract."

Carver calmly stood at the other side of the desk. "He was no longer in danger. He has his own team to handle the day to day."

"You were supposed to secure him long-term."

"Mark, if Walter got his way I'd be working for him right now."

His boss conceded the point with a harsh grunt. "I suppose that's a win, of course. Sit down, will you? You're making me anxious."

Carver ignored the offer and interlocked his fingers before him. "But I don't think I can continue working at DSS all the same."

"What?" he cried in exasperation. "Why not?"

"My eyes have opened a little bit. You know Special Agent Gunn of the FBI was really Officer Gunn of the CIA."

"Yeah?" He arched an eyebrow but only appeared mildly surprised.

"I realize Gunn wanted to scare Lachlan with that attack in Arizona. But he didn't really want to kidnap him. He wanted to push him into securing his secrets in our data vault."

Mark was more than anxious now. "I don't know what you're talking about."

"Of course you do, Mark. How else would Gunn insert himself into the sale?"

He pressed his lips together. "Okay, you're right. He strong-armed me."

"You're not that weak."

He leaned forward with an emphatic swipe of his hand. "You call that weak?!? He's the CIA."

"He *was* the CIA. He's dead now."

Mark Marino blinked in astonishment.

"You wouldn't have gone along with something illegal just because someone threatened you, Mark. I know you too well to believe that. You know why you let Gunn strong-arm you? Because you were already culpable, neck deep in the data theft business. You've been making money on the side for a while, haven't you? Only this time, Gunn discovered your plot. How am I doing so far?"

Marino swallowed nervously and his robust posture slowly deflated.

"Except Gunn didn't just turn you in. He wanted a piece for himself. So he forced you to cut him in at risk of prison time."

Mark burst out of his chair with fists clenched and primed to spring. As soon as he met Carver's intrepid gray eyes, he froze. He saw the death in them and knew it was coming for him. The man sagged back into his chair, knowing he wouldn't stand a chance in a fight.

"What were you thinking, Mark? This wasn't just proprietary information. It affects our national security. I had no choice but to tell the CIA about you. But I owed it to you to be straight, even if you weren't with me."

His boss stared at the top of his desk, unable to meet Carver's eyes.

"You used me," he continued. "You got Davis killed. And Lachlan's men in Arizona."

"I didn't know about that! All right?" exclaimed Mark. "Jeez, what kind of person do you think I am? I saw my chances of securing Lachlan's data dwindling, yes. Our contract was ending in Arizona and Walter was stubborn as all hell. But Gunn wouldn't take the loss. He staged the attack behind my back. He saw it as a way to secure Lachlan's trust and keep you on the job. He set up the Taipei trip. It was all him..."

Mark shook his head in defeat. "My God, I couldn't believe it when I heard what happened. It was so outrageous it took me a while to piece together, but that's the CIA for you. That's how they insert assets. And Gunn's plan worked. Thankfully you thwarted the attack. Protection is what we do, right? You're the best at it, Vince."

Carver nodded away the nostalgic bonding. "I hate to break it to you, but I've been doing a little more than protection over the last week." He patted the SIG in his belt holster.

"Whoa, slow down, Vince."

"They label us mercenaries," he replied with scorn. "People who ditch ethics for money. And look at you, Mark... You're everything they hate about us."

Mark put pleading hands up. "I'm not a killer, Vince..."

"You sold out your country for a nest egg."

"Come on! We were both soldiers once. We got shit on and used. We saw brothers killed in action. I couldn't put up with that anymore. I saw an opportunity, Vince. I saw an opportunity to make some money on the side and I took it. What I was doing benefited us all. We could still get the money, you know. Call Lachlan back and half is yours."

Carver's hand rested on his weapon. He watched the pathetic man he once called a friend groveling before him and nodded. "You were a soldier once, Mark, but you're right. You're not a soldier anymore."

Mark Marino began to whimper. "Please... We're friends..."

"I'm not going to kill you. But you're ruined, you hear me? You're ruined. The CIA's seizing your assets. DSS will be dissolved. You have nothing to look forward to except prison time. And I quit."

Carver spun around as Mark sobbed. He almost left the office before turning around, withdrawing his pistol, and placing it on Mark's desk. "I believe this firearm is company property."

Carver left his boss to his own devices.

27

Mark Marino was too much of a coward to face the music. He skipped town and actually made it as far as Ensenada before he was picked up after a week. Carver didn't ask about him and he didn't care. That chapter of his life was closed.

Dynamic Security Solutions was closed too, but Carver's equity in the company and then some had been cashed out and pivoted into a new venture. He strolled into a small office in a strip mall that used to host a failing dental practice. A few moving boxes were set on the floor, and Carver slid the last symbolic item into place in the private office in the back: his Eames office chair. There wasn't even a desk to go with it yet.

"So what do you think?" Carver asked as he returned to the main entry.

Juliette Morgan looked around, unimpressed, before suddenly snapping her fingers. She dug through a box of office supplies and took a black sharpie to a piece of copy paper before taping it to the front door. It read, "Kinetic National Security."

They stared at the sign wordlessly before Morgan

mentioned having to go.

"You sure about this?" Carver asked. "Joining arms with me again?"

"You're gonna do it right, aren't you?" she asked.

"You're damn right I am."

She smiled. "Then I'm sure."

Shaw marched into the place lacking his usual pomp. "Truck's empty," he announced. He frowned at the sign and the rest of the environs. He wanted to say something, but held back.

"I'm..." started Morgan, breaking the silence, "I'm gonna head out. Believe it or not, Frank and I are trying *another* marriage counselor. Third time's the charm, right?" She snorted but the comment didn't bring the intended levity. After a second she said, "See you first thing Monday, Vince." Morgan punched Shaw's arm on the way out, but he held his tongue.

Carver crossed his arms and waited.

"This is a far cry from DSS," muttered Shaw. "Seems like a step down from your previous operation."

"It's going to be a step up before I'm through with it. I wish you would commit to joining us, Nick."

The man stroked his beard in a rare moment of hesitation. "I'm not so sure, boss. I would've followed you into the breach if only you were straight with me."

Carver winced. "It was the CIA's call."

"Since when?" he scoffed. "Guys like us don't trust the CIA, and with good reason." He grimaced and said, "You didn't follow your own rules, Vince. You left me on the outside. You didn't tell Davis what he needed to know. Maybe—"

"Don't say it," Carver urged.

They both took a breath and traded a pitiful stare.

"You don't think I've thought about that," said Carver, "every single day since it happened?"

Shaw shook his head again. "You did your best, Vince. It was a damn good op too. You're a hero. I just... I think this is where our paths diverge." He held a fist up to his friend in solidarity.

Carver worked his jaw and nodded softly. He pounded Shaw's fist. "If you ever—"

"I know, boss."

He turned around and left Carver alone with his guilt.

* * *

Bringing the office to some level of respectability made for a long day, but a cathartic one. This was a new start for Carver, an opportunity to refocus. No computers, no data, no techy stuff. He would stick with what he was good at. The world spun on its axis only at the behest of men like him, and he intended to do something worthwhile with that skill set.

That didn't include scrounging through Silicon Valley upstarts for clients.

His discussion with Officer Lanelle Williams had broached the subject of doing future intelligence work. The proposition was an iffy one, but making a real difference beat a surefire gig protecting rich businessman any day of the week. Carver now had the national security itch.

Except he would do it his way or not at all. There was no guarantee he would find work, but what he did would be on his terms. It didn't matter who hired him. The CIA, the FBI, or anyone else. If the job came with the slightest hint of deception or greed, he would turn them down. Carver was the new boss, and he was determined to put in the work only if it was the right thing to do, for the good of his country.

The sentiment was idealistic, but holding yourself to impossible standards was the entire point of ideals in the first place.

Carver locked up, returned to his apartment, and showered. He shaved and put on a nice button-up and the nicest jeans he had. Then he drove the Dodge Ram to a nearby hotel where Yi-An waited wearing a low-cut ensemble for a night on the town. She excitedly hopped in the truck and they embraced.

"How long do you have?" he asked.

"A week." She laughed. "Now that my private security career is over, they don't know what to do with me."

"My situation isn't so dissimilar."

She faltered under his look and her mirth faded. He kissed her long and hard. The car in the driveway behind them honked but he ignored it. When Carver pulled away from her, Yi-An Su watched him with large, longing eyes.

"You doing anything now?" he said with a smirk.

She hiked a slender shoulder. "I suppose it's too late to see what California lunch is like, but how about dinner and dancing?"

"Dinner's good," he said, commanding gaze never wavering from her own, "but I was thinking about staying in. You don't have a problem with that, do you?"

Her chest rose and fell rhythmically. He wasn't entirely convinced they'd make it to dinner.

Afterword

That's all for the first chapter in Vince Carver's new career! I hope you enjoyed the story I crafted. If you're new to my books, it should be obvious I'm a fan of intricate plots, layered characters, and overall happy endings with a gut punch or two to keep my heroes honest. I'll let Carver shoot the bad guys while I shoot for delivering a story you can believe in.

As for believability...

Sometime in 2010, China cracked the online protocol used by the CIA to communicate with their assets embedded in the government and military. In the following years the CCP rolled up the entire spy network. Dozens of officials were executed. This was the opening salvo of an ongoing bulk-intelligence data war that China appears to be winning.

This existential competition between the two wealthiest governments in the world is the basis for *National Security*, an exploration of the emerging Cold War in the digital age.

It's no accident the book's central plot to steal data turns out very different from a physical dead drop. Today, legitimate companies like the fictional Dynamic Security Solutions and Asia Pacific Quartz engage in espionage for the CCP. Intelligence collection and processing are written into official Chinese policy. Real-world counterparts like Huawei, Alibaba, and China Mobile have already been implicated, and that's just the tip of the iceberg.

AMD, to bring this discussion to the semiconductor market, has famously entered a joint venture with a Chinese military contractor. Although the deal was approved by US authorities and was presumably above board, that military contractor has now been placed on a list of companies barred from accessing US computing technologies. This so-called "Entity List" is reserved for known risks to national security. It's no stretch on my part to imagine the layers of spycraft that are surely occurring in this sector.

Taiwan is a key player here. Taipei Semiconductors is a fictional stand-in for Taiwan Semiconductor Manufacturing Company. The most important chipmaker in the world, TSMC works closely with US and Japanese allies. It is a partnership fraught with uncertainty. Zhen Sheng's honeypot comment reflects CIA fears that anything shared with Taiwan eventually ends up on the mainland.

On the American front, bringing strategic supply chains back home is officially big business. An expanded TSMC fab is underway in Arizona. If war ever were to come to our island ally, their escaping technicians could flee to the US and resume their vital work unfettered.

Which brings us to our very own national resource, the quartz deposits at Spruce Pine, North Carolina. Honestly, I'm blown away a place like this actually exists. The importance of high-purity quartz to the global market is not exaggerated in my novel. *National Security* merely asks the question: how might this homegrown resource be targeted, and for what gain?

I began the novel with the PLA definition of intelligence, which Zhen Sheng repeats. Vince Carver's response about whether that gathering of knowledge is motivated by greed or protection is topical in an age where big data is king.

This is my first espionage thriller so I'd love to know what you thought! My goal was to keep things exciting without endless repetitive gun battles. What good is a spy story without intrigue anyway? If you'd like to chat, or if you have a special skill set yourself and would like to set me straight about an error in my story, feel free to email me at matt@matt-sloane.com. Writing is a lonely business, and I welcome collaboration and corrections from readers.

On that note, if I did a good job, you can share in the book's success by leaving an online review. Simply put, your opinions are powerful. The more you give voice to good stories, the more of them you'll find. Whether it's a few words or an essay, every five-star rating increases our visibility. Think of it as a vote of confidence in me and Vince.

Thank you for reading.

-Matt

Read Next:

Ghost Soldiers
Vince Carver Book Two

Continue the Vince Carver series
where Matt Sloane books are sold.

Matt-Sloane.com

Be notified when new Vince Carver
thrillers are released, right to your inbox.
Sign up at the website and never miss another book.

A Favor

It's not always easy to ask for a favor, even a small one, but I'm going to do it.

As an author, it's impossible to understate how much my career relies on you, the reader. Every purchase supports me. Every kind word helps my work flourish.

For that all I can say is thank you, from the bottom of my heart.

I know you're ready to dive into the next book, the next adventure, whether by me or another author, but it would be an incredible kindness if you could spend another single minute in the world of Vince Carver to leave me a review wherever you bought the book.

I guarantee that your words will make a difference. Not just to me, but to a random stranger stuck deciding what to read next and wondering if an author they've never heard of is worth their valuable time.

For that one guy, your input means everything in the world.

Preview:

Ghost Soldiers
Vince Carver Book Two

Government work is generally seen as a vessel for steady pay, solid benefits, and unmatched job security. The downside, of course, is the government part, that of participating in a slow-moving, wasteful bureaucracy.

Government *contracts* are a different story. You get the best of both worlds, the agility of private enterprise with the backing of limitless funds. Defense contracts are the proverbial golden geese of the financial world.

That was the theory, anyway.

In the real world, the act of catching said geese requires connections, and in the real world, Vince Carver only had one.

His fledgling security outfit was currently a two-man operation—one man and one woman to be precise—and the absence of legitimate espionage opportunities meant there was nothing to do. He didn't have the staff to take on side jobs, or the inclination for that matter. The best he could do was drop hooks in the water and wait for a bite.

So it was a welcome sight when Lanelle Williams of the CIA strolled into his converted dentist's office perusing his own business card.

"Kinetic National Security," she read in a tone that could plausibly doubt the sky was blue. "Providing top-end executive protection and investigations with special operations expertise."

"It's been two months," said Carver gruffly. "I expected a call by now."

She flashed a sardonic smile. "Intelligence walks to its own drum."

Williams wore her garnet leather jacket and black skirt like a uniform. She was full-bodied, bordering on stocky, yet seemed capable of gliding across the room to strike at a moment's notice. Appearances aside, the threat was misleading. Williams had no military or combat experience. Her true strength was her calculating nature. Her hair was close-cropped, she wore modest earrings and minimal makeup coverage, and had a resting bitch face that would make her mother blush.

"There's some disagreement within our community about using you again," she said leadingly.

"Averting a national disaster not good enough for Uncle Sam these days?"

"I'm referring to what happened to one of our own."

Carver chose not to give the accusation merit. Instead he said, "You and I both know justice was served."

"We're not in the business of justice, Vince."

"Speak for yourself. The CIA was the one side-dealing with China."

She huffed. "I don't condone what Officer Gunn did. And

the Agency appreciates your discretion in the matter. It's one reason I've convinced them to give you a shot."

Carver leaned into the vintage tan leather of his Eames office chair and motioned for Williams to sit across from the desk. If there was one quality he liked about the case officer, it was her straight shooting. "I appreciate the good word, Lanelle. How about we get down to it?"

"This is about the bombing in Rome last week." She sat, somehow looking more stiff in the chair. "Twelve dead after a suicide bomber drove into a crowd and detonated. Terrorists affiliated with the Libyan National Army took credit, releasing a statement condemning cooperation with the West."

Carver knew something of this world. He'd served six years in the US Army's 1st Special Forces Operational Detachment-Delta, much of that time in Africa dealing with various Salafis and jihadis. Officially, the Government of National Accord runs Libya, sanctioned by the United Nations Security Council. In truth the country is a hotly contested war zone. Various sectarians vie over territory and idiomatic influence in a resource-rich state. Larger powers, serving their own interests, back them by proxy. Russia and the United Arab Emirates outfit the rebels while Turkey and Italy support the interim government.

"They call Libya the Gateway to Europe," said Carver, revealing to Williams his knowledge of the area. "Migrants cross into Italy to gain access to the EU. While the vast majority simply want a better life, they don't all have good intentions. You need help tracking a terrorist cell?"

"Interpol has a handle on that aspect. We would like your cooperation, however, with protecting someone who escaped the blast."

Williams slid a phone over the desk. It was a standard CIA burner, and it currently displayed a picture of a young woman. Carver picked up the screen to study it.

"Her name is Katarina Litvinenko, a Russian figure skater in the Beijing Olympics. She spoke out against the abuses of her country and was ordered to return before the commencement of the games. She refused and eventually received a humanitarian visa from Poland."

Carver bristled. "This kid was the target of a bombing?"

"She's not a kid. She's twenty-three, rich, and has a well-connected family. She speaks publicly about leaving her country, and she barely escaped the blast in Rome as her outdoor speech concluded. Frustratingly, Katarina refuses state protection. She's currently employing private bodyguards in Berlin. Officially, the CIA can't get involved. Katarina is too open about her dealings with government agencies. That transparency is why she's so popular, and why we can't push her too hard. We also can't risk a confrontation with Russian interests that apparently wish her dead."

"But private security like me is okay."

"Off the books, of course."

"More proxy battles," he chortled.

"It's the way today's wars are fought."

There were only three photos of the girl on the phone, and in two of them she was holding a large handbag with a pampered dog sitting inside like an accessory. It was a Russian toy terrier, which resembled a black-and-brown chihuahua except its ears and mane were fluffy. Katarina's hair was decidedly less fluffy. It was long, blonde, and expensively done. Carver was already yearning for his previously barren work schedule.

"So the largest complication is the client," he summarized.

"In more ways than one. Katarina doesn't publish a planned speaking circuit so her movements are difficult to predict. Her appearances are mostly driven by on-the-fly social media activity. But we did find mention of an important future stop in Kyiv. I don't need to remind you that Ukraine is a non-NATO country and tensions on the eastern border are ripe. The USA's mandate in the region is increasingly specific. We provide military training and economic support, but we're no longer conducting official operations on the ground. The State Department issued advisories clearing out all non-essential personnel. The embassy was relocated to Lviv in the west, and the latest thinking is to move them clear to Poland."

"We're conceding Ukraine to Russia?"

"C'est la vie. Let the powers that be worry about geopolitics. Your mandate is Katarina Litvinenko."

After seeing there was nothing else of consequence on the burner phone, Carver slipped it into his pocket. "Sounds straightforward enough, if a little far-fetched. Why is the girl so important? And how can you be sure she was the target of the bombing?"

"Because her uncle is Arkady Malkin, Russian oligarch and right hand of the president. He's one of many corrupt businessmen currently sanctioned by the US. His fingers are in casinos, restaurants, and politics. He funded the Internet Research Agency, famous for coordinating sophisticated cyberattacks against us. He also has a hand in running the Wagner Group."

That was the mercenary outfit that took Crimea, nicknamed little green men at the time because of their non-affiliated army uniforms. In reality they were private military contractors with heavy sponsorship by the Russian state. US forces recently skirmished with them over an oil field in Syria. More notably, the Wagner Group put boots on the ground in Libya, training and supporting the Libyan National Army.

"It all comes full circle," said Carver, unsurprised. "Proxies training proxies."

"Just another facet of Russian unconventional warfare. They're brewing a perfect storm of aggression in Eastern Europe. A worsening gas war, weaponized migrants, political assassinations, and an increased troop buildup bordering Ukraine. The Kremlin is cultivating right-wing sentiment to fracture the European Union and protect their buffer states. They're constructing a renewed Iron Curtain."

"When do we start?" asked Morgan.

Very little was able to unsettle the CIA officer, but the silent approach of Carver's coworker to his doorway had a noticeable effect.

"Juliette Morgan," said Williams icily. "How much of that did you hear?"

"It's okay, Lanelle. Jules works for me, and I don't keep secrets from my team. Not anymore."

"There are national security implications at play here..."

"And there's only the two of us. You have nothing to worry about. Jules is the sole member of my security advance party, necessary to secure my arrival, collect and prep my equipment, and perform initial recon of the situation. That includes technical surveillance countermeasure sweeps of our forward-operating bases to protect your secrets."

"I'm aware of her role on your team, Vince."

"Good. Then you're aware that she needs to arrive before I do, which means the sooner you get on board with this, the sooner we can start."

Morgan leaned on the doorframe with crossed arms. Her straight brown hair curved like talons at her chin and framed a sideways smirk. Williams was markedly less amused.

"I can already see I'm going to regret this," she muttered.

"I beg to differ," countered Carver. "You give me your trust, continue being straight with me, and I'll do everything I can to deliver a win. That's what you're paying me for. That said, you're not my boss and I don't take orders. Once you hand this off, this is my show. It's the only way this works."

The CIA handler clicked her tongue. "Such is the price of

deniability. Fine, we'll do it your way."

"Thank you. But I need to know the end goal here. What do your bosses see as the ideal conclusion to Ms. Litvinenko's unofficial protection services?"

A shrug. "It's simple. Katarina is young and thinks herself invincible. She doesn't yet see reason. Your job, while keeping her alive, is to convince her there are only two outcomes in her future: she defects to the West, comes in out of the cold, so to speak, or she's eventually assassinated. The only variable is the timeline."

"The Libyans are coming after her again?"

"We've picked up chatter that indicates as much. Katarina will eventually see the light. We need the CIA in her ear when the revelation hits. Otherwise we're looking at another dead Russian dissident and who knows how much collateral damage."

Pick up GHOST SOLDIERS
where Matt Sloane books are sold

Also by Matt Sloane

VINCE CARVER THRILLERS
National Security
Ghost Soldiers
The Service of Wolves
Project Sundown

The latest books and information will always be on
Matt-Sloane.com

Made in the USA
Monee, IL
02 September 2024

65028169R00177